ALSO BY BARBARA FISTER

In the Wind

On Edge

THROUGH
THE
CRACKS

THROUGH

BARBARA

THE

FISTER

CRACKS

MINOTAUR BOOKS ✹ NEW YORK

This is a work of fiction. All of the characters, organizations, and events portrayed in this novel are either products of the author's imagination or are used fictitiously.

THROUGH THE CRACKS. Copyright © 2010 by Barbara Fister. All rights reserved. Printed in the United States of America. For information, address St. Martin's Press, 175 Fifth Avenue, New York, N.Y. 10010.

www.minotaurbooks.com

Library of Congress Cataloging-in-Publication Data

Fister, Barbara.
    Through the cracks / Barbara Fister.—1st ed.
        p. cm.
    ISBN: 978-0-312-37492-1
    1. Women detectives—Fiction.   2. Rapists—Fiction.   3. Rape—Investigation—
Fiction.   I. Title.
    PS3556.I81466T48 2010
    813'.54—dc22

                                                                    2009047479

First Edition: May 2010

10   9   8   7   6   5   4   3   2   1

For Rosemary and Tim,

Tim and Rosemary

ACKNOWLEDGMENTS

This story was inspired in part by the work of the Center on Wrongful Convictions at Northwestern University and Adalberto United Methodist Church in Chicago, where immigration rights activists facing deportation have been given sanctuary. Books that I found particularly useful (and well worth reading) are *Surviving Justice: America's Wrongfully Convicted and Exonerated* compiled by Dave Eggers, James M. Doyle's *True Witness: Cops, Courts, Science, and the Battle Against Misidentification*, Susan J. Brison's *Aftermath: Violence and the Remaking of a Self*, and Kevin Davis's *Defending the Damned: Inside Chicago's Cook County Public Defender's Office*. Thanks are due also to Dan Mandel, and to Gina Scarpa for her intuitive grasp of how stories work. I also owe a special debt to Maddy, DJ, Nicole, Sherry, and the community of readers they have fostered.

There is a crack, a crack in everything.
That's how the light gets in.

—*Leonard Cohen,* "Anthem"

THROUGH THE CRACKS

ONE

knew I couldn't run much farther. Blood pounded behind my ears. The sinews of my legs sang with a fine pain like high tension wires humming in the wind. I was past the point of rational thought when I noticed motion at the far edge of my peripheral vision. A car was approaching from behind. As it closed in, I checked my mental map of the area. There was a vacant lot ahead that I could cut through. But before I could reach it the car accelerated sharply, swinging around the corner to block my path. I could barely stop before careening into it, my palms smacking against the hood as I tried to keep my balance. Only then did I see who was inside, leaning over to throw open the passenger door of his Jeep.

"Jesus, Dugan. Trying to run me over?"

"Get in." It was a sharp command.

"Why?"

He had his jacket pushed back to clear his holster as his eyes scanned the street, on full alert. "Who's chasing you?"

"Nobody." Breathing hard, I wiped sweat out of my eyes with the heel of my hand. "Just getting some exercise."

He stared at me. "Looked like the hounds of hell were after you."

I leaned on the open door, a little dizzy from the sudden stop, and massaged a calf muscle that had tightened painfully. "Not unless you're talking about that obnoxious dachshund down the street, but he's tied up."

"Sit down a minute, anyway, catch your breath." I hesitated, then climbed in. He turned to rummage in a duffel bag on the backseat and handed me a bottle of water. I cracked it open and drank half of it in thirsty gulps.

"When I see people running like that in this neighborhood, it's usually not for exercise," Dugan said.

"So I should drive over to the lakeshore and use the jogging path like normal people?" I said. "This is where I live."

"I know." His affable response felt like a rebuke. Of course he knew where I lived. He'd spent hours all summer helping me transform the neglected scrap of land behind my West Side two-flat into a real garden with a brick terrace and raised flower beds overflowing with color. "You look tired," he said. "Still having trouble sleeping?"

I drank the rest of the water and set the empty bottle on the floor. "I just ran three miles."

"As if the dachshunds of hell were after you. Haven't seen you in a while. How's it going?"

"The garden's a mess. Everything's dying."

"Guess I should have warned you. That happens in the fall."

"All that work, then you get one lousy frost and all that's left is a bunch of dead stalks. What's the point?"

"You get to do it all over again in the spring."

The sun had gone down and the October air was crisp. I rubbed my arms, feeling chilled. My fingers unconsciously found the places on my upper arm where a bullet had passed through, leaving a dimple on the front, a welt of scar tissue where it exited. It had been a minor injury, quickly healed. My closest friend hadn't been so lucky. Though over a year had passed since Jim Tilquist had died, it hadn't gotten any easier to deal with.

I realized Dugan was watching me. Like most cops, he was good at taking things in without giving anything away. Still, I felt exposed, so I untied the hooded jacket I had knotted around my waist and slipped it on. It hid the scars from view, but I could tell Dugan knew what made it hard for me to sleep, what made me run until my thoughts shut down.

Though our careers with the Chicago Police Department had overlapped, Dugan's path hadn't crossed mine until after I'd resigned and took out a private investigator's license. He had taken advantage of the opening at Harrison Area Violent Crimes to transfer from an administrative post at headquarters to a position where he could spend more time on the street. He was a good detective, and unusually free of cynicism given he'd been on the job for seventeen years. Though he was dedicated and hardworking, his true passion was growing things. The moment he first saw the neglected wasteland that was my excuse for a backyard he started imagining the possibilities.

Six months earlier, we had bumped into each other at a Division Street café. Though it was a wintery day, with snowflakes squalling out of a leaden sky, he pulled out an envelope and started sketching out what I could do with my small patch of weeds and dirt. A few days later, in the midst of a sloppy thaw, he showed up at my place with tools and a six-pack of Leinenkugel's, putting me to work until I had blisters on my hands, dirt wedged under my fingernails, and a close acquaintance with back muscles I hadn't even known were there. He came by most Saturdays, but once the growing season came to an end, our get-togethers grew less frequent. We hadn't seen each other for almost a month.

"What brings you up here on a Wednesday evening?" I asked. "One of my neighbors misbehaving?"

"No doubt, but nobody's reported it yet. I had an errand to run. Stopped by your place to see if you had time to grab some dinner. You weren't home, so I figured you must be busy with one of your kids."

"*My* kids? What a horrible thought."

"Figure of speech. The wayward youth you specialize in."

"I was never convinced I was cut out to be a parent. Now I know for sure I'm not."

"That bad?"

"Not really. They're good kids, just messed up. We only had two crises this month. One of them is in the hospital. The other one's in rehab. Again."

"The one in the hospital—it's not Jim's kid, is it?"

"No. Sophie's been doing fine lately."

By chance, I had found a strange niche in my new profession. After helping the Tilquists find their daughter, who had bipolar disorder and tended to disappear from home during manic episodes, word of mouth led to my working for a handful of North Shore families with troubled teenagers. Whenever they lost track of their offspring they'd give me a call. I wasn't always able to find the kids before they did something stupid or got themselves hurt, but it gave their desperate parents the sense they were doing something. There was no shortage of potential clients. It wouldn't be hard to make it a full-time specialty, but it was emotionally taxing work, so I balanced it with more routine investigative jobs, most of them for Thea Adelman, a lawyer who specialized in civil rights cases. We didn't get along very well, but her dry irascibility was a refreshing contrast to parental anguish.

"I might have a new client," I told Dugan. "This woman e-mailed me out of the blue a couple of days ago asking if I was free to work on something."

"Another wayward youth?"

"I don't think so. But she didn't tell me what it was about and hasn't responded since. Maybe the rates scared her off." Which was disappointing. I wasn't sure my aging furnace would last through another Chicago winter, and replacing it wouldn't be cheap.

"What about dinner? There's a new Puerto Rican place not far from here that—" His cell phone rang as he spoke and he grimaced. "Shit." He had a cryptic conversation, mostly grunts, before punching it off. "Great timing. Sorry, I—"

"No problem. I know how it goes."

"A guy who's given me decent information before just got picked up on a drug beef. Says he used to run with Diggy Salazar, wants to deal. He probably doesn't know anything, but . . ." He shrugged.

"You're working on the Miller case?"

"Everyone is. Highest priority, according to the chief of detectives."

It wasn't surprising, given that the controversial case was getting national attention. Kathy Miller, a young woman living on the North Side, had disappeared six months ago. Though her body had never been found, the police were treating the case as a homicide; the blood, bone fragments, and brain matter found in an alleyway near the bar where she'd last been seen made it unlikely that she had survived the attack. That didn't stop her family and friends from holding out hope. Her face had become an icon of innocence: blond hair ruffled by a breeze, a wide smile, eyes squinting against the sun in a family video that ran over and over on the television news. The search for Kathy Miller gripped the city. In September, an undocumented Mexican immigrant was arrested and charged with her murder.

Digoberto Salazar had been caught on a surveillance camera as he left the scene of a liquor store holdup only blocks from where Miller had been attacked. Police believed he'd jacked Miller's car and bludgeoned her to death when she resisted. He'd hidden her body, then abandoned her car in a vacant lot in Cicero, where it was stripped almost to the chassis before the police spotted it.

That was the theory, anyway, but it wouldn't be easy to prove without the body. Still, the arrest of an illegal immigrant for the murder, after months of speculation and agonized appeals from the girl's family, had caused a furious outcry. The Cook County state's attorney, Peter Vogel, was prosecuting the case himself and making the most of the media attention, assuring the public the case against Salazar was solid and that justice would be served. He had plenty to gain from the publicity, given he was rumored to be a hot pick for the next gubernatorial race.

"Area Three detectives are running the show," Dugan added, "but Salazar's from our turf, so we're working all his connections. The SA's going to need every piece of evidence we can find to make this case stick. Not that we don't have other things going on. I got four unsolved homicides on my desk, but they're just kids shooting each other; business as usual. No overtime for that." There was a hint of jaded sarcasm in his tone, unusual for him.

"I warned you what it was like to work at Harrison."

"It's good to get back to the streets, but sometimes . . . like, I got this call just before I left work. This woman's son was killed in a drive-by eight months ago. No leads, no wits, nothing. She checks in every week. I never have any news for her."

"She just needs to know you haven't forgotten."

"I suppose. I better get going. Can I drop you off at home?"

"No, I need to finish my run. Thanks for the water."

"Anni—" He looked at me, searching for the right words. The ones he came up with were like him, straightforward and direct. "You doing okay?"

I missed Jim. His loss was a wound that wouldn't heal, and I ached with a feeling of guilt I could never explain. "I'll be all right," I said, answering as honestly as I could. Dugan nodded, understanding what I meant. It would never be okay again, not really, but I would find a way to get by.

We made vague promises to get together soon. He drove off to interview his potential source and I jogged the eight blocks back to my house, unlocked the side gate, and went through the gangway to the back garden, where I found not everything was dying. Three pots were grouped near my Adirondack chair, bronze and gold chrysanthemums hardy enough to take a little frost. That must have been the errand Dugan was running before he rescued me from imaginary pursuers.

There was a folded piece of paper tucked in among some of the flowers. I reached for the note, feeling apprehensive. I liked Dugan. I liked the easy way things were between us, but there was just enough attraction there that things might get complicated. It was a relief to see it was just a few words scrawled on a sheet of notebook paper: "I opened your gate with a paper clip. Get yourself a decent lock, Koskinen."

I smiled to myself, picturing Dugan with his crooked nose and cockeyed smile, carrying the pots from his car and arranging them around my chair. I stuffed the note in my pocket, then sat for a moment under the walnut tree, looking up at the sky, a pure, deep blue through the lattice of the nearly leafless branches, a few stars showing like pinpricks in the darkness overhead. The three-legged stray cat, who lived in the alley and liked to pretend he belonged to nobody but himself, yet expected his food bowl to be filled on a regular basis, peered through a tangle of dried vines, annoyed that he had to share his night garden with an interloper.

The chill finally drove me inside. I switched on my phone and found a message waiting. I returned the call. The conversation was brief, but promising. A woman named Jill McKenzie had something confidential she wanted to discuss with me. She was willing to pay me for my time and travel, even though she lived some four hours from Chicago, just across the Iowa border. I agreed to drive over to see her the next day; I figured I could be there around noon. As soon as she finished giving me directions to her house, she hung up so abruptly it was almost rude.

I had no idea what she wanted me to do, but it would cost her a lot to bring me to Iowa to talk about it. Maybe if our meeting went well I would be able to afford a new furnace after all.

Toward midnight, I set my alarm clock and went to bed. Of late, I had grown used to jerking into an alert state just as I started to drift off, or being roused within a few hours by dreams that made me reluctant to go back to sleep.

But this time it was screaming that woke me up.

TWO

n my befuddled state it took a moment to realize it wasn't part of a nightmare. That high-pitched wail had to come from Daniel, the toddler who lived in the apartment downstairs, but I'd never heard him sound so terrified, so frantic. Sirens in the distance were howling along with him. I blinked at the bedside clock: 4:23. As I disentangled myself from the sheets, I heard feet pounding up my back steps. "Federal agents! Open the door!" A fist hammered on it. "*Abre la puerta!*"

I was wearing nothing but a faded Chicago marathon T-shirt from five years ago, so I groped in the dark for a pair of sweats. As I slipped them on, my door shuddered under blows from a fist. "Hang on, I'm coming!" I called out. I sidled to the window. There was enough light from a streetlamp to see three shapes in bulletproof vests and blue windbreakers clustered on my porch. One man had turned to guard their rear; there were large white letters on his jacket spelling out POLICE, and under that, ICE. Immigration and Customs Enforcement.

"I'm opening the door, okay?" I called out. I switched on a light and worked the bolts, my hands clumsy with tension. As soon as the last bolt was unfastened, the door flew open, banging hard against the wall, and a man pushed past me into the room, his eyes scanning from side to side. I reached for his arm. "Hey, what're you—"

It was a mistake to touch him. He reacted automatically, knotting the back of my shirt in his fist and shoving me hard against the wall, twisting my arm up behind me in a practiced move. The other two men who followed him in had their weapons drawn. "What the hell's going on?"

"José Guerrero. Where is he?"

"I don't know. I don't know who you're talking about."

"He's on our list. He lives here."

"Nobody named . . . wait, are you talking about Joey? He used to live downstairs. He moved out over a year ago."

I didn't like the pleading tone that I heard in my voice. With the man's weight braced against me I felt trapped and had to draw on everything I had to resist an impulse to struggle. There was a trembling eagerness traveling like a current through the hand that gripped my wrist; he was just waiting for an excuse to hurt someone.

One of the men checked the closet, another kicked my bathroom door open, his gun held up in both hands beside his cheek like a character in an action movie.

"Where'd he go?" The breath of the man holding me was hot on my neck.

"I want to see your warrant."

"We don't need a warrant. Just answer the fucking question."

"You damned well need a warrant to enter my house." The angle of my arm was notched up, pain shooting across my shoulders, making sparks go off behind my eyes. "I was a cop for ten years," I said between my teeth. "I know what I'm talking about. You're breaking the law."

"Just calm down and answer the question. Where'd Guerrero go?"

"I don't know. He didn't tell me." My skin crawled from his touch, my muscles spasming with an almost overwhelming urge to fight free.

"Check her for weapons," the man who held me said over his shoulder. I saw a blue latex glove move toward my ribs. I closed my eyes as hands felt around my hips, down my legs to the ankles, then up toward my crotch. I clamped my teeth down on my lower lip. *Don't struggle. Don't resist. . . .*

The hands went away and my arm was released. I turned around to face the agent, blinking away tears of pain and rage.

"So you're not gonna help us?" he said.

I swallowed my anger and spoke calmly. "I told you, I don't know where he went. He didn't leave a forwarding address."

Another agent jabbed his finger at my face. "We find out you're lying, that he's still hanging around here? We'll be back."

The floor shook as the three men headed for the door. I caught a glimpse through the window of their heads bobbing past as they tromped down the stairs. I leaned back against the wall and slid into a crouch, trembling.

focused on taking deep and steady breaths until the tremors subsided. Then I pulled on shoes and a jacket and stepped out onto my porch. The dead hour before 5:00 A.M. was usually the quietest time of the night, when the clock ran slower for officers working the first watch. But not this night. There was palpable tension in the air. I heard frightened voices raised somewhere down the blocks. Sirens called to each other from every direction in the dark. I went down the stairs and tapped my knuckles on the back door of the apartment downstairs. "It's me, Anni."

A bolt turned, the door opened. My tenant, Adam Tate, stared at me, his eyes wide with shock. He was holding his fourteen-month-old son, Daniel. The baby had handfuls of his dad's T-shirt bunched in his fists and his legs were clamped tightly around his father's waist, clinging so hard, I had the impression that if Adam let go, he would still hang on, like a determined crab. "You guys okay?" I asked.

Adam nodded, as Daniel looked at me suspiciously. The skin under his eyes was stained a fierce pink from crying; even his forehead was flushed. He breathed a heavy, shuddering sigh, then buried his face against his dad's chest with a little whimper. Adam patted his back distractedly. "Come in out of the cold. That was freakin' weird. Never had police bust in like that before. Can they do that?"

"They're the ones with guns." I followed him inside. For a moment I thought the agents had trashed the place, but then remembered it always looked like this. Toys, papers, empty Red Bull cans, and clothing were scattered everywhere, and the kitchen counters were cluttered with dirty dishes and crusted carryout containers. Adam was able to write elegant computer code and played both chess and classical guitar with professional skill, but he was strangely oblivious to basic domestic tasks. His apartment always looked like a frat house for geeky toddlers.

"Isn't it, like, illegal?" he asked.

"Yup. They don't need warrants to stop and search non-citizens, but suspecting an illegal immigrant is in someone's home doesn't cancel out the fourth amendment." I rubbed my shoulder, still aching from having my arm twisted behind me. "They were pretty pumped up. I think they'd kind of lost track of the legalities."

Adam tried to shift his son to one hip, but that only made the little boy cling tighter. "I don't think Daniel is going to let me put him down anytime soon."

"Poor little guy. He must have been terrified."

"We were asleep when they started banging on the door. Soon as I opened it, they ran in, waving guns and shit, like in the movies. They asked who else lived in the building, and three of them went up to your place. Sorry, I didn't—"

"It's not your fault. Best thing to do with guys like that is to cooperate."

"They told me they were looking for some dude with a Hispanic name, that they're rounding up gang members all over the city. Guess they got the wrong house."

"Sort of. There was a guy who was born in Mexico living in your apartment last year. He wasn't in a gang, but apparently his name and this address was on some kind of list." Joey's parents had brought him across the border without papers when he was not much older than Daniel, so he had grown up under constant threat of deportation to a country he didn't remember, where they spoke a language he barely knew. I only found out he was undocumented after police and FBI agents had flooded the neighborhood the previous year, looking for a fugitive and, fearing deportation, he abruptly packed up and moved out.

"Soon as they realized we were, you know, white, they backed off and apologized," Adam said. "But man, it's weird to see guns pointed at your baby."

"No kidding. Well, I just wanted to make sure you guys were okay."

"We're fine," Adam said, but as I let myself out, he was rubbing his little boy's back as if to reassure himself that they really were.

There was no chance I'd get back to sleep; my nerves were fizzing with adrenaline. Back in my flat I started a pot of coffee, then picked up my cell phone and scrolled through my contacts until I found Azad Abkerian's number.

Az was the senior reporter on the courts and cops beat at the *Chicago Tribune*. I'd first met the portly legend, dressed as usual in a ketchup-stained tie and rumpled suit, at a crime scene during my first year on the job. Over the next ten years, we'd helped each other out from time to time. Even though I was no longer with the police, he checked in regularly for tips or comments. I wasn't sure if he'd thank me for waking him up, but if this really was a citywide operation, he wouldn't want his counterpart at the *Sun-Times* to get it first. "Hey, Az. Sorry to call so early, but—"

"I'm up anyway. Whatcha want?"

"My house was just raided by ICE agents."

He laughed. "No shit? That's what you get for living in a Hispanic neighborhood. They been sweeping places from Logan Square to Back of the Yards. Right now, I'm in Little Village. Feels like the place is under siege." From his tone, you'd think it was the best entertainment he'd had in years.

"What's this all about?"

"Part of a nationwide operation, in the works for months, according to Homeland Security. They're supposedly arresting dangerous criminals in six cities. Far as I can tell, all the people they picked up haven't committed any crimes apart from being undocumented. The CPD was involved because of the gang angle, but now the superintendent is denying any responsibility for this mess. The feds apparently failed to update their lists of targets even when CPD gang specialists told them it was way out of date. A narcotics detective I talked to told me one of these cowboys actually drew a weapon on *him*. He was disgusted, said they were totally unprofessional. And this is a Chicago cop talking, not Miss Manners."

"The agents who came to my house were really aggressive. One of them actually told me in my own living room that he didn't need a warrant."

"They must have some of those Washington lawyers busy making up new definitions for 'search and seizure.' I called D.C. Ever try getting through to anybody there outside office hours? What a joke." I heard a rustle of paper. "Finally got a quote from some assistant to an assistant to the special agent in charge of the raids . . . where is that? Oh, yeah. 'These people move around a lot. We may have to go to six places before we find them.' Like, it's okay to raid homes without warrants because one of these times we'll actually find the guy we're looking for. So, what were they doing at your place?"

"I rented the apartment downstairs to a man who, it turned out, was undocumented. He moved out over a year ago, though. They practically tore the door off its hinges when they came in."

"How you feel about that? Gimme a juicy quote."

"I would, but I don't think you're allowed to use those words in the paper."

"So, translate."

"This isn't how a democracy is supposed to work."

"Gee, thanks. A civics lesson. I already got the ACLU for that. This is putting the mayor in a hell of a tight spot. The city doesn't do immigration enforcement; that's been the policy since Harold Washington's day, and Hizzoner doesn't want to change it, not when almost a third of the city's Hispanic. But he's got to pay attention to the other two-thirds, and given how people are responding to Diggy Salazar's arrest, he's between a rock and a hard place. The fact Salazar's an illegal—" He broke off abruptly. "Whoa, hear that? Could be gunfire. I gotta go."

So long as I was wide awake, I decided to head out for my meeting, even though it wasn't much past 5:00 A.M. I would be early, but at least I would avoid the worst of rush hour traffic. I showered, dressed, poured coffee into a travel mug, and filled the cat's bowl with Little Friskies. The neighborhood was still crackling with tension as I walked to my car, people huddled together on porches talking nervously.

Once in the car, I switched on the local NPR station. In between news from the Middle East and financial reports, there was state and national coverage of the raids. The DHS secretary was already calling the operation a success, with over a thousand lawbreakers detained across the country. An unnamed Chicago police officer disagreed, describing a chaotic operation, poorly coordinated and dangerous, netting few if any serious criminals.

"Man on the street" reactions were mixed. Some said it was wrong, others said it was about time. "Illegals have no reason to expect the same rights as citizens," one man sputtered. "They're illegal, period." Another voiced a more pointed criticism: "Look at what they're doing to the crime rate. If the authorities had cracked down earlier, Diggy Salazar would have been in jail, or back in Mexico, instead of here in Chicago killing innocent women."

I kept the radio on at a low mutter as I headed west, turning it up when, shortly after 6:00 A.M., Peter Vogel, the Cook County state's attorney, issued a statement that sounded like a campaign speech. He congratulated Homeland Security on the success of its efforts and urged local law enforcement to cooperate with all federal agencies as a matter of policy. It was time for Chicago and Cook County to drop outdated practices that protected illegal immigrants and made the city a sanctuary for criminal gang members.

The mayor, too, held a brief press conference, typically pugnacious and uninformative. They were looking into it, they'd get to the bottom of it, and the media was blowing it all out of proportion. It sounded word for word like previous mayoral responses to law enforcement bungles.

The radio started to crackle as I reached the limits of the reception area. I switched it off and watched farm fields roll past as the sun rose behind me.

THREE

When I reached Jill McKenzie's sleepy college town, nestled against the bluffs of the Mississippi River, I stopped at a café and killed time reading the local weekly paper cover to cover. The sparse police reports included a vandalized mailbox and the theft of a pumpkin off someone's front porch. It made me more curious than ever why a woman who lived in a place like this wanted to hire a Chicago investigator.

All I knew about Jill McKenzie were the few tidbits I had found on-line: she was forty-three years old and had no criminal record. She owned a modest two-story home, built in 1912, according to the county assessor's records. She was an associate professor of sociology at St. Vincent's College and had published several academic papers and a well-received book on ethnic change in rural Iowa. She served on several college committees and was a tough grader, but fair, according to ratemyprofessor.com. None of it gave me any hint about what we would be discussing.

Though it was still well before our appointed time, I left the café and drove to the address she had given me over the phone, a few miles out into the countryside, so remote that my cell phone could barely pick up a signal when I tried to phone ahead. I bumped over some railroad tracks, passed a grain elevator, and followed a washboarded gravel road to the top of the bluff overlooking the town. Her home was a weathered frame farmhouse surrounded by open pastureland. The setting would have been bleak if it weren't for its spectacular view of the river valley, brilliant with fall colors.

When I knocked on the front door there was no answer. I could hear the whine of a power tool coming from an outbuilding behind the house, but as I started around to the back, the noise ceased. I called out a greeting and stepped through the wide-open doors of what looked like converted stables. A pickup truck was parked on one side. The rest of the space was taken up with carpentry equipment: tools hung neatly on a Peg-Board, a workbench holding planers, sanders, and chisels, shelves filled with cans of stain and finish. A plank of wood lay on a table saw, fresh sawdust spilled around it, the air scented with resin. The room was perfectly still, except for motes of dust that swam lazily in the sunlight that slanted through the open door. There was something eerie about the dead silence in the room, as if whoever had been working there mere moments ago had been swept through some cosmic vortex, leaving behind nothing but spinning flecks of light.

I turned to peer into the shadows on the other side of the room and my throat seized up. Two brindled mastiffs the size of Shetland ponies were standing, still as statues, behind the pickup truck. They watched me with lowered heads, eyes unblinking, identical ruffs of fur bristling across muscular shoulders, not making a sound. As we stared at each other, the silence was broken by the familiar *snick* of a hammer being drawn back. I glanced toward the sound and saw a .38 Detective's Special trained on my chest. The woman holding it moved out from the shelter of the truck's cab. She was as silent as the dogs and had the same aura of lethal competence.

"You're early," she said, turning the barrel to one side and easing the hammer down with a practiced move before holstering the gun. Apparently that was an all-clear signal to the dogs. One nuzzled her hand as she came around from behind the truck; the other came up to sniff my crotch with interest. "Leo, don't be rude. Just push him away."

I let Leo have his sniff, feeling the aftereffects of adrenaline wash through me until even my fingertips tingled. The dog seemed friendly now, but those jaws were big enough to take my hand off at the wrist. I wasn't any less nervous about Jill McKenzie. She was graceful and slim, with an attractive fine-boned face and strawberry blond hair cropped short as a boy's, but there was nothing delicate about her. In spite of her slight build, she was fit and muscular, and she studied me with the same cold, unreadable expression of a street-hardened cop.

"Do you usually wear a gun when you do carpentry?" I asked her.

"Always." She held out a hand. Her grip was firm. My fingers were shaking, a difference she noted by raising an ironic eyebrow. "Let's go inside."

L eo followed us into the old-fashioned kitchen, his nails clicking on the hardwood floor, while his twin settled on the back porch, as if they had divvied up the guard duties in advance. Jill McKenzie pointed me toward a seat at the kitchen table, then slipped off the down vest she had been wearing in the chilly stable, unclipped her holster from her belt, and set the holstered gun on the counter.

"I wasn't expecting you for another hour," she said, her words as clipped and controlled as her actions.

"I wasn't expecting to have a gun drawn on me. For the second time today," I said as I realized it was true. "There was a big immigration sweep in Chicago early this morning," I explained. "Some agents showed up at my house looking for a guy who'd moved out a long time ago."

"I heard about it on the news. What a mess. They actually had their weapons drawn?"

"They were a little overheated."

"We had a big raid last spring on a meatpacking plant in Postville, one of the communities where I've done my research. It caused a lot of hardship for hundreds of families."

"Sounds as if most of the people who were detained this morning weren't the gangbangers they were supposedly looking for, just undocumented. But there's a lot of anti-immigrant feeling in Chicago right now because the guy arrested for murdering Kathy Miller is Mexican."

"I haven't been able to stop thinking about that case. They still haven't found her body?"

"No, and that's making it tougher for the police. They're under a lot of pressure to make a conviction. There's been so much press coverage."

"Naturally. She was young and white and pretty. Her family threw themselves into keeping her in the public eye. High-profile crimes like this one become big stories because they tend to focus and amplify the fears people have about race and class." She made a face. "Sorry. You can tell I'm a sociologist."

"It sounds familiar. My grandfather taught sociology." Leo came to sit beside me, after sniffing around the perimeters of the room, checking for intruders, bombs, or stray crumbs. It was time to get down to business. "The gun you're carrying, does that have something to do with this job you want to talk about?"

She opened the refrigerator and peered inside. "I guess you could say that."

"Look, I'm not a bodyguard. If you're looking for someone who can provide personal protection—"

"I'm not. Coffee?"

"Thanks." Leo rested his big head in my lap as she shook beans into a grinder and filled a carafe at the sink. I tentatively scratched behind the dog's ears and he sighed happily.

She punched the coffeemaker on and sat across the table from me. Leo immediately switched allegiances, padding over and slumping to the floor beside her chair. "The reason I carry a gun goes back more than twenty years," she said. "When I was an undergraduate I was raped. For months I was totally disabled by fear. I realized I had to do something to recover some sense of control, so I bought a gun and learned to use it. I took self-defense classes and still work out every day. I started wearing my hair short so that nobody can grab it and drag me into the bushes. When I moved into this house, I rooted out the lilacs planted around the porch so now I can see for half a mile in every direction. All of these precautions are superstitions, really, like touching wood, but they give me the illusion of safety."

"Leo probably helps, too," I said, and his tail thumped against the floor, hearing his name.

"He and his brother look impressive, but they're not trained as attack dogs." She reached down to scratch his ears and he drooled happily.

"What's happened recently that has you on edge?" I asked. She gave me a puzzled look. "You looked prepared to shoot me out there."

"That's how I respond when someone sneaks up on me." She narrowed her eyes, reading something in my expression. "I have a right to defend myself."

"Look, I don't want to get into a debate over the second amendment, but—"

"You just happen to think civilians shouldn't be armed. But I have a permit, and I practice at a shooting range regularly. I haven't shot anyone yet."

There's always a first time, I thought, but I'd already pushed the boundaries with a potential client. "Must be tough, living on constant alert all these years."

"It's better than constant fear. You wore a gun every day when you were a police officer; it's just as automatic with me, part of getting dressed to go out."

"Even to go into your own backyard?"

"I like living out here in the country, but it's isolated. Building furniture is my hobby. I wouldn't be able to do it if I didn't feel safe."

"Do you wear your gun to work?" I asked, curious.

"I take it with me, but lock it in my car. College regulations."

"What made you contact me? There are a lot of investigators to choose from."

"Nancy Tilquist told me about your work. We know each other professionally. I respect her opinion." I nodded, having already guessed that might be the connection; Jim Tilquist's wife, Nancy, taught anthropology at a small college on the North Shore, and academia is a small, tightly knit world. "I was sorry to hear about her husband's death. I understand you were with him when he was shot."

"Yes. We were close friends."

Her eyes were not blue as I had originally thought, but gray, almost smoky in color, the only thing about her that wasn't sharply-defined and decisive. She studied me for a moment, and I waited for the usual platitudes, already feeling the prickly irritation that came when people who didn't know me offered sympathy. But she simply nodded and moved on. "You work for Thea and Harvey Adelman, that was another factor. They wouldn't hire anyone who wasn't well-qualified. But it really came down to the fact that your grandfather talked about you all the time."

"You knew my grandfather?"

She allowed herself a brief but genuine smile. "He's the reason I'm still a sociologist. He introduced himself after I gave my first paper at a national conference. I was a nervous wreck, and the audience threw me some tough questions that made me want to scrap my dissertation and drop out of grad school. He sensed how shattered I was, and took me to a diner nearby for a cup of coffee. We talked for hours, and after that I didn't feel so stupid and useless. He became my mentor and friend. He talked about you a lot, you and your brother. He was proud of everything you'd accomplished. So when Nancy told me you were working as a private investigator, it made sense to call you. I need someone I can trust."

"Okay. Let's talk about what you want me to do."

Her lips tightened before she spoke again. "This is confidential, right?"

"Confidential, yes. Privileged, no. If I were served with a subpoena—"

"I'm not worried about that. I just don't want to lose my privacy." She stared out the back window, her hands folded, one thumb rubbing a knuckle on the other hand. For the first time she appeared uncertain, even fragile.

"I'll be discreet," I said. "Of course, if you need more time to think about it—"

She took a breath and squared her shoulders. "No, I'm ready to go ahead with this. I want you to find the man who raped me."

FOUR

The man who . . . you mean, twenty years ago?"

"Twenty-three years ago. I'm not saying it will be easy."

"I'm sorry, but it's not just the lapse of time, though that's going to make it difficult." I groped for words, trying to soften my response. "Even if I could find him, it's almost certainly too late to prosecute. I'm not familiar enough with Iowa law—"

"It happened in Chicago."

"Then I know there's a problem. Illinois has a ten-year statute of limitations. And besides . . . Look, I realize there are reasons people sometimes avoid reporting assaults to the police, but if it wasn't a police matter then—"

"It was. They arrested a man within forty-eight hours. He received a thirty-year sentence. His conviction was thrown out two years ago."

Her words were matter-of-fact, spoken without any apparent emotion, but it was painful to see how tightly the skin was drawn across her cheekbones.

"I'm sorry. I can only imagine how that feels."

"The guilt?"

"No, having everything you believed for all those years pulled out from under you. You think the guy really was innocent?"

"The prosecutor insists it was a solid conviction, but I'm pretty sure I identified the wrong man."

"There is one exception to the statute of limitations. If DNA obtained at the time of the assault was entered into a database within ten years of the crime—"

"There is no DNA. This happened before they used DNA routinely in criminal cases, and most of the evidence went missing from storage years ago."

"I hate to be so discouraging, but without that evidence, there's no way we could get any firm resolution, let alone a conviction."

"Unless he's raped other women." She took a breath. "What he did to me—I'm sure he'd done it before. And he was going to keep doing it as long as he could. That's not just a personal opinion. All the research suggests a rapist who makes the kind of attack he made on me is going to offend again."

Her chair scraped against the floor as she stood abruptly. She filled mugs with coffee, then set a sugar bowl and quart of milk between us and got spoons out of a drawer. Leo raised his head and watched until she sat again and wrapped her hands around her mug. When she spoke, her voice was steady though her knuckles were white from gripping her cup so tightly.

"Look, I'm a demographer. I use numbers to study groups of people. Numbers cut through all the clutter, they help you see patterns. It's like when you're on an airplane: as you lift off, things look neater and tidier the further away you get. You can see the shape of the land, figure out how things relate to each other. Most of my research has been about ethnic change in rural communities, but after the conviction was thrown out I wanted to work on something else. If numbers give you a way of seeing things more clearly, why not use them to understand my situation?"

Leo nudged her leg and she absently reached down to scratch his neck. "I teach an upper-level course on the sociology of gender, and one of the things we talk about is sexual violence against women. I disclose to my students that I was a rape victim, though I don't go into details. I need to let them know it happens to people like them, that they can trust me to understand if they want to talk. I know what a difference it makes, given my experience with your grandfather. For a long time he was the only friend I was able to talk to about what had happened to me. That may seem strange, but Golly was . . ." Her voice trailed off, at a loss for words.

"I know," I said.

"Oh, I talked to therapists, to rape counselors. Professionals. They knew what to say, and I suppose it helped at the time. But they weren't like Golly. He was an amazingly good listener, and even though he was so low-key and gentle he was . . . what's the word?" She squinted up at the ceiling as if it might be written up there in tiny print. "Rigorous. You'd get to where you thought you had your understanding all worked out, and he'd ask a probing question. And you'd realize there was a whole new layer there to think about. You know what I mean?"

I nodded. Gerasim Golovkin, known to his friends as Golly, adopted my brother and me when my search for the mother who'd abandoned us led to a man who'd been abandoned by his teenage daughter. When he took us in, I was eleven years old and Martin was thirteen. We'd shuttled from one foster home to another for most of our lives. Martin's odd habits—rocking, flapping his arms, putting things in obsessive order—and his frequent outbursts of frustration put him at risk of being institutionalized. I was determined that we would stay together, and as a result developed a rare talent for manipulating our case workers. But when we moved in with Golly, it didn't take long to realize I couldn't put one over on this rumpled old man with basset-hound eyes and gravelly laugh. He was kind and patient, but his unerring lie detector caught every one of my fabrications.

"He was pretty amazing," I said.

"You must miss him."

"Every day." He had died six years earlier of a stroke, thanks to decades of chain smoking and a diet too rich for his sedentary habits. I felt a sudden pang that was a combination of old grief and the persistent longing for nicotine that hadn't gone away after I quit smoking myself. I never caught a whiff of fresh tobacco without thinking of his Chesterfield-scented hugs.

"I couldn't go to his funeral." She looked at me, stricken. "I wanted to, but . . . I haven't been to Chicago since—"

"It's okay. There were a lot of people there."

"I'm sure. Golly was a mentor to generations of students. I missed him so much when I found out the man they'd locked up all these years was most likely innocent; he could have helped me understand it. It shook me up, but the last thing I wanted was to let my emotions take control of my life again, so I decided to apply my research methods to the issue. Create a picture of rape victims and their circumstances, see what the numbers could tell me. I wrote a grant so I could hire some students to work with me over the summer and made a formal request for records from the Chicago Police Department. It took a long time, but we eventually got copies of all the incident reports for aggravated criminal sexual assault cases for the past decade. Thousands of records. The first step was to sort them into two categories: known versus unknown assailants. Then we looked at circumstances. I thought I would be able to remain dispassionate, but it was harder than I'd imagined, trying to code variables that come so close to my own experience."

"Some things are hard to intellectualize."

"Researchers are supposed to be objective. It's part of our training, but I'd never tackled a project like this. I was a little worried about exposing my students to it, especially since I knew at least one of them had been assaulted herself. But they were able to handle it. We had great conversations. Maybe that was the greatest benefit of the whole project. It taught them to see the patterns, to recognize there were people behind them, people who felt alone but had something in common—and it kept me from flaking out. Because even though all of these crimes were committed at least ten years after my assault and the majority of them involved known assailants, it was disturbing to see so many incidents that reminded me of my rape. Oh, I knew I would likely have flashbacks, nightmares. All the research suggests that's common, so I was prepared for it. But . . . some of the assaults were so strikingly similar I couldn't help thinking: What if it *is* him?"

"When you say similar—"

"The places the women were attacked, the time of day. The violence of it. I pulled some records to show you." She rose and went into the next room, came back with a stack of manila folders. She selected a file and handed it to me. I noticed her hands were no longer so steady. "These are the ones that had the most features in common. None of them have been solved."

I skimmed through the reports. Though the crimes spanned ten years, they were surprisingly similar. Seven sexual assaults, all committed on the West or Northwest Side during the early morning hours, all against women in their late teens or early twenties. Two of the women were white, three black, two Latina. All of them had been on foot when attacked, and all of them had been threatened with a knife and battered ferociously. Two of the women either had no memory of the attack or were too badly injured to provide a description. Those who were able to recall it described their assailant as a light-skinned black man between thirty and forty-five years of age, with short hair and a wiry build. Guesses at height and weight were fairly consistent, putting him at around five foot ten, in the neighborhood of 170 pounds. The women's names and home addresses had been blacked out to protect their privacy. Between the lack of names and the repetitious formality of the language, it gave me the unsettling impression that the same woman had been attacked again and again. I flipped a page to look at the last report and drew in a breath.

"Is that the woman who was found in Garfield Park?" Jill asked, trying to read upside down.

"She was walking her dog."

"Right."

"He killed the dog."

"And nearly killed her."

"I know. I didn't mean . . . It just reminds me of the Lincoln Park Rapist."

"That's why I pulled it out to show you."

"In fact, they all kind of . . ." My words faded as I realized what she was saying. "Wait. You're—?"

"I'm Jill McKenzie," she said sharply. "A teacher and a scholar. Yes, I was assaulted and left for dead in Lincoln Park half a lifetime ago, but that's something that happened to me, it's not who I am."

I wasn't processing her angry words. I was thinking about what it meant.

The Lincoln Park Rapist.

It was one of those crimes that seizes newspaper headlines day after day and comes to symbolize the anxieties of an era. An attractive college student took her cocker spaniel for a walk in one of Chicago's most popular public parks early one spring morning, before the sun was up. She was spotted an hour later by a jogger, who thought at first she was dead. Her spaniel was found a few yards away with his throat slit.

Press reports did not identify the victim, other than to say she was twenty years old, a sophomore attending a local university, that she had come from a small town on a scholarship, and that she was undergoing surgery after identifying her attacker from her hospital bed. Chase Taylor was arrested two days later. He had just turned sixteen, but was already well known to the police. He and some friends had spent the evening before the assault attacking people at random while high on a new crystalline form of cocaine that was ravaging the East Coast.

The violence of the crime shocked the city. The fact that the accused had been running wild with friends hours before the rape, robbing nearly a dozen people in a part of town normally considered safe, fueled fears that the crack epidemic had arrived in Chicago. That a dog was killed in the course of the crime—"tossed aside like a blood-soaked rag" in the words of one of the responding officers—added to the viciousness.

What the news reports didn't say in so many words was that the victim was white and the accused was black, but that fact colored everything.

My memories of the crime were tinted with my own awakening awareness of race. It was the year we moved in with Golly, trading a chaotic household in the city for a quiet bungalow on the affluent North Shore. We were in a secure and loving home for the first time in our lives, but I felt out of place. On the first day I attended my new school, a girl was pushed forward out of a giggling group in the cafeteria to ask the question they all were whispering about: "What are you?" At first I didn't know what she meant. Then I didn't know how to answer. My brother, Martin, had our mother's fair skin and light brown hair, but I had inherited features of a father I'd never met: dark eyes, curly hair, skin the color of milky coffee dusted with cinnamon. I didn't know what I was—only that I wasn't like them.

I knew it wasn't good to be different. Martin was different. He hummed and rocked and made clicking noises at the back of his throat when he was happy. Teachers assumed he was stupid because he wouldn't talk and didn't pay attention in school, but he was smart in his own way. He could put broken things back together so they worked, and when he played speed chess against the hustlers in the park he almost always won. When people left him alone, he was fine. When they didn't, he would get upset. Sometimes he would get so worked up that he threw things or hit himself and screamed. When we moved to Stony Cliff, well-meaning friends advised our grandfather to send Martin to a place where experts could look after him, but Golly had promised me he wouldn't, and he kept his word. He found a therapist who helped Martin adjust to the new situation, made allies among the special ed teachers at our new school, read all the books about autism that he could get his hands on, and spent hours studying the way Martin approached the world. Within six months he understood my brother's moods and ways of communicating almost as well as I did.

But even Golly couldn't help me interpret the alien culture of sixth-grade girls. I didn't understand the references to clothing brands or music that my classmates used, but I grasped all too clearly what they didn't even realize they were saying. It made me acutely aware of the ways people talked about race without ever naming it. That secret code was threaded throughout the news accounts of the Lincoln Park Rapist.

Chase Taylor was described as a "wolf on the prowl," a rogue member of a pack of feral kids who terrorized people just for kicks, part of an aberrant subspecies emerging from the underclass. A prominent businessman was so outraged by the crime he took out a full-page ad in the *Sun-Times* calling for authorities to impose the death penalty on "this animal" and others like him. There was a backlash, with black activists criticizing the lynch-mob mentality spurred by the press, others questioning the judgment of a woman walking alone in a city park before sunup. Nobody came right out and said "she was asking for it," but that was the implication.

In spite of the controversy, the trial was swift and conclusive. The "animal" was charged as an adult, found guilty at trial, and sentenced to thirty years in prison. Chase Taylor's name faded from public consciousness, but the Lincoln Park Rapist didn't. It remained a symbolic crime, a touchstone for a moment when crime reached a new low of senseless violence—or when racism clouded the public's perception, depending on your perspective.

When I read in the paper the verdict had been overturned I wasn't surprised. Over three hundred criminal convictions had been thrown out since DNA testing became a reliable tool, and many of the exonerated were young black men who confessed under duress to crimes they hadn't committed. Chase Taylor's photo was on the front page of the *Tribune* again, having turned from a shifty-eyed kid into a bewildered-looking man in his thirties. Columnists and talk shows rehashed the original incident, spinning off discussions about violence against women, about race and criminal justice. But within days it was old news; Chase Taylor faded back into obscurity, a symbol turned into a statistic, just one more overturned conviction to add to the list.

realized Jill McKenzie was waiting for me to speak. I closed the file and asked the first question that came to mind. "You said the DNA evidence was lost. Why was the case thrown out?"

"The confession Taylor signed before he got a lawyer was coerced. The lawyer who eventually represented him was incompetent. Key witnesses recanted their testimony and others came forward who could place Taylor miles from the crime. And, of course, the most common reason for a wrongful conviction: the victim identified the wrong man."

"You sound sure of that."

"I was shown photos of six men shortly after the attack. One of them looked more like my assailant than the others, so I pointed him out. By the time of the trial, I had seen that picture so many times I was utterly convinced that was the man who attacked me."

"But now . . ."

"Now the only thing I can be sure of is that I don't know. It's a phenomenon psychologists call contamination of memory. It wasn't deliberate. The police were using a standard protocol. It's just that once you've seen the picture of a suspect, it fills in a troubling gap in your knowledge. Every time you revisit that memory, the image grows clearer and clearer. You forget that you were ever unsure. Whatever you originally saw is overwritten by a substitute."

She took a shaky breath. "You know what I said in my testimony? 'I'll never forget that face.' And it's true. Even now, knowing it was almost certainly someone else, when I have flashbacks of the attack, it's Chase Taylor's face I see."

"God," I said. "I'm sorry you—"

"I don't want sympathy. I want this man stopped." She spoke so fiercely Leo scrambled up on his haunches and fixed suspicious eyes on me.

I took a sip of my coffee. It had grown cold and tasted bitter. "Look, you aren't going to want to hear this, but I need to be honest with you. I'd like to help, but it's unrealistic to think I could catch this guy two decades after the second-largest police force in the country failed to find him."

"They quit looking too soon."

"What about these cases?" I tapped the file. "I'm just one person. There were a lot of detectives working on these."

"Over fifteen hundred criminal sexual assaults were reported in Chicago last year. How much attention do you think each one really got?"

"These cases? Plenty. Stranger attacks on young women, an extreme level of violence—these are the ones that keep you awake at night. They were investigated aggressively, trust me, and the detectives doing it had access to a lot more information than I have. I don't even have the names of the victims." She started to interrupt but I went on. "It would be unethical of me to take a case that I have no reasonable expectation of solving."

"I'm only asking you to try."

I closed my eyes and rubbed my temple where a headache was starting to form. That last incident report, with its typos and awkward formal phrases, cockeyed because it had been photocopied hastily, seemed to have imprinted itself somewhere behind my eyelids.

"I'll write a check for five thousand dollars," she said. "That should be enough to give you an opportunity to assess whether there's anything in it."

"Look, I don't want to waste your money when—"

"What I do with my money is my choice."

"I don't want to waste my time." I sighed, wishing I'd found words that weren't so harsh. "There's something else you need to consider. You said you valued your privacy. What if your name got out? The media would be all over it."

"I'll just have to trust you, won't I?"

"Trust has nothing to do with it. If I do what you're asking, I'll have to talk to the detective who led the investigation, to Taylor, to his defense team. No matter how careful I am, it wouldn't take much for a reporter to get wind of it and connect the dots. Are you ready for that?"

She looked at me, her gaze unwavering. "Not really. I dread the thought of being hounded by journalists, of everyone knowing I was that famous victim. But there's a chance the man who hurt me has attacked other women the same way and he might do it again. I can't stand by and do nothing."

"All right," I said at last. "I'll see what I can find out, so long as you realize—"

"That you expect to fail, I got it. I'll write that check."

"Make it for fifteen hundred. That will cover my trip out here and the initial research. If it looks as if it's worth going forward, we'll talk about how to proceed. If it doesn't look promising, I'll refund whatever money is left over." I pulled out a notebook and opened it. "To start with, I need to get some basic information from you about the assault."

"I figured you would, so I wrote it all down." She pushed the stack of files across the table. "I also have some news clippings and court documents. These are copies you can take with you."

"Good. Let me read through your statement and then I'll have some questions for you."

"You mean . . . right now?"

"Do you have something else you need to do?"

"No, I just— It's all there, everything I can remember." She looked at the printout in my hands, at the wall, toward the door, her eyes skittish. She had geared herself up to get this far, but it had been a strain and now her well-oiled gears were starting to slip.

"There may be things I need clarified."

She stood, swept up the holster from the counter and clipped it on her belt. "Fine. I'm going to get some work done." She picked up her down vest and slipped it on.

"I'll let you know when I'm finished." I massaged the aching spot in my temple as Leo scrambled to his feet to follow her. "Just one thing—"

Jill paused, her shoulders rigid. "What?"

"Do you have any aspirin?"

FIVE

Her statement was concise and to the point. It only took a few minutes to read it. A copy of the original police incident form was attached, as was the preliminary medical evaluation that detailed her injuries: extensive vaginal tearing and bruising, fractures, internal bleeding from a ruptured spleen. Multiple superficial cuts from a knife on her neck, breasts, torso, and abdomen, apparently more to terrorize her than anything. The life-threatening injuries, inflicted after the rape, came from a more primitive weapon: her assailant's fists. The list of her broken bones read like notes for an anatomy exam: infraorbital foramen, zygomatic, sphenoid, maxilla, occipital, clavicle, scapula . . .

The aspirin wasn't working. I rubbed my forehead.

I looked through the other files, sat thinking for a while, then got up and went out the back door. She hadn't gone back to her workshop. Instead, she was sitting on the steps playing with the ears of one of the dogs while the other snuffled around the yard. There was a rigidity in her pose that made me think she would prefer to have plenty of space between us. I sat at the far end of the step. Some black-and-white cows were grazing near the fence. One lifted a head to stare at us, then went back to chomping grass.

"How long were you in the hospital?" I asked.

"Six weeks, the first time. There were two more surgeries later. No, three."

"You must have had good surgeons."

"The scars are there, you just have to know where to look." She touched a scribble of scar tissue beside her eye, another small white thread that followed her jawline. Then she wrapped her arms around her chest and leaned forward. "We told everyone at home I was in a car accident. I missed a year of school, transferred to a small college closer to home. It was hard on my parents. They still . . . It's been hard. They don't think I should do this."

"They know?"

"We've talked about it in general terms. I haven't told them I'm going ahead."

"Have you spoken to anyone else about it?"

"One close friend. That's all."

"There's not much description of your attacker in your statement. Can you tell me anything more about him?"

She took a tight breath. "Not really. I wrote down everything I remember."

"You said he was wearing dark clothes. I'm wondering about the color. Black? Brown?"

"Dark blue or black. I can't be sure."

"Pants or jeans?"

"I don't know. Not jeans."

"Buttoned shirt or a T-shirt?"

"Buttoned, I guess. It wasn't a T-shirt." Her voice was growing frayed.

"Same color as the pants?"

"No idea. I had my mind on other things. Does it even matter?"

"It might. You say he smelled as if he had been sleeping outdoors. Do you mean he smelled dirty, like he hadn't washed in a long time? Like the way the stairs smell at an El station?"

"No, like outdoors. Earthy. Leaves, grass. If he smelled like urine I would have said so."

"His hands were rough. You mean his palms were calloused, like someone who does manual labor?"

She sighed with impatience and nodded.

"You wrote that he told you to 'stop fussing.' Were those his exact words?"

"You think I made it up?"

"No, I'm just—"

"That's what he said."

While pressing the point of a knife just under her eye, according to her written statement. "What did his voice sound like?" I asked.

"Just a voice. Not especially deep, not high. Just . . . ordinary."

"Did he sound African-American?"

"As opposed to white?"

"Or West African, or Haitian, or—"

"African-American, I suppose. He only spoke a few words."

"His face. The general shape, was it long or round?"

"He grabbed my hair from behind before I knew he was there," she said, her voice shaking with iron control. "He hit me on the side of my face so hard my eye socket was fractured. I could barely see, and I was terrified. You think I'd be able to recall every detail under those circumstances?"

"I need to ask these questions."

"To prove to me this is a bad idea? I spent all that time writing it down so we wouldn't have to do this. Are you trying to catch me in a lie?"

"No. I just—"

"There's a voyeuristic aspect to this, you know. I found that out when all those people from the prosecutor's office wanted to hear my story. They acted all sorry and shit, but they wanted to hear every detail, just like you, even though I'd already told it over and over. You have no idea how invasive it is." She glared at me. "Were you ever attacked by a man?"

"On the job, sure. Things could get physical."

"I'm not talking about that. Before you had a gun, before it was your job. Were you ever sexually assaulted?" Her eyes narrowed, seeing something in my face. "You were," she whispered, sounding oddly pleased about it.

"No. Not really. It was nothing like what happened to you."

"Because he was your boyfriend? You were both drunk so it doesn't count?"

"He wasn't my boyfriend and I wasn't drunk."

I took a breath, looked down at my notepad and read the last word I had written: "ordinary." I set the pad and pencil beside me on the step and rubbed my palms against my knees. I sensed her eyes on me as she waited.

"I was ten or eleven years old," I said. "We were in foster care before we moved in with Golly. This was one of those homes where they're in it for the money, so they had as many kids as they were allowed and didn't pay a whole lot of attention. An older boy was always messing with me. One afternoon I was reading a book on the couch in the basement. I didn't see him coming until it was too late. He got on top of me, pulled my pants down. He was only a couple years older than me, but he was big and heavy. I wasn't strong enough." My words sounded as if they were coming from one of those documentary narrators with a steady, calm voice. I hadn't thought about it in years, but the memory had rushed back so vividly I could feel his weight trapping me, smell the sour stickiness that I felt against my skin for weeks, no matter how many showers I took. "But in the end, nothing happened. He was too excited, he went off before he could get inside. He was just a stupid horny kid."

"Did you tell anyone?" Her voice sounded subdued, now, all the triumph gone out of it.

"The foster mother. She just said boys were like that; I shouldn't lead him on."

"Jesus. You had to go on living with him in the house?"

"Not for too long. Something happened, he got sent to juvenile detention. I don't even remember his name." *Clayton Brown*. It came to me suddenly, as clearly as if he'd crept up behind me and whispered it in my ear. I wiped my palms again and picked up my notepad. "Listen, I need to get clear on some other stuff. When did you find out the case was being challenged?"

"I got a call from Peter Vogel." Her voice sounded different, now, softer, tired, no longer defensive and angry. "I guess it would have been almost four years ago, now. He told me the Center on Wrongful Convictions at Northwestern University was looking into it. He wanted to warn me in case it got into the news."

"He called you personally?"

"Yes. He was just an assistant state's attorney when he prosecuted the case."

"Wait, it was *his* case?"

"His first big starring role."

That wasn't going to make things easier. Vogel had advanced through the ranks and was now the state's attorney for Cook County, director of the second-largest prosecutor's office in the country, overseeing the work of more than 900 attorneys. He'd been on the national news frequently of late, talking about the Kathy Miller case, with his square jaw and marine-short haircut looking like law and order personified. No wonder he wasn't happy when the conviction against Chase Taylor was thrown out. It not only threatened to put a crimp in his political ambitions, it cast doubt on his skill as a prosecutor.

"He couldn't have been much over thirty at the time," Jill said. "He looked even younger, like a high school nerd, but he was already a rising star. I thought he was a jackass. He acted all concerned and outraged, but every now and then I'd catch him grinning to himself, like I was the best thing that ever happened to him. The detective in charge of the case was all right, though. He seemed to genuinely care about what had happened to me. I guess some of the things he did may have been wrong, but it wasn't to advance his career. He just wanted to find the bastard and lock him up. I've often wondered how he feels about the way things turned out."

"If I find out, I'll let you know. Do you remember his name?"

"Jerry Pozorski." She spelled it for me and I jotted it in my notepad. It wasn't familiar to me, but he might have retired before I went on the job.

"Did the people working to free Taylor ever contact you?" I asked.

"I contacted them, actually. Peter Vogel said not to worry about it, they were just activists latching onto a famous case to get attention. He didn't come right out and say it, but I think he wanted me to keep quiet, not give anything to the other side that they could use. That was fine with me; I didn't want anything to do with it. But a few months later I came across an article about their efforts. They had turned up witnesses. It laid out all the things the prosecution did wrong. It was pretty obvious that there were serious problems with the case, that the only thing that held it together was my eyewitness identification. So I decided I should get in touch with them."

"Who did you talk to?"

"At first, a student. There were several law students working on it under the direction of one of the Northwestern faculty and a team of pro-bono lawyers. I didn't tell her who I was, just said I had information. She connected me with Thea Adelman."

"Thea Adelman?"

"Thea and Harvey did most of the work. That's one of the reasons I have such a high opinion of them."

That took me aback. I had been doing occasional investigative jobs for their law practice in the past year, but this case had never come up. It fit their specialty, though—cases that had to do with race, inequality, and failures of the justice system. Chase Taylor was lucky. Given Thea's strong media contacts, her involvement would automatically raise the profile of any case they took on.

"That's good, isn't it?" Jill asked, picking up on my hesitation. "You already have a working relationship with them. Won't that make things easier?"

"It should." But I had my doubts. Harvey was easygoing, the dictionary definition of a nice guy. His wife, Thea, was another matter. She was often in the public eye, an eloquent and sharp-tongued spokeswoman for the oppressed and unfairly accused. Though we worked together on a regular basis, we'd rubbed each other the wrong way from the start. Chances were she'd give me a hard time for taking money from a traumatized woman for a case that was most likely hopeless. "Would you mind if I let them know you're my client? They'll keep it confidential."

"Sure. And Jerry, too. The detective. You can tell him you're working for me."

"If I can find him, and if he's willing to talk to me." That was another thing that would be tricky. "I should have probably warned you before we got too far into this. I don't have particularly good relations with the police."

"I'm not surprised, after the way you testified in that brutality case."

"How'd you know about that?"

"What do you think? I Googled you. Found all kinds of stuff."

"Yeah, well, I noticed you haven't scored any chili peppers on ratemyprofessors dot com," I said.

She laughed. "Thank God. Tells you something about the state of higher education when 'hotness' is a factor in teacher evaluation."

"Seriously, my past is going to be a problem, and not just with Pozorski." Two years earlier I'd seen a cop lose his temper with a teenager. The kid ended up with permanent brain damage, his family sued the city, and I was called as a witness. The city settled with the family for a large sum without admitting responsibility—and I was ostracized by most of my colleagues. After failing to get swift backup in a volatile domestic situation where lives were at risk, I finally faced reality and turned in my badge.

"It's going to be hard for me to get information about those cases you found, the ones like yours," I told her. "Cops don't appreciate it when one of their own testifies against an officer."

"Is that why you resigned?"

"More or less." I felt an urge to defend the profession, even though it still hurt that cops closing ranks had forced me to leave the only job I'd ever wanted. "Look, most police officers are good people, but they deal with crap constantly and nobody else understands what it's like. It gets to a point for a lot of them where it's 'either you're with us or against us.' I crossed that line, and it made it hard for a lot of them to work with me after that." She started to say something, but I cut her off, not wanting to hear someone who didn't know anything about it criticize the community I'd once been part of. "It's just going to make this investigation more difficult, that's all."

"Well, since you tell me it's already impossible, I'm not too concerned." She gave me a lopsided smile, gone as soon as it appeared, then looked over at the pasture. "Look, I need to apologize."

"For what?"

"Being a jerk. I shouldn't have reacted the way I did. Shouldn't have put you on the spot like that."

"Hey, at least you didn't shoot me."

"It pisses me off that I still have so much trouble talking about what happened to me. About being raped. But that's no excuse."

"I'm used to it. Crime victims get angry, and the person they're angry with usually isn't handy. I'm sorry I had to ask so many questions."

"It shouldn't bother me, but it does. These weird things happen, physiologically. I get short of breath, my muscles cramp up. It's frustrating, being unable to control my reactions even when I know what to expect." As she spoke, the dogs suddenly grew alert, their heads swiveling toward the road as they both noted something beyond my hearing. I tensed and she smiled. "Relax, it's a friend."

"How can you tell?"

"The dogs know." I finally heard the sound of a car with a faulty muffler approaching in the distance. Leo made a soft "wuff" sound. The two mastiffs rose and started around the house, tails waving like metronomes.

"His name is Tom Farrell," she said. "We've been together for nearly eight years now. He knows about all of this."

As she spoke, I heard the crunch of tires on the gravel driveway, a door slam, a male voice muttering affectionate small talk to the dogs. Leo and his brother came romping back into the yard, circling a man in jeans and a battered leather jacket. He had sun-bleached tangled hair, a weathered face, and an easy smile. Jill introduced us. "Tom lives just up the road. He bought the local shooting range a few years ago."

"Not that it makes any money," he said. "But if you need your house painted or your gutters cleaned, I'm your man."

"He's also a fine carpenter," Jill added. "Not to mention a capable electrician and plumber."

"References provided on request," he said, deadpan.

"How are you with furnaces?" I asked him. "Mine needs replacing, though I don't suppose you include Chicago in your service area."

"A little too far for me."

"She's taking the case," Jill said to him.

"Well, okay," he said. He rubbed the side of his nose with his fist and looked away at the cows.

"I'm checking into it," I said. "We'll see if there's any reason to dig

deeper." My cell phone started to trill in my pocket as I spoke. I took
it out and checked the number. "Excuse me. I need to take this."

I walked away toward the barbed wire fence as I listened to one of
my clients. She was sobbing so hard she could hardly tell me what
was wrong. Apparently her son, Ryan, had banged out of the house
last night after an argument. She was afraid he hadn't been taking
his medication lately. Her husband thought they should stop cod-
dling him, let him take the consequences this time, but she couldn't
stop worrying. I asked a few questions and made comforting noises
in response to her outpouring of frustration and anxiety. As we
spoke I glanced back at the house, Jill murmuring something to Tom
earnestly. She reached out to hook her little finger in his. His face
softened into a smile as they shook, as if they were children sealing a
truce.

Feeling as if I'd intruded on a private moment, I turned away and
listened to my distraught client a while longer, then told her I would
be tied up for a few hours, but I'd start looking for Ryan as soon as I
could. I ended the call and walked back to the porch.

"I have to get back to town," I said. "But I think I have enough
information to get started."

"Let me get those files for you. Tom, there's coffee inside. Help
yourself."

In the kitchen, Tom filled a mug as I gave Jill a copy of my standard contract and went over it. She signed it and wrote out a check.
"What's the best way to contact you?" I asked her. "Should I use your
home phone number, or—"

"E-mail would be best. You have my address."

I nodded. It wasn't the most secure medium for sensitive information, but I sensed she was more comfortable with computer commu-
nication than the intimacy of the phone. "One other thing," I said as
I started to pack the files into my bag, realizing I'd neglected to ask
an obvious question. "When you first noticed the similarity between

those recent cases and yours, did you talk to anyone about it? Anyone official?"

"I tried to get hold of Jerry Pozorski," she said. "That's when I found out he had retired and moved out to Plainfield. I didn't want to talk to some detective I'd never met. I finally decided to write Peter Vogel a letter. I gave him the case numbers, explained my concerns. Three weeks later I got his response by mail. Their investigators had looked into it. They remained confident these cases were unrelated, that my assailant had been behind bars when these other crimes occurred. He wanted to reassure me that he and his office remained committed to justice, blah blah blah. It was so patronizing. I would have included it with those files, but I got so mad I ripped it up. Sorry."

"That's okay," I said, though it wasn't good news. I expected the state's attorney to resist any efforts I made to dig any deeper into these cases. Now I knew he'd been forewarned.

As I said good-bye, Tom drained his mug and set it in the sink. "You're not staying?" Jill murmured to him.

"Got a job in town."

"Stop by after work."

"Could be late," he said.

"That's all right. I'll be up anyway; I have a pile of papers to grade."

They gave each other a simple kiss, the kind that's had plenty of practice. I hoisted my bag and walked with Tom to the driveway, where his car was pulled up behind mine. He didn't seem in any hurry to get out of my way as he dug a set of keys out of his pocket and sorted through them.

"I know it's none of my business," he said finally.

"You're right," I said gently. "It really isn't."

He looked up at the sky where a ragged V of geese was winging its way south, following the river valley. "She's the smartest woman I ever met, and the bravest," he said. "I don't want her hurt."

"Neither do I."

"I knew her when she was a little girl, she tell you that? We went to the same school in a little town about fifty miles west of here. She was smart, and pretty, too. I was just a dumb farm kid. I couldn't wait to finish school. Scraped through a couple of years of community college so I could take a job with the state patrol. Didn't last, though. I wasn't good at taking orders and I got sick of dealing with what happens to people when they get drunk or start yakking on their cell phones when they're doing eighty on the interstate. This one time, a car full of teenagers . . . well, I went home after my shift ended and the next day I couldn't make myself go back. Just couldn't."

He turned away from the geese and gave me an affable shrug. "I took a leave, made it permanent when it ran out. Found work as a fishing guide in Canada during the summers. Friend of mine has a camp up there, some cabins and boats. It's nothing much, but I like being miles from so-called civilization. Rest of the year I get by with odd jobs. Guess it was ten years ago that I got a job on a building restoration at the college. Found out Jill worked there, but I figured I wouldn't have anything in common with a college teacher. Then one day I went out to the range to let off some steam, and there's Professor McKenzie, firing away, intent as hell." He laughed. "Just like she used to be in school, dead sure of herself, only this time it was putting holes in the center of a target, all clustered up tight. She's a hell of a shot. I think she can do anything she puts her mind to—except forget what happened to her."

"No, you don't forget something like that."

"It took years before she could tell me about it. But I knew something had happened to her, something bad. She came through it, but it was like coming through a fire. Burned away a part of her and left the rest scarred. You know that saying about what doesn't kill you makes you stronger?"

"I've heard it before."

"It's bullshit. What doesn't kill you hurts like hell, and it doesn't ever stop hurting. She's strong, all right, but that's her doing, that's sheer willpower. When she found out they'd locked up the wrong man, it was like she was having to go through it all over again, only this time carrying a huge load of guilt. She hates it that an innocent man spent most of his life in prison over this. But shit, they showed her his picture in the hospital. The doctors weren't even sure she was going to live, and the cops are pushing photos in her face asking her, 'Is this the guy?'"

He bent down and picked up a chunk of gravel, narrowed his eyes at a fence post across the road, and threw the rock. It missed and he gave a little sigh. "I was in northern Ontario, taking tourists out fishing, when she got those police records in the mail and started going through them. She didn't tell me till I got back what she'd found, what she thought she had to do about it. I don't think this is a good idea, raking it all up again. Far as I'm concerned, she doesn't owe anybody anything. But it's her decision to make, and I'll stand by her."

"It's good to know. Whatever happens with this investigation, she'll need support."

"Don't let her hear that. She thinks she's Superwoman." He bent to pick up another piece of gravel and weighed it in his hand. "You think you'll find this guy?"

"All I can do is try."

"Glad I'm not in your shoes."

"Because you wouldn't want to let her down."

He took aim and threw. This time he hit a fence post with a hollow *thwock*. "Because if I found him," he said, "I'd kill him."

SIX

As soon as I got on the highway, I started making phone calls. Over the past months I had developed networks of contacts for each of the kids whose parents had hired me. Technically I was employed by the parents, but only on the condition that everyone understood I wouldn't make the kids do anything they didn't want to do, and I wouldn't reveal anything they didn't want me to share other than a general report on their state of well-being. In practice, it didn't always please the parents that I couldn't just handcuff their children and drag them home by force, but most of the time they saw the wisdom of this approach. Once the kids realized they could trust me, they were more likely to cooperate. When they were okay, I served as a buffer between them and overanxious parents. When they weren't okay, I was less likely than their parents to freak out about it.

I was stalled in rush hour traffic on the Eisenhower when I finally reached someone who knew exactly where Ryan was: a few feet away, sleeping on a couch. Ryan's voice was gummy with sleep when he took the phone. He told me he'd taken the train into town after his dad ripped into him again over something stupid. He'd hung out all night with friends, talking and listening to music, and had fallen asleep a few hours ago.

"Your mom's worried."

"Shit." He didn't sound surprised.

"She thinks you haven't been taking your meds lately."

"Jesus. Why doesn't she ever trust me?"

"I'm not sure that she doesn't trust you. It's just where her thoughts go when she's worried."

"She's always worried."

"That's what moms do. Part of the job description. Sounds as if you and your father aren't getting along too well."

"He's an asshole. Want to hear his job description? Boss everyone around, act like you know everything, make stupid rules. He gets mad at me over nothing."

"How much of a problem is it?"

"It's not that big a deal. I just get pissed off sometimes and need to get out for a while. But that's good for you, right? You get paid."

"Don't do me any favors, Ryan," I said lightly, and glanced at my watch. It was just past 5:00 P.M. "So, you want to call your mom, or you want me to?"

He thought it over. "I'll call her."

"I can give you a ride home if you want." He didn't say anything in response. "You have my number, anyway?"

"Yeah."

"Use it if you ever need to."

"Yeah, yeah."

He sounded on the verge of death by boredom, but I trusted him to make that call, and I could tell from our conversation he wasn't off his meds. He was just being a kid, a normal sixteen-year-old who argued with his dad and left home to hang out with friends. But his mother had been through a lot and was now constantly anticipating the next crisis.

I was approaching my exit when it occurred to me I could do a little work on Jill's case and pick up some dinner while I was at it. Olivia Jackson had always been a reliable source of information about whatever was going on in the East Garfield Park neighborhood. She also made some of the best food on the West Side. A natural-born entrepreneur, she cooked mountains of traditional soul food in her small kitchen and enlisted a network of relatives to take boxes of chicken and okra, beans and corn bread to work sites or busy corners at lunchtime. It wasn't strictly legal, since she didn't have any permits or inspections, and I doubted she reported the income to the IRS, but that didn't seem to bother any of the patrol officers from the 11th District who stopped by her house routinely to pick up a home-cooked meal.

I parked on a side street off Homan. There weren't many businesses in this part of town, at least not the kind that were on the tax rolls, but the streets were always humming with activity. On this early evening, a cluster of men were gathered around a car with its hood up while a group of boys hung out nearby, laughing and exchanging rabbit punches. An ancient man with a porkpie hat squashed on his head was limping from one person to another asking if anyone could spare some change for the bus. As I parked and climbed out of my car, a man relaxing on his front stoop with a can of malt liquor and a cigarette nodded at me. "How you doing today?" he asked politely.

An average day in the 11th district would see a dozen arrests for battery, theft, prostitution, and narcotics. It was a dangerous neighborhood, and most of the residents had difficult, hardscrabble lives. But in spite of all that, people had small-town manners and were more likely than in North Side neighborhoods to smile at strangers and say hello.

I knocked on Olivia's door. A child opened it. Olivia's elderly father, settled on the couch in a nest of blankets, recognized me and gave me a grin as jagged and gapped as a jack-o'-lantern's. "Who called the *po*-lice?" he joked.

Olivia came out of the back, wiping her hands on a towel. "How you doing, gal? Ain't seen you in ages."

"I was passing by. Wondered if you might have something on your stove."

"You know I do. Look at you, all skinny. Ain't taking care of yourself."

I followed her into the steamy room. "I got chicken, greens, black-eyed peas," she said. "Only corn bread I got left is from yesterday, but it tastes okay if you warm it up. I'll throw it in for nothing. You ever met Aisha? She helps me out after school. Aisha, this is Miz Anni Koskinen. She's a detective, but not with the police no more. She's a private eye, ain't that right?"

"Let me give you a card." I got one out of my wallet, a simple white rectangle with my name, phone, e-mail address, and the word *Investigations*.

"It's awful plain," Olivia said, frowning as she took it from me. "You ought to have a picture of a magnifying glass or something." She showed it to Aisha before setting it on the windowsill over the sink.

"I was going for the discreet look. Something that would tell people 'confidentiality is guaranteed.' Also, it was a lot cheaper without a logo."

The girl, who couldn't be more than fourteen years old, gave me a brilliant smile as she scrubbed a pot in the sink. She was at an awkward age: half child, half woman. But her face was strikingly attractive, like an Ashanti sculpture, with huge doe eyes slanted over prominent cheekbones, framed by a beaded curtain of braids. She had the pudgy figure common to kids who lived in neighborhoods where playing outdoors was dangerous, but her face could have belonged to a fashion model, if it weren't for crooked, oversized front teeth. She must have been self-conscious about them, since she immediately closed her lips over her smile and turned away, as if keeping a secret to herself.

"What you working on now, Sherlock?" Olivia asked.

"Today, a missing kid, but I already found him. Turned out he wasn't exactly missing, just hanging out with his friends. I'm about to start on another job, though. In fact, I was hoping I could ask for some private advice about it."

"Aisha, honey, leave them dishes for a minute. I want you to take some supper to Mrs. Stevens up the street." She filled a container with food and handed it to the girl. "She gets lonely, living by herself, might be wanting to talk some. Spend a little time with her, okay?"

I didn't speak again until the girl had left the room. "Is she a relative?"

"Naw. I just let her help out 'cause her momma has a hard time. Can't pay the girl much, but least this way I know Aisha and her brothers got something to eat. What can I help you with?"

"I need to find someone. A man attacked a woman in Garfield Park four years ago. Raped her, beat her up, killed her dog."

She was shaking her head before I even finished. "Let me 'splain something to you, Miz Detective, if I knew who was responsible for that—"

"He'd be locked up."

"He'd be crippled first." She picked up a handy paring knife and brandished it. "I'd do a little surgery on his you-know-what 'fore I turn him over to the police. That kind of evil behavior, there ain't no excuse. That girl was hurt bad."

"Thing is, another woman may have been attacked by the same man."

Olivia frowned. "This just happen?"

"She doesn't live in this neighborhood, but she got beat up the same way," I said, avoiding a direct answer. "The police don't believe there's any connection. I think there is, but they aren't going to listen to me."

Olivia nodded. She knew why I had resigned. It wouldn't surprise her that I'd have a hard time getting the police to take anything I said seriously.

"The woman who got attacked in the park, here, her name was

kept out of the papers. I don't know how to get in touch with her. I was hoping you could ask around, tell her I'd appreciate a chance to talk to her. I'd like to stop this man."

"I can make a few calls."

"Great. Let me give you something to help out with the phone bill."

It was an old routine, but it still worked. Seven dollars for the food, another forty for information. Olivia knew everyone in the neighborhood, and all of their business. I had no doubt she'd be able to pass my message along.

The real question was whether the woman she gave it to would be willing to talk to me—and if she would be able to provide any useful leads.

I t was getting dark as I carried my food up the back steps and into my flat. I hadn't stopped for lunch and was hungry after driving home in a car aromatic with fried chicken and ham-flavored greens. But my apartment seemed too empty, too quiet. I had a sudden, vibrant memory of Jim Tilquist sitting at the kitchen table, loosening his tie and giving me a tired smile. The finality of his absence filled my chest with a thick, choking emptiness. I put the food into the fridge, my appetite gone. I stood for a few minutes, paralyzed by memories. Then I drank a glass of water, changed my shoes, and went out to run.

It felt good to be outside, to pay attention to nothing but the whoosh of blood through my veins, the thud of my feet against pavement. Lights glowed inside houses. A dog barked, a car door slammed, a car trolled by with a thumping musical sound track. Everything seemed normal in the neighborhood, the raids of the morning just a bad dream. Stray thoughts brushed past me as I ran. At one point I flashed on the memory that Jill had pried out of wherever I'd hidden it years ago: the book I was absorbed in knocked out of my hands, my wrists gripped tightly as I fought to get free. It rushed at me, a feeling of fear and fury and utter helplessness.

I ran faster.

Down streets, past alleys, pushing myself as hard as I could until once again the only thing I was conscious of was the breath rasping in my chest. But as I followed a footpath around the lagoon in Humboldt Park, something shifted subtly.

My awareness of surroundings had always been finely tuned. When I was young, a caseworker called it hypervigilance, as if it were a disorder, but it had served me well as a police officer. As I ran through the park it seemed as if a dial had been twitched a notch higher, picking up a different frequency, one that broadcast a constant, high-pitched whine of danger. Sounds, movements, a shadow shifting under a tree—things that I would normally register, assess, and dismiss—were now charged with ineffable menace that I couldn't identify and couldn't outrun.

I got home and headed down the gangway to the backyard, breathing hard. It was a symptom of how frayed my nerves had become that I nearly screamed when a dark shape slithered past my feet to disappear into the darkness. Just the cat, I realized, a familiar shadow in the yard, but the same chemical response flooded my senses as on that day when a boy in a basement pinned me down and tried to rape me.

I climbed the stairs, went inside, and bolted the door behind me, my muscles quivering. Only after I switched on lights, opened a bottle of wine, and put on some music to chase out the silence did I start to feel normal again. In control.

Safe.

SEVEN

The next morning I called Thea and Harvey Adelman's law office and asked if I could speak with one of them. They were both in meetings, but their assistant put me down for a fifteen-minute slot with Thea at 10:00 A.M.

I arrived a little early at their modest Uptown office, a collective shared with four other attorneys who had the same politically progressive interests. I'd learned through experience that it didn't do to keep Thea waiting, though she often did it to me. I wasn't surprised when the office assistant explained something had come up; I'd have to reschedule or wait.

I opted to wait, picking up a discarded copy of the *Trib* to read Az's front-page story about the raids. As usual, he reported the incident with an even hand, but managed to slip in a police officer's criticism of the feds' bungling and several accounts of innocent citizens being caught up in the sweep. The ACLU was threatening legal action, but Homeland Security proclaimed it a successful operation that had led to the detention of scores of dangerous criminals throughout the country.

Twenty minutes later, Harvey stepped through a door and beckoned me over. He was a lean man with curly hair that habitually needed a trim, and wrinkles that deepened when he smiled. "Looks as if we're going to be tied up for a while. We may have to reschedule."

Through the partially opened door, I glimpsed a familiar face, one that was square and blunt, with a nose that had been broken once or twice and now looked like a misshapen potato. "What's Father Sikora doing here?" I asked.

"He's got a bit of an emergency on his hands. Can we postpone your appointment until Monday?"

"I only need a few minutes," I said, wondering what kind of emergency the old priest was having. He was the pastor and sole priest at St. Larry's, a Catholic church in my neighborhood. It was probably related to the immigration raids. The majority of his parishioners were Latino, and it was likely some of them had been detained.

"What's it about?" Harvey asked.

"A case you worked on a couple years ago, Chase Taylor's exoneration." I lowered my voice. "Jill McKenzie wants to know who was really responsible for that crime."

Harvey stared at me, then shook his head as if to clear it. "Why? It's way past the statute of limitations."

"I know, but doing some research she came across records of seven unsolved crimes that are similar to hers. She thinks the guy who attacked her may be an active serial rapist."

"Did she tell the cops?"

"She told the state's attorney, Peter Vogel. He dismissed it. Sounds like he doesn't want to open the door to any speculation that women are being attacked because he screwed up his first high-profile prosecution."

Harvey stared past my shoulder, gnawing his lip. "On second thought, maybe you'd better join us." He opened the door to the conference room wider and waved me in.

Thea frowned at the interruption. She had long, dark hair that fell nearly to her waist, and a slender elegance that had something severe and crisp in it. That aura of cool confidence was an advantage in court for a woman of color—she was an enrolled member of the Grassy

Lake Band of the Ojibwa tribe—but in person it made her seem humorless and forbidding.

"I think you two know each other," Harvey said to the priest.

Father Sikora answered by climbing to his feet and wrapping his arms around me in a big Polish bear hug. "How have you been, Anni?"

"Fine. How about you?"

"Can't complain." He held me out at arm's length, frowning as if I'd failed a lie detector test. "Why don't you come talk to me anymore?"

"You're a busy man." Though he was getting on in years, he had a punishing schedule. He attended to all the usual parochial duties of a busy urban parish and also oversaw the activities of the community center in the old rectory next to the church. Somehow during the past year he'd also found time for me, even though I wasn't a churchgoer. He was the only one I'd entrusted with my deepest feelings about Jim Tilquist's death.

"I'm never that busy," he said sternly. "Come see me."

"All right. What are you doing here, anyway?"

"Seeking free legal advice. I should be talking to the diocese's lawyers, but I thought these folks might give me answers I'd like better. Turns out, I'm wrong."

Harvey seemed to notice Thea's irritated look at last. "Anni has an interesting situation," he said. "And, speak of the devil, it involves Peter Vogel."

"And a client to whom I promised confidentiality," I added quickly. I wasn't worried about Father Sikora, but wanted to be sure everyone understood the need for discretion.

"Right. Twenty years ago Peter Vogel convicted an innocent man for a particularly brutal crime against Anni's client. We helped get the case overturned. Several other crimes may have been committed since, possibly by the person who attacked Anni's client. She's trying to find out if they're connected." He repressed a grin without much success. "Right now, Vogel has supporters who think he's going to defend us from the tidal wave of illegal immigrants. He might lose some of that support if it turns out he was wrong about this case."

A complicated eyebrow tango went on between Thea and Harvey. She gave me a thoughtful look. "How credible do you think it is?"

"I've only seen the initial police reports, but there are enough similarities I'd say it's worth investigating. I'd like to get whatever information I can about the original case."

"As it happens, Father Sikora has brought us a problem this morning that has similar political repercussions and in a tangential way, it involves Peter Vogel, too."

"Tangential?" Father Sikora snorted. "It's got his name all over it."

"What have you been up to now?" I asked the priest.

"A woman facing deportation came to St. Larry's early yesterday morning asking for sanctuary for herself and her baby."

"Sounds like Elvira Arellano," I said. A couple of years earlier, a woman who had been ordered to report for deportation had taken shelter with her eight-year-old son in a storefront Methodist church on Division Street, not far from my house. Authorities had avoided confrontation by ignoring her presence in the church, where she remained for over a year; it wasn't until she flew to Los Angeles to give a speech to immigration rights activists that she was seized by federal agents and deported.

"There are differences," Thea said dryly. "Arellano was an undocumented immigrant who was otherwise a law-abiding citizen. The woman who has asked for sanctuary at St. Larry's has permanent residency status, but because of a previous drug conviction she's subject to deportation. That's why we believe Peter Vogel made sure she was targeted in the raids yesterday. He wants her detained so he can use her as leverage."

"For what? Who are we talking about?" I asked.

"Her name is Esperanza Ruiz," Father Sikora said before Thea could answer. "The baby's name is Alexis."

"And the father is Diggy Salazar," Thea said, "the man recently arrested in the most notorious murder case in years. If the press find out his girlfriend is seeking sanctuary at St. Larry's, anti-immigrant activists will demand action, Peter Vogel will go on record as being outraged that a leftist priest is standing in the way of enforcing the law, and ICE will be forced to act, whether they want to or not."

"They're so good at acronyms," Father Sikora said. "Immigration and Customs Enforcement sounds dull and bureaucratic, but ICE—it's so northern and pure."

Thea drummed a pen on a yellow pad in front of her, impatient with his interruptions. "The last thing the feds want to do is break down the doors of a church to arrest a woman with a baby while the cameras are rolling, but they will if their hand is forced. And Vogel's in a position to force it."

"It doesn't make it any easier that Ruiz has gang connections and a criminal record," Harvey said. "She's hardly a poster child for the cause."

"She's not a poster, she's a person," the priest objected mildly. "She's being persecuted because she had a child with a man Peter Vogel is trying to convict of murder. He's pressuring Diggy to confess to something he says he didn't do."

"You're not taking on Salazar's defense, are you?" I asked Thea.

"We'll be providing some assistance, but Simone Landry's handling it."

That was good news for Salazar—and for those who attended the public gallery of the Cook County Courts as a hobby. Landry had been legendary among Cook County public defenders before she left to join the law faculty at Northwestern. The classroom didn't give her the same charge as the courtroom, so recently she'd started a free clinic in Little Village, representing indigent immigrants charged with criminal offenses but ineligible for public defenders. She was a short, fat, flamboyant force of manic energy, a highly intelligent and theatrical attorney who bedeviled and badgered her opponents mercilessly. I'd been on the wrong end of one of her cross-examinations once. It wasn't pleasant, but I had to admire her skill and her commitment to her clients.

"Wow. Landry versus Vogel," I said.

"King Kong meets Godzilla," said Harvey, obviously relishing the thought.

"More like David and Goliath," Father Sikora said dryly.

Thea nodded her agreement. "Landry has a lot of experience defending capital murder cases, but it's an uneven fight. Last time I talked to her, she was juggling twenty-six clients, two of them facing the death penalty. Her clinic employs a handful of investigators; compare that to the thousand or so detectives working for the CPD. But that's another matter. We need to advise you on the legal implications of offering sanctuary."

"You already have," Father Sikora said. "Turns out it's not a legal issue at all. Just a moral one."

"With significant repercussions for you and your congregation," Thea said. "I don't want you going into this blindly."

"I've done it before. It wasn't legal then, either." I had forgotten that Father Sikora had been involved in the Sanctuary Movement in the 1980s, when thousands of refugees from Central America sought asylum. Churches around the country had given them shelter, and St. Larry's had been one of them.

"Times have changed," Thea said, "and the laws haven't changed for the better. Noncitizens can be arrested or searched without a warrant. Any noncitizen convicted of a felony drug offense even as minor as the one on Ruiz's record, can be detained and deported without any chance of returning to this country in the future. And the Aguilar decision in 1989 established clearly that the free exercise clause isn't grounds for a legal claim for sanctuary."

"I understand." Father Sikora gripped the arms of his chair and hauled himself forward, as if he was getting ready to leave. "Thanks for your time. I'll do what I can for her."

Thea spoke with exaggerated patience. "What we're saying, Father, is that there's really nothing you *can* do for her."

"But at least there will be witnesses. She won't be spirited off to some detention center in Texas or Oklahoma without anyone but Vogel knowing where she's gone. It might end up on YouTube." He smiled with a glint of mischief in his eyes. "You know the slogan from the '68 convention, 'The whole world is watching?' "

"The whole world watched people's heads getting busted." Thea sighed, exasperated. "You could be arrested again."

The priest shrugged, acknowledging the possibility.

"What will you say to the archbishop?"

"That he'd better get ready for a press conference."

"You're a stubborn old man, you know that?"

"I do my best."

Thea pinched the skin at the top of her nose, closing her eyes as she rallied her energy. "All right. If you want to avoid violence, we'll need to plan carefully. You two start working on a strategy while I copy some files for Anni."

Thea opened the door to her office and waved me inside. The small room was lined with crowded bookshelves and mismatched filing cabinets. She sat at her desk, opened the laptop in front of her, tapped a few keys, and frowned at the screen. "Did you explain to Jill McKenzie that her assailant, whoever he is, is protected by the statute of limitations?" She started to hunt around her desk, stacking up files, opening drawers.

"Of course. I tried to talk her out of it, actually, but she feels responsible."

Thea looked up from the drawer she had been peering into. "Responsible? That's absurd. As soon as she knew the case had problems, she did everything she could to correct the record. If anyone's to blame, it's Peter Vogel. That was a very shoddy case he put together."

"It sounds like it. What are you looking for?"

She slammed the drawer shut, frustrated. "A disk for these files."

"Use this." I dug a flash drive out of my bag and handed it to her.

She inserted it into her computer and started copying files. "I can't give you anything that might be privileged, of course, but some of this should be helpful." She watched her screen for a moment, then added, "I have mixed feelings about what you're doing. Like Harvey, I'd like to see Peter Vogel held accountable for his mistakes. I also sympathize with Jill McKenzie's concern that other women could be at risk. But I have to consider the welfare of our client. Digging all this up won't benefit him. It may well harm him."

"Why? If the real Lincoln Park Rapist was identified—"

"What would Chase Taylor gain? He already has his freedom, for what it's worth. Convicting someone else won't make up for the two decades he spent in prison. He certainly doesn't need any more media attention. He has enough problems as it is."

Something in her face gave me a glimpse of insight. "You think he might actually have been guilty."

"That's neither here nor there. The burden of proof is on the state, and the only real evidence they had was an eyewitness identification made by a woman who was being treated for life-threatening injuries."

"She told me she could hardly see her attacker. The first thing he did was punch her so hard it broke her eye socket."

"There you go. Though even without impaired sight it's a questionable form of evidence. Eighty-five percent of wrongful convictions involve faulty eyewitness identification."

"But you had evidence. You dug up witnesses who put Taylor elsewhere."

"You'll find their statements in the files." She clicked a few keys, pulled out the flash drive and handed it back to me.

"Were they lying?"

"I have no reason to believe so."

I rolled my eyes at her lawyerly response. "But you think they may have been."

"Twenty years after the fact, it's hard to be certain of the accuracy of anyone's memories. All we could do is raise doubts. Which we did, successfully, with Jill McKenzie's help."

"If you think Taylor could have committed that crime—"

"What I *think* is that it would have been nice to have the DNA evidence the police conveniently lost, then maybe we could have cleared Taylor's name once and for all. All we had was a man who spent twenty years in prison on the basis of a coerced confession and next to no evidence." She sighed and pushed a strand of hair behind her ear. "Without absolute proof of his innocence, he'll be at risk as you rake all this up again. As it is, the police have been trying to pin something on him ever since he was released, and he's the kind of guy who makes it easy for them."

"What do you mean?"

"He has less than average intelligence, emotionally he's a mess, and he's easily manipulated by people who don't have his interests at heart. His family tries to keep him out of trouble, but it's too little, too late. It's just a matter of time before he'll get into something that'll send him back inside. Look, I need to get back to Father Sikora." She glanced at her watch and winced. "Try not to do too much damage."

EIGHT

spent the afternoon poring over the files Thea had copied for me: scans of police reports, witness statements, court documents, and investigators' notes.

The witness statements included ones from the five teens who had been running wild with Chase just hours before the rape. They had smoked crack for the first time that night; one of them had a cousin who had been visiting from New Jersey who had brought it with him. I could see from the records that crack cocaine was a novelty in Chicago in 1986, but it had made enough of an impact on the East Coast that *Time* magazine had named it the "issue of the year." Some news clippings about crack included among the files sounded eerily similar to the press reports on the Lincoln Park Rapist, laden with racial code words and simmering anxiety that young black men would burst out of the ghetto and wreak havoc.

The five witnesses were all residents of the Cabrini-Green public housing project, at the time a vast maze of high rises and row houses on the Near North Side. When the five boys were picked up they all were found to have cash, credit cards, and jewelry they'd taken in half a dozen muggings. Having criminal charges hanging over them provided a strong incentive to testify against Chase Taylor.

Twenty years later, investigators working for the Adelmans tracked down the five witnesses. One had died in a car accident, another had been shot and killed in a gang incident only months after Chase's conviction. The surviving three described the time they spent with detectives as a terrifying nightmare. They had been first threatened by the cops, then pressured to paint Chase as a violent predator. None of the witnesses now believed Chase was guilty of the rape. But in those days police were known to beat suspects, administer electric shocks, even suffocate them with plastic bags or typewriter covers to get a confession. All three wanted nothing more than to do whatever it took to get out of there.

One of the witnesses in particular insisted that Taylor had been the victim of a concerted effort to find a black man—any black man— guilty as quickly as possible. Raymond T. Ashe now worked for the Chicago Transit Authority as a bus driver. His name seemed familiar. I ran a search of the *Tribune* archives and found that he was a union official and a community organizer who had recently launched an unsuccessful bid for a seat on the City Council. He also appeared in every photo of the exonerated man that had run in the paper, a stately presence at Taylor's side, acting as a spokesman for the family. And there was one other news story, nearly ten years old now, a short item in the crime reports. After a long-standing dispute with a neighbor over a noisy dog, he had shot the animal. There was no follow-up story. I pulled up a database I used for background checks. No criminal history listed for Raymond Ashe. It seemed odd. With Chicago's strict handgun laws, I expected him to have been charged with a weapons offense.

There were other witness statements. The most damning had come from a man named Otis Parchmann, who lived in the same building as the accused man. He said he'd overheard Chase Taylor bragging about how he'd jumped a white woman who was walking her dog in the park. The story Parchmann told was suspiciously detailed, including Taylor's boast that he'd broken her jaw, cheekbone, and shoulder blade. In my experience, men rarely cataloged in detail the damage they did to women. More often, they would dismiss the effects of an assault, saying "gave her a little tune-up" or "smacked her a couple of times, is all." And the police had no corroboration for the conversation Parchmann claimed to have overheard. A good defense attorney would have demolished it, but Chase Taylor didn't have a good attorney.

His family would have qualified for a public defender, but they opted instead to scrape money together and borrow all they could from friends and relatives to hire a "real lawyer." It was a bad choice. Though the attorneys who worked for the public defender's office were overworked, they knew criminal law and court procedure inside out. Those who took on heater cases like the Lincoln Park Rapist were the most zealous. The lawyer the family hired was inexperienced in defending anything more serious than DUI charges and seemed unwilling or unable to put in the time and resources the case required. Again and again, as I read the transcript of the trial, I saw that he failed to raise objections or ask the right questions in cross-examinations.

Though the prosecution's case was not particularly strong, the records kept by Jerry Pozorski, the detective who led the investigation, were well-organized and informative. Skimming his case notes, I was impressed by the intelligence and single-minded determination they showed. He had organized a smart and agile investigation, made an arrest within forty-eight hours, then nailed down whatever evidence he could find like John Henry in a rail-driving competition. He must have been running on adrenaline; it looked as if there had been hardly any time for sleep in the two weeks following the crime. That hadn't stopped him from documenting each step meticulously. The handwritten notes he had submitted with the official record were thorough, with dates, times, and details all clearly indicated, though some entries were blotted with coffee stains.

After hours of reading and note taking, my eyelids felt gritty. I decided to take a break and see if I could find Pozorski and set up a meeting. Jill had mentioned he had retired to the suburbs; I had to stare at a map before I remembered she had mentioned Plainfield. There were three Pozorskis listed for Plainfield. Only one had the right first initial.

A woman answered the phone. When I asked to speak to Jerry, she said "Christ, is this about the leak again?"

"Uh, no. I have a problem with a furnace, but—"

"Look, there's no point in calling here." She sounded exasperated. "He's probably at the building on North Park. Try there."

It sounded as if Pozorski had gone into real estate in his retirement. "Sorry, but I don't know where that is."

"What, are you subletting? Someone should have explained all this. Corner of Eugenia and North Park. The red brick, on the north side. It's the basement apartment. Lean on the bell; he doesn't always hear it. Who gave you this number, anyway?"

"This was the only one I had."

"He hasn't lived here in two years. Do me a favor. Don't call here again."

checked the map and found that the apartment building she'd mentioned was in Lincoln Park. Apparently, when he went into real estate, he chose the high end. I drove there and spotted the building, a handsome 1920s-era block with bay windows and ornate brickwork. It took ten minutes to find a parking place among all the cars that were far flashier than my battered Corolla. When I finally made my way to the front door of the building, a young woman was unlocking it to go inside. I explained I was looking for Jerry Pozorski and she pointed to the bank of doorbells. "Try the one for the manager."

I pushed it and waited. She went inside and got out her mail, giving me a curious glance through the glass front door. I pushed again and left my finger on it for a few seconds, following the advice of the cranky woman on the phone. The girl pulled the door open. "Any luck?"

"He doesn't always hear the bell."

"You know Jerry?"

"He's a friend of a friend."

"You can try knocking on his door if you want. It's in the basement. Down those stairs, first one on the left. Only he might be . . ." I waited for her to finish the sentence, but she just shrugged. "Good luck."

"Thanks." I opened the door she had pointed out and switched on the light, a feeble low-wattage bulb that didn't penetrate very far into the basement. At the bottom of the flight of stairs there were storage closets and signs pointing to a laundry room. I knocked on the door that had "Manager" stenciled on it and waited. Just as I was about to give up, I heard a thump and a muttering voice before the door opened.

He was unshaven and bleary-eyed, dressed in wrinkled chinos and a faded Cubs sweatshirt. His gray hair was tangled and stood up in uneven wisps. The room smelled of stale food and unwashed clothes.

"I'm looking for Jerry Pozorski."

"Yeah? Whatcha want?"

"I'm sorry. Did I wake you up?"

"If you're looking to rent, call the number on the sign outside," he said. A calico cat crept past his legs to sniff the air in the corridor. He nudged it back with a foot. His sock had a gaping hole in the heel.

"I'm not looking for an apartment. I need to ask you about one of your cases." I handed him one of my cards. "My client suggested I talk to you. Could I come in?"

He blinked at my card. Behind his legs I saw a tabby kitten with big ears peeking at me. "What client?" he asked. This time I caught the smell of bourbon on his breath.

"Jill McKenzie. You investigated an assault against her in 1986. I've been going through your case files; you did a good job. But as you know, the case has been thrown out, and there have been more recent assaults that may be related. It would be very helpful if I could talk to you."

He bent to scoop up the calico as it started to wander into the hallway, then turned unsteadily and walked into his apartment, the tabby kitten scampering in front of him. I started to follow him, catching a glimpse of a recliner and a coffee table crowded with bottles and fast food containers, but had to step back quickly to avoid getting hit by the door as he slammed it behind him.

I knocked again, but the only response I got was the sound of a bolt being fastened.

NINE

As I emerged from the basement, the girl I'd seen earlier was coming down the hallway with a sack of laundry. "Any luck with Jerry?"

"Not really. He wasn't in a mood to talk."

She nodded knowingly. "That happens a lot. I had this leaky faucet once? I went down there to ask him about it, but he was totally hammered. So, whatever. Guess I'll just have to put up with a dripping faucet, right? Next day, he came up and fixed it. He was all quiet and polite, like nothing had happened. I didn't say anything, but I kinda hope I never have a real emergency, you know? 'Cause half the time he's wasted."

It was getting dark as I walked to my car. I'd known police officers who had a hard time with retirement, dealing with the yawning emptiness of a day with nobody to chase down, no court appearances to prep. Twenty-year marriages fell apart under the pressure of too much time together, and often the very people who talked most enthusiastically about what they'd do with their freedom were the ones who would be waiting in the bar when the guys stopped off for a drink after the second watch. The contrast between the detective who'd written the reports in the case file and the current reality was stark. On an impulse I pulled out my cell phone.

"Hey, Dugan. You up for that dinner?"

"Damn. I'm on my way to Wisconsin for my nephew's wedding.

Attendance is required. I'd blow it off and meet you somewhere, but then they'd have to kill me."

"Well, we don't want that," I said lightly, but I felt a sharp pang of disappointment.

"Thought I'd be working this weekend, actually. All the political fallout after those raids, there's a lot of pressure to make progress on the Kathy Miller case. Like, if we can prove Diggy Salazar's a killer, it will somehow cancel out that mess."

"My house got raided."

"*Your* house? Why?"

"They had a list that included one of my tenants who moved out over a year ago. He wasn't a criminal, anyway."

"Couldn't be worse timing for us. We're trying to get people in the community to come forward, and now—forget it."

"Did that guy you were going to talk to give you anything?"

"Guy? . . . Oh, the drug arrest the other night. No, he was just trying to get out of a crack. Waste of time. My boss told me to take the weekend off. Has to be my mom's influence. She's got connections everywhere." Dugan came from a large family, and all of his siblings worked in law enforcement, as had their father before them. His mother had been opposed to Dugan's transfer to the dangerous West Side from his safer gig at headquarters. He attributed every move that took him out of harm's way to her influence.

"Say, those plants look nice," I said, realizing I hadn't thanked him yet.

"Figured you could use something to brighten the place up. Just throw a sheet over them when there's a frost predicted, and they should last for a while. Did you get a new lock for that gate yet?"

"No, mother. I'll do it this weekend."

"What about your furnace? You said you might have a chance to replace it."

"That job came through. I've been working on it all day, in fact.

Say, there is one thing I want to ask you. Do you know a retired detective named Jerry Pozorski?"

He hesitated before answering. "What about him?"

"He's working as an apartment manager up in Lincoln Park."

"Yeah." His tone had grown reserved.

"So, I just went to see him about something. He's not in very good shape."

"What do you mean?"

"Looks like he's been hitting the bottle pretty hard."

Dugan's tone had definitely shifted now, into icy anger. "The man put in over thirty years of honorable service. If Thea Adelman has some kind of beef with him—"

"No. This is nothing to do with Thea." I was baffled by the turn the conversation had taken.

"He's one of the best detectives I ever worked with, okay? He didn't do anything wrong, except maybe care too much. If this is part of some civil rights crusade of yours, you're going after the wrong guy."

"Dugan, I have no idea what you're talking about."

"This isn't about Dante Russo?"

"I don't even know who that is."

He sighed. I waited. "Around five years ago, Jerry was downstairs at Belmont, talking to the watch commander," Dugan finally said. "This guy came in, Dante Russo. An EDP. We'd had problems with him before. Mostly D and D, but sometimes his parents asked for assistance when he was delusional and doing weird shit, which happened a lot."

I had a sudden jolt of memory. "Was this the guy with the machete?"

"That's the one."

EDP was cop-speak for "emotionally disturbed person." I remembered hearing the news and thinking, as every cop must have, *that could have been me*. A man had burst through the doors at Area 3

Headquarters on Belmont. He was holding a machete and yelling something that made no sense. A detective tried to talk him down, but it didn't work. When the man started swinging the blade, the detective shot him four times in the chest.

"So it was Pozorski who put him down?"

"He took it hard," Dugan said. "Retired a few months later. I thought maybe you were going after him for being, you know . . . insensitive to the mentally ill or something."

"No. Christ, it worries me one of my clients' kids will get into a situation like that. But under the circumstances—he didn't have a choice."

"I haven't talked to him in ages. I should go out to Plainfield one of these days, see how he's doing."

"He's not there. I talked to somebody, his wife probably. The phone's still listed in his name, but she told me he hasn't lived there for two years."

"Shit. I didn't know."

"He lives in the basement of that building in Lincoln Park with some cats."

"Oh, Christ."

"What?"

"*Two years*, you said? That's when he moved out?"

"Yeah."

"One of his cases got thrown out by a judge two years ago. The Lincoln Park Rapist."

My stomach lurched. I hadn't made the connection. "That was a big case," I said cautiously.

"Before my time, but I heard stories about how hard he worked to put that one down. He didn't talk much about it, but I know he really felt for that woman who was attacked. He has two daughters himself. Come to think of it, it was your pal Adelman who went to court to get Taylor out of jail."

"Before my time," I echoed. It felt wrong, not telling Dugan I was working on that case, but I had promised Jill I would protect her privacy.

"It's got to hurt when a case you put your heart and soul into gets overturned. All so a scumbag like Chase Taylor can walk. Tell you what, if you wanted evidence that prison doesn't work as a deterrent, he could be exhibit A. After twenty years in the slammer, you'd think he'd bother to keep his nose clean, but not him. He's got to keep up with his Four Corner friends."

"He's in a gang?"

"He wants to be, but he's so stupid it's bad for business. In fact, the only reason he hasn't been rearrested is that his potential business partners can't trust him to make correct change. When it hit the news that Taylor was getting out, I called Jerry to say . . . I don't know, just to show support, but he wasn't home. I talked to Maureen, his wife. She didn't say anything about them having problems. He might have already moved out by then. *Shit.*"

"I'm sorry to dump this on you when you're heading to a family thing."

"No, that's . . ." His voice trailed off for a moment, preoccupied. "Can you give me his address, though?"

"Sure. I think he could use a friend." I gave him the cross streets and described the building.

"I'll check on him when I get back to town. What case were you asking him about?"

"An old ag assault that might be connected to something more recent," I said vaguely, feeling like a jerk.

"For your new client, huh? Well, I'd better make time or I'll be late for the groom's dinner and my mother will claim justifiable homicide."

We said good-bye. I got into my car and stuck the key in the ignition, but didn't turn it. I thought about going back to my empty apartment; I thought about taking a run, doing something physical to get some distance from the image of a good cop turned into a lonely, shambling drunk. But the streets were filling with evening shadows, and I felt that weird, indefinite sense of vulnerability again.

I pulled my phone back out of my bag, called my brother, Martin, and told him I'd be joining him for dinner.

TEN

Martin worked as a lab technician at Stony Cliff College, where our grandfather had taught for four decades. He was also the caretaker for the science building and, as a perk of the job, had a small apartment in the basement. Martin's studio was clean and neat, with potted cactus plants lined up on the windowsills, a small collection of physics textbooks with their spines neatly aligned, the Berber carpet precisely parallel to the couch, everything in its place. He would have been disturbed by the disorder I'd just come from. It wasn't just that the dirty glasses and trash were distasteful, the chaos it represented would have been physically painful to him.

We ate in the student union, then went back to his apartment, where Martin switched on his laptop computer and showed me the latest photos he'd uploaded to a photo-sharing site. I sat beside him and typed in tags for each photo, since words were not Martin's forte. "That's the hallway in the Fine Arts building, right? I like the way those doors line up." I tagged the picture with relevant terms. "That person way at the end of the hall—he looks kind of lonely." Martin nodded. I added the tag "lonely" and we moved on to the next picture.

He'd grown interested in photography during the past year, so I'd given him a good digital camera for his birthday. He'd started by taking pictures at the lab—close-ups of equipment and geometric images of computer boards. He'd since branched out, looking for images around the campus and town that offered unusual shapes or satisfying patterns. Recently, a student showed him how to upload pictures to Flickr, and it had opened a new world to him. He'd developed a cadre of "friends" around the world who left comments on his pictures.

We finished up and I left close to 8:00 P.M., just as one of his favorite History Channel shows was coming on. I drove out of the parking lot, planning to head back to the city, but I found myself turning down a familiar street instead, as if the past had laid down tracks that my car had no choice but to follow. My tires crunched on leaves as I pulled up outside a modest frame house.

Martin and I had lived nearby in our grandfather's small bungalow. It was a funny little house, with only one bathroom and not enough closets, but I loved my bedroom, tucked up under the eaves. It was the first time in my life that I'd had a room all to myself, my private sanctuary. I pictured Golly's study, the shelves crowded with books, a threadbare oriental carpet on the floor, a blue haze of cigarette smoke over his head as he worked among a clutter of papers and coffee cups. His desk was the only thing I still had to remember him by. I'd sold the property for an absurd amount of money after our grandfather's death and used it to set up a trust for Martin. The new owners liked the location, but not the inconvenient little house; they tore it down to build a bloated McMansion in its place. Ever since, I avoided driving down our old street.

But the Tilquist's house, just around the corner, hadn't changed in all these years. Nancy had bought it when she was a young single mother, recently arrived from England and just starting her teaching career. Stony Cliff hadn't yet become the exclusive North Shore address it was now. I often babysat Sophie for Nancy, and before long there was a path beaten between our backyards. I was the one who introduced Nancy to Jim and schemed to bring them together, designing the perfect family. And it was, for a while.

Coming here always felt like coming home, but it was a complicated homecoming these days. Jim had been my mentor, my best friend, my role model. But just before he died I had learned things about him that left me hurt and confused. And I still missed him so badly it felt like the deep bruise that was left after a bullet went through him and struck my Kevlar vest. A constant ache, just over my heart.

I realized Nancy had come out onto the front porch and was hugging herself for warmth as she peered at me. "Everything all right?" she asked as I climbed out of the car.

"Yeah, I just . . . I dropped my keys." I held them up to show that I'd found them, feeling a familiar pang of guilt for lying to her.

"I've just put Lucy to bed. Can you come in for a cup of tea?"

"Sure. I can't stay long, though."

I got mugs out of the cupboard while she rinsed out the teapot. Sophie and Alice were out with friends, she told me. Alice was busy with rehearsals for the school play. Sophie was doing well, working part-time and finishing her high school requirements in an alternative program. If all went well, if her meds kept working and she stayed out of trouble, she could start college next year. "Thank goodness we have tuition benefits," Nancy said. "I'm not sure what I'd do for money otherwise. I could sell the house, I suppose." She found a tin of cookies and put some on a plate. She turned to set them on the table and must have seen something in my expression because she added hastily, "Don't worry. I'm not planning to."

"Good."

"I couldn't uproot the children from their schools, their friends. They've had enough to deal with in the past year. How have you been lately? We haven't seen you in a while."

"I've been busy with work."

"Oh, that reminds me. A woman I know asked for your contact information last week. She's a sociologist, teaches at St. Vincent's in Iowa. Did she get in touch?"

"She called a couple of days ago," I said evasively. "Had a question about some research she's doing."

"How disappointing. I thought I might be bringing you some business."

"I'm pretty booked up at the moment, anyway."

"That's good, I suppose." She looked at me, hesitating.

"What?"

"Nothing. Only you look worn out. Maybe you're working too hard."

"No. Work's not a problem. I just haven't been sleeping well." I filled my mug, added some milk and watched it swirl through the dark liquid. She kept her eyes on me, gently probing for more. "I thought . . . It's been over a year. I thought it would get easier. But it doesn't."

"I know what you mean. Sometimes I can forget, for a bit. And then, *wham!* Ambushed by something trivial, out of the blue. I had to leave a committee meeting the other day. I was flipping through a file of papers and found an old shopping list mixed in among them. In Jim's handwriting. Potatoes, bread, milk. And for a moment it felt as if he was still here, it all had been some horrible mistake. Luckily, I made it to the ladies' before I started bawling."

"It must be much worse for you."

"I don't know. You'd known him most of your life, and he had a lot to do with who you are." She gave me a tentative smile. "I see a lot of him in you, actually. But we were so different, and we'd been arguing so much at the end, I thought we were headed for a separation. We'd somehow lost the knack of talking honestly with each other. Which . . . I don't think I ever thanked you properly. If you hadn't—" She broke off and pinched her nose, took a breath, and tried again. "It seems so stupid, now, arguing about his work. The thing is, if we hadn't made it up before, before . . . oh, damn." She reached for a box of tissues, exasperated with herself. "What I'm trying to say is I'm grateful you got us back together before it was too late. Because otherwise, I'd feel even worse."

I felt words I could never say well up in my throat, burning as I held them back. I closed my eyes tight, too, as if I had to try and dam my tears up in case all the regrets I felt escaped with them, but some leaked out anyway, hot on my cheeks. I felt Nancy's hand on mine, a warm, forgiving pressure. After a while, I blinked and sniffed. "Sorry."

She pulled out a tissue for me. "Here, blow," she ordered, and I laughed because it was exactly what I'd heard her say to her girls when their noses were stopped up like mine.

We talked for a while longer about the girls, about Martin, about safe things, and then I left for home. I had just put my bag down on the kitchen table when I heard my cell phone ring. I dug it out. "Did you know about this?" an angry voice demanded.

"Hello?"

"That crazy priest! Turn on your TV. I don't believe this shit."

By then, I had identified the growly voice with extra-strength Chicago vowels: Az Abkerian, the *Chicago Tribune* reporter. "Which channel?"

"Any of the affiliates. They're all leading with it."

I switched on my television and saw a reporter standing in front of the familiar façade of St. Larry's. The steps were crowded with parishioners holding candles. More were joining them, making the steps look like a rack of flickering votive candles. Their faces glowed with reflected light as they shielded their flames with cupped hands.

Blue and red lights pulsed against the stone columns behind them, thrown by the light bars of nearby squad cars. Thea and Harvey stood in the center of the crowd beside Father Sikora. Her brown skin and straight black hair made her blend into the mostly Latino crowd, but Harvey, towering over his neighbors and trying to diminish his height by slumping his shoulders, looked pallid and nerdy. The reporter was speaking to the camera, but I couldn't concentrate on what she was saying; Az was still giving me an earful. "You knew about this, and you didn't tell me? What kind of friend are you?"

"I think you're confusing 'source' with 'friend,' Az. And anyway, what makes you think I knew about this?"

"It's in your neighborhood, you're tight with that commie priest, and you work for Thea Adelman. What can you give me about this?"

"For background, not for attribution, okay? No direct quotes." It wouldn't do Father Sikora any good to have my name associated with his latest project, given my touchy relations with law enforcement.

"Sure, whatever. Just cough it up."

"Esperanza Ruiz and her baby, Alexis, went to the church sometime yesterday and asked for sanctuary. DHS has a deportation order out on her. She's Diggy Salazar's girlfriend, and she has a green card, but she also has a record, some kind of drug offense. She may have gang connections." As I spoke, I was staring at the television. A restless crowd was gathering and a shoving match erupted. Two uniformed officers waded in to break it up. "From what I hear," I added, "Peter Vogel wants her detained so he can ratchet up the pressure on Diggy. You might want to talk to his lawyer, Simone Landry."

"Like that wouldn't occur to me. I already have all this shit. Except for the drug offense and the gang angle. Which gang?"

"I don't know. It's just a rumor."

"What's the drug charge?"

"Must be a felony if it makes her deportable, but I don't know the details."

"Is this—ah, fuck me! There's a stringer for *The New York Times* up there on the steps with Sikora. Doesn't that priest have any hometown loyalty? I gotta go."

I put my phone down and turned up the television volume. ". . . the growing crowd. It looks as if Father Sikora is about to make a statement."

The camera focused on the priest as he walked with his rolling gait to a makeshift podium with a bristling fringe of microphones. He opened his mouth to speak, then closed it as flashes went off like a burst of fireworks. He waited for them to subside.

"Good evening," he said in a low-key conversational tone. "Esperanza Ruiz has asked if she and her little girl, Alexis, could take shelter at our church. We have agreed to provide them a place to stay for as long as we can. The Bible tells us that when we offer hospitality to strangers, we may entertain angels unaware." He grinned. "Technically speaking, little Alexis isn't an angel, but she's cute as a button." He grew sober and coughed. "Here at St. Larry's we try to turn our principles into action. We have a food shelf for the hungry, we provide clothing for the poor, we help families find shelter. In years past, we were a place of refuge for victims of violence in Central America. Today, we offer sanctuary to two victims of our country's immigration policies. This isn't about politics. This is a matter of faith." He paused. When he spoke again his voice was deeper, more resonant. " 'For I was hungry and you gave me food; I was thirsty and you gave me drink. I was a stranger and you welcomed me.' So we welcome Esperanza and her baby. I'll answer a few questions."

The crowd of reporters in front of him erupted into a chaotic babble. Father Sikora leaned forward to pick out the words of one of the speakers, then said, "No, that is incorrect. Esperanza is not an illegal alien. She has a green card." There was another burst of incomprehensible clamor. "Yes, she has been told by the Department of Homeland Security to report to them." He listened, head cocked. "I don't know the answer to that. You'll have to ask them." Another explosion of questions. "That's right, Digoberto Salazar is the child's father. I can't answer any questions about him because I've never met him." He paused to listen to the cacophony. "We'll cross that bridge when we get to it." He pointed to someone in the crowd and listened intently, then answered the question in Spanish. I had to concentrate to make out what he was saying. "She's doing as well as can be expected. She's worried about being separated from her baby. Sometimes *la migra* sends detainees to faraway states, and that's a hardship for families. We hope that won't happen, but we don't know."

He stepped away from the microphones as the reporters competed to outshout one another. Someone among the people on the steps started to sing in a warbling voice, and others joined in. It was an iconic tune, "We Shall Overcome," but the words were sung in Spanish. Just as their voices were rising—"*O, en mi corazón*"—some of the singers broke off and ducked, raising their arms protectively. A moment later, Father Sikora's head jerked back. He took a handkerchief out of his pocket and wiped a trickle of blood off his forehead, his slightly out-of-tune voice carrying through as the song faltered, until the other voices found the chorus again.

The camera cut to the rowdy crowd, where uniformed police were bent over a man they had tackled, then swung back toward the nervous-looking reporter. "To recap, a woman with a connection to accused murderer Digoberto Salazar has taken sanctuary at St. Lawrence Catholic Church in the largely Hispanic Humboldt Park neighborhood. It appears that Homeland Security has issued a deportation order for this woman. The police are dispersing the crowd that has formed here." She paused as a police bullhorn blared out an order. "As you can see, the situation is volatile, but the police are out in force and are, at this very moment, clearing the street. We'll be following this story as it develops. Live from the West Side—"

I didn't have any desire to walk the four blocks to the church to join in the fray. Instead, I watched the rest of the broadcast while simultaneously scanning news sites on-line. A number of blogs sympathetic to immigrant causes had already posted well-developed commentary, making me think Thea had primed them with advance information. Anti-immigration blogs were also picking up the story, voicing outrage that a church would help a murderer's family evade a legal order. Angry comments were popping up on news sites, many of them filled with bigoted slurs and suggestions that Catholics should concentrate on punishing their pedophile priests instead of sheltering criminals. I cruised around blogs a bit longer, then shut my computer off, unsettled by the depth of anger being expressed.

It was harder to shut my thoughts off. There were voices calling out in the street. Sometimes blue flashing lights washed over my walls as squad cars prowled by. It began to grow calmer after midnight, but I couldn't shake the sense that the neighborhood was simmering on the edge of violence.

With a glass of wine and a book, I tried to shift gears, but my mind kept drifting to other things—to Father Sikora wiping blood off his face, to Nancy Tilquist trying to smile as her eyes brimmed with tears, to Jerry Pozorski and his cats in that dark, cramped apartment. My thoughts kept circling back nervously to the inadequate lock on my gate. I hadn't paid much attention to the note Dugan had left about it, but since he'd mentioned it again during our phone conversation earlier in the day, it nagged at me, like an annoying splinter. Once, hearing a noise outside, I went out on my back porch to see if someone was in the yard, but I saw no one there.

Around 2:00 A.M. I finally went to bed. Though I usually turned the porch light off, I left it on. The yellow light that leaked in through the blinds cast stripes that fanned out across the wall over my head. It was a long time before I was able to drift off into a restless slumber.

ELEVEN

woke early from a dream that always left my chest feeling bruised with sorrow. It was as familiar as an old song, a ballad with words I could never quite grasp, one that ended with plain pine boxes in a lonely trench. It was a version of a story I'd pieced together with Jim Tilquist's help years ago when he helped me find out what had happened to my mother. Now that I'd lost him, too, the dream carried a doubled load of grief.

I needed to run.

I dressed, splashed water on my face, pulled on my sneakers and a hoodie. Rather than take my usual route, I jogged down the sidewalk toward St. Larry's. Though it would be some time before the sun would peek over the eastern edge of Lake Michigan, the sky was filled with a faint pearly light. A bedraggled group of people was camped out on the front steps of the church. A couple had sleeping bags pulled around their shoulders for warmth as they drank from steaming mugs. One of them told me they would hold a vigil there so long as Esperanza and her baby were inside. I could sign up for a shift if I wanted.

"What will you do if ICE agents come for her?" I asked.

They looked at each other and shrugged. "We won't try to stop them."

"But we'll get it on record." A young woman lifted a camera from her lap to show me. Her fingers looked red and chapped from the cold.

Lights glowed in the windows of the old rectory next door, which had been converted into a community center. I went inside and found a group of women chatting in the kitchen. They broke off, startled, when I appeared at the door, but one of them knew me from my volunteer work with their homeless outreach program and offered me a cup of coffee. I took it, knowing it would be a cut above what you usually got out of church urns, the beans purchased from a sister parish in Guatemala. So far, they told me, everything was quiet. The office behind the sacristy had been furnished with a crib and mattress from the stock of furniture they stored in the basement for needy families; toys and clothes had arrived by the boxful from sympathetic families. They hoped I didn't want to talk to Father Sikora. He had two baptisms that day, and a steady stream of appointments, not to mention the 7:00 P.M. mass to prepare for. They wanted to let him sleep for as long as possible. He wasn't getting any younger, after all.

As we chatted, their eyes were drawn to the hallway behind me. I turned and saw a teenager with a baby on her hip. The baby had that red-eyed zombie look children get when they've been awake too long; the teen looked tired and sullen. She had the naturally full, pouty lips that people tried to achieve with Botox injections, and wore a low-cut T-shirt over tight jeans. Her long straight hair was dyed a color that looked metallic and unnatural. "Can somebody take Alexis for a while? She kept me awake all night, I swear."

None of the women moved for a moment; then one of them held out her arms. The baby put up a token resistance, mewing a weary protest before she nestled into the woman's cushiony chest, sucking sleepily on her fist. "You shouldn't leave the church, Esperanza," the woman scolded.

"Ah," the girl waved a hand dismissively. "I used the side door. Nobody saw me. Besides, there ain't any cops around." She went over to the refrigerator and peered inside. "What are you, a reporter?" she asked me.

"A cop." She looked around at me. "At least I used to be."

"Yeah? What happened, they kick you out for being too short?"

I couldn't help smiling. Considering she was facing jail and deportation, she seemed amazingly self-assured. "No, I quit. Now I'm an investigator for Thea and Harvey Adelman."

"You should investigate who really killed that Miller woman, 'cause it wasn't Diggy."

"You sound awfully sure of that."

"'Course I'm sure. Sheesh, who buys the groceries around here? No Diet Coke." She sighed and pulled out a liter bottle of generic cola. "Look, they say he killed her for her car, right? But that's crazy. She drove an ugly two-year-old Chevy. It was *beige*. If he was going to kill someone for a car, it would have to be something really nice, you know?"

"He was fleeing an armed robbery."

"'Fleeing'?" She giggled. "Shit, you still sound like a cop. Nobody talks like that."

"What I mean is, he couldn't afford to be picky."

"Don't matter. Diggy would never do that to a girl," she said firmly. "He would have just took it from her, she wouldn't have got hurt. Want to know what this is really about? That state's attorney wants to be governor, so he arrested a Mexican."

She set the bottle on the counter and started opening cupboards, banging doors shut until she saw what she was looking for. She had to stand on her toes since she was, if anything, even shorter than I was. Her shirt rode up and I noticed a tattoo on her brown skin just under her belly button, words in gothic script, but I couldn't make out what they said. She must have noticed me looking at it, because when she finally retrieved the plastic cup she was reaching for she turned and lifted her shirt up with one finger, tilting her hip provocatively: NOTHING TO LOSE.

"Nice tat," I said.

"You should see the one on my ass." She picked up the bottle, swinging it between two knuckles as she headed for the door. "I'm gonna get some sleep," she said over her shoulder.

The women exchanged looks. "That one's going to be on the news," one of them muttered. "You'd think she'd have some sympathy for that poor girl, but all she does is joke around."

"She acts tough," another one said. "But she's scared. Here, let me hold that baby."

After my run, I showered and put on fresh clothes. I slipped my cell phone in my pocket, packed up the case files and my laptop, and headed down the back stairs. A light was on in the kitchen of the first-floor flat. I tapped on the window and waved to Adam, who was sleepily filling a bottle for the baby. He gave me a grin and waved back.

I went to Café Colao on Division Street, where I ordered a cup of strong Puerto Rican coffee and a guava pastry still warm from the oven, then took a corner table and got to work. I took notes and made a spreadsheet of similarities in the seven cases. All of the attacks had occurred between 5:00 and 7:00 A.M. and were against young women going to or coming from work, walking the dog, or starting what seemed like an ordinary day. All the victims reported that their attacker threatened them with a knife, but only two were actually slashed. I used the café's Wi-Fi to pull up a map of the city and mark the sites of the attacks. All fell within a five-mile radius, and each of the crimes happened in or within a few blocks of city parks.

Several mugs of coffee later, I had extracted all the information I was going to get out of the reports. I leafed through them again before putting them away, my eyes drawn to the blacked-out names. I hadn't heard back from the woman Olivia Jackson was going to find for me, but she wasn't my only route to the victims. I'd worked with rape-victim advocates based in hospitals and staff at crisis intervention programs. Some of the women whose names were under black ink might have been referred to their services. If I could identify even one or two linked cases that were fresh enough to fall within the statute of limitations—

My cell phone rang. It was Adam Tate. "Sorry to bug you, but are you planning to be home anytime soon? Some kids are here, waiting for you."

"Kids?"

"Three black kids, sitting on the front steps. Two of them are little guys. One of them is older, a girl. Maybe twelve? Beaded hair, pretty face, big teeth like a gopher. I said they could wait inside if they wanted, but she said no."

"Did she say what it was about?"

"She wouldn't say much of anything. Thing is, they've been there twenty minutes. They look pretty cold sitting out there."

Adam was intelligent in his own way, but usually unobservant when it came to practical matters. The children would have had to be nearly frostbitten for him to notice. I told him I'd be there in a few minutes.

TWELVE

The girl sitting on my front steps was the one who had been helping in Olivia's kitchen the other day. Small boys sat on either side of her. One had his head burrowed turtlelike into his coat and his arms pulled inside so the empty sleeves dangled loosely. The other one was restless, jumping up and being pulled back down by his sister. As I approached he was hollering and trying to wriggle away from her grip.

"Hello, there," I called out.

"Hey, Miz Koskinen," the girl said, standing up and giving me a wide smile before remembering to pull her lip down to hide her oversized teeth. She was wearing a faded floral dress and an outsized windbreaker too thin for the weather. "Don't know if you remember me. I'm Aisha LeTorneau."

"Of course. We met at Olivia Jackson's house."

"These are my brothers, Rashid and Omar."

"How you doing?" Omar said politely, his voice muffled inside his coat as he worked his arms into his sleeves. When his head poked out, I realized he was older than I had originally thought, probably eight or nine, though small for his age. Rashid had retreated behind his sister's legs, peering at me warily. He looked about four years old, though he had the random kinetic energy of a younger child.

"I was wondering if I could talk to you about something," Aisha asked.

"Sure. Let's go inside, though. It's pretty cold out here."

"I don't want to put you to no trouble," she said.

"We want to go *in*," Omar corrected her under his breath. "My butt's frozen."

"How about some hot cocoa. That sound good?" I unlocked the gate and herded them through the gangway. Rashid, the smaller boy, rushed ahead when he saw the cat, who flattened himself in a panic, then scurried in his lopsided way into the undergrowth to hide. Rashid tried to follow, thrashing his way through a bed of flower stalks until Aisha scooped him up in her arms.

"He only got three legs!" Rashid squealed.

"And he still got away from you," his brother said scornfully.

"Hush, you two," the girl said. She carried Rashid up the steps and sat in a chair at the kitchen table, holding him in her lap as he squirmed. "I apologize. He's kind of excited, taking the bus and all."

"How did you know where I live?" I asked, curious. She'd seen my business card, but it didn't have my home address on it.

"Olivia mentioned you lived near here. I just kind of asked around."

"We walked for, like, a hundred miles," Omar said—just a statement, not a complaint. As he spoke, I noticed he was staring behind me at a basket of fruit.

"Want a banana?" I asked.

He nodded shyly. His little brother started to whine and kick his heels against his sister's shins, so I pulled one off from the bunch for him, too. Aisha declined, looking embarrassed. Omar peeled one for Rashid before starting on his own, wolfing it down with quiet intensity. I remembered what Olivia had told me: she gave Aisha a job so she could take leftover food home. These kids were hungry.

I put a pan of milk on the stove for cocoa and pulled bread and cheese from the fridge. "It's getting close to lunchtime, so I'm making sandwiches. Hope you like grilled cheese."

"I like it," Omar said.

"You live in Olivia's neighborhood, right? I used to work near there, at Harrison Headquarters."

"You a cop?" Omar squinted at me, suspecting a trick.

"Not anymore."

"What, you get fired?"

"Omar," Aisha hissed. "Don't be saying rude things."

"I wasn't fired, I just wasn't getting along with people I worked with, so I changed jobs." I heated a pan for the sandwiches, then dropped some chunks of Ybarra chocolate into the hot milk. "Speaking of jobs, I need someone to stir the cocoa while I grill the sandwiches. Be careful. I don't want you burning yourself."

I pulled a stool over to the stove for Omar to stand on and showed him how to roll the handle of the wooden *molinillo* whisk between his palms to make the cocoa frothy as I toasted the sandwiches. I kept an eye on him as I sliced some apples, then set the food on the table and poured the cocoa into mugs. Omar had whisked with enthusiasm and the cocoa was nicely frothy. The three of them ate quickly, hardly taking time to breathe between bites.

Rashid's eyes started to droop shut as he chewed sleepily on the last apple slice. Aisha put him down for a nap on the couch as Omar and I washed up. Then I settled Omar at my desk with the laptop, showing him a game to keep him occupied so that Aisha and I would finally have a chance to talk.

She waited politely, looking at framed photos hanging on the wall. "That's my mother," I told her. "The other photo is me with my brother and our grandfather. I had just graduated from the Academy. My hat was way too big." She smiled, dimples forming beside her tightly closed mouth. We sat at the kitchen table. "So, what did you want to talk about?"

"Olivia said you was wanting to talk with a woman who got

attacked in the park. I don't know that lady, but I know somebody else got attacked near there."

"Who is that?"

Her hands were clasped in front of her, fingers tightly intertwined. "My sister, Amira. It was just like that woman who got her dog killed, only Amira was over by the railroad tracks and she didn't have no dog with her. But she got messed with the same way. You know. Took advantage of."

Aisha's eyes slid away from mine as she spoke. I looked over at Omar. He seemed absorbed in his game.

"When did this happen?"

"Last April."

"How old is your sister?"

"Seventeen. She was sixteen when it happened. A man who works for the railroad saw her laying in the weeds by the tracks, called a ambulance. She was beat up real bad. She told the police this man came up behind her when she was walking home from a party, but they didn't believe her 'cause her boyfriend beat on her before. He's in prison now, but not for that."

"The railroad tracks. Do you mean the Metra line that runs near the conservatory?"

"That's right. By Hamlin Avenue."

Only a block or two from Garfield Park, then. It fit the pattern of the other rapes. "Do you think she might be willing to talk to me about this?"

"Maybe, but I don't know where she's at right now. She was living with her boyfriend, but after the police said he was the one messed her up, he got mad and kicked her out. She stayed with a girlfriend for a while, but that didn't work out. I don't know where she lives these days." Aisha turned to fumble in the pockets of her windbreaker hanging on the back of her chair. "This picture was from when she was fifteen. She got it done professional."

She handed me a studio picture in a cardboard frame. The girl in the photo looked a lot like Aisha, with the same Ashanti face and slanted doelike eyes, but instead of braids, she had relaxed hair pinned up in a twist and wore a skimpy satin blouse with a plunging neckline that would have shown cleavage if she'd had any. Her head was turned to one side to give the camera a knowing, sophisticated smile, her lips pursed in invitation.

"Did your sister tell you anything about the man who attacked her? How old he was, what he looked like?"

Aisha shook her head. "She didn't like talking about it."

"How long has it been since you've seen her?"

"She came by on Omar's birthday, end of July. I ain't seen her since then."

"And she hasn't called?"

"We don't got a phone."

I studied her. She was staring at her hands folded in front of her, her face pensive and private. "Looks as if I need to find your sister," I said. She didn't look up, but her shoulders seemed to relax in relief. "Why don't you tell me everything you can about her."

"Like what?"

"Like when she was born, who her friends are, where she liked to hang out, where she went to school."

"She stopped going to school a while ago."

"Her last school, then. Anything that might help me find her." I got a pad of paper and started taking it all down.

Aisha told me her sister was smart and got good grades, but dropped out of school and left home for good when her boyfriend got her a job as a hostess at a club. Amira had been planning to earn a GED and then enter a nursing program, but it was hard to save up for college because the family was always running short and borrowing from her.

"Our momma has difficulties," Aisha said softly. "She tries real hard, but she can't always manage."

"And you haven't seen Amira since July? It must be tough not to have that extra support anymore."

"We're fine," she said quickly. "I can work, too, when I'm not at school."

I started to say something, but she glanced over at Omar and I sensed she didn't want to talk about the family's problems in front of him. Instead, I took the names and addresses of all the friends and acquaintances that Aisha could think of.

"Okay, this gives me something to work with," I said at last. "I'll make a copy of that picture. Omar, maybe you can help me with this."

He quickly finished up the game he was playing, then I had him arrange the photo on my scanner and showed him which buttons to push. He stared as his sister's picture appeared on the screen. "Hope you can find her," he said.

"I'll try my best."

"She's gonna be a nurse. They make good money."

It made something hurt inside my chest, hearing the simple trust in his voice. It wasn't likely his sister would ever become a nurse, and I had a sinking feeling nothing good would come of my search for her. But I didn't have any words for explaining that to a boy still young enough to think things might work out in spite of everything. Instead, I asked if he would mind keeping an eye on Rashid for a minute. "I want to introduce you to my downstairs neighbor," I told Aisha. "His name's Adam. He's a single father, and a good dad, but he's a total slob."

"Where's the baby's momma at?"

"I never heard the whole story, but apparently she walked out not long after the baby was born. Adam has no idea how to keep a house tidy. Think you could come by once a week and clean for him?"

"I could do that. Olivia don't need me on weekends."

"Let's go talk to him, then."

If Adam had been reluctant about the arrangement, I was prepared to become a hard-assed landlady and insist he take better care of my property, but he was all in favor of the idea. Aisha's eyes grew big as he showed her around the messy flat. He owned hardly any furniture besides their beds, an expensive leather couch, and a huge flat screen TV. The floor was an obstacle course of toys and junk, and there was flora growing in the corners of the shower that made me wince. He tentatively suggested fifty bucks for each Saturday cleaning. "Is that enough?" he asked anxiously, seeing her eyes grow even bigger.

"So long as you provide transportation and the cleaning supplies," I said. "Pay her double the first time, since it's going to be a lot of work. Cash, no checks. She can bring her brothers if she has to, right?"

"No problem. Daniel will like it."

Adam was about to take his son to a playdate, so he gave her a twenty-dollar advance and they agreed he would pick her up tomorrow afternoon so she could give the apartment a going-over. Then we went back upstairs and woke up Rashid. As I drove them home I was glad the Corolla was a two-door, since Rashid was pushing every button and lever within reach, drumming his feet against the back of my seat when he ran out of other mischief to do.

Aisha gave me cross streets instead of a specific address, but as we neared the corner, Omar leaned forward. "Right here," he said, pointing. "This is where we live." He seemed oblivious to the sudden humiliation showing in his sister's face. The building was a decrepit three-flat surrounded by vacant lots. It looked abandoned, with broken windows on the top floor and trash littering the front yard.

"Why don't you take your brother inside," I said to him. "I need to talk business with your sister for a minute."

Omar blew air out of his cheeks. "Come on, Rashid," he said in a long-suffering tone. We watched him steer the boy toward the building, holding tight to his wrist. It wasn't easy, with Rashid dragging behind, at one point flopping right down on the ground and yelling.

"That little boy's a handful," I said.

"He gets too wound up," Aisha said. "Always been that way. I don't know what he'll do when he gets to school."

I was moved by her prematurely adult tone, but I steeled myself. I had things to say that she wouldn't want to hear. "Aisha, you remember those pictures hanging in my apartment?" I asked her. "The ones of my family?"

Aisha nodded, visibly confused by the change of subject.

"I barely remember my mother. I was only two years old when she took my brother and me to Union Station, sat us down on a bench, and told us she'd be right back. She was lying. We never saw her again."

"That's tough," Aisha said awkwardly.

"For years I was mad at her for leaving us like that, but I finally understood why she did it. She was a drug addict and a prostitute and she knew she couldn't take care of us, so she did something really hard: she walked away from the only two people in the world who loved her. But she had to do it, no matter how much it hurt. What I'm trying to say is that sometimes it's better if a family doesn't try to stick together."

"I know," Aisha said in a small voice.

"You said your mother has difficulties. What are we talking about?"

"She just has trouble finding steady work, is all." There was more to it than that, but Aisha's expression had grown closed. Whatever problems there were at home, she didn't want to share them with me.

"We went into foster care," I said. "Me and my brother. It wasn't great. We moved around a lot, and Martin had problems, like Rashid, only worse. I was worried they'd send him to an institution, and I didn't want to be left all alone, so I decided I had to find our mother.

Even if she couldn't take us in, maybe she had family who would. All I had to go on was that picture you saw, but I took it to the police station over on Harrison to see if they could find her."

I had to pause for a minute, remembering how Jim Tilquist had taken that photo from my hands, holding it carefully as he asked me questions. I cleared my throat and blinked.

"Things don't always turn out like you expect. We found our grandfather, and he adopted us, so that was good. But we also found out my mother was dead. And that . . . I didn't think I would care what had happened to her. I was mad at her for leaving us, I was *furious*, but there was this little part of me deep down inside that always hoped she was looking for us all those years, that it was all some mistake. But that's not how it was. She lived a hard life and she died on the streets and nobody even knew her name when they buried her."

I stared out at the street, thinking about the few memories I had of her: a warm lap, an Indian block-print skirt with a mysterious spicy scent. A string of blue glass beads that I rolled between my fingers and held up to the light to see their clear, sapphire glow.

Much clearer was the memory of the day Jim drove me to the cemetery in a suburb south of the city where, we'd learned, my mother had been interred with other indigents in an unmarked grave. I'd bought a bunch of flowers with my own money. When we drove through the cemetery gate, my heart lifted to see such a beautiful place, shady and green. Jim asked for a map at the front office and we drove to the area at the far end of the cemetery that was labeled "Garden of Peace." But when we got there, it wasn't a garden at all. Weeds grew up through disturbed earth; rocks and dirt lay in piles. I got out and walked across the uneven ground, a bitter wind blowing hair in my face as a backhoe carved a trench near the back fence. I remembered feeling Jim's hand on my shoulder, hearing him ask if I was ready to go home, shaking my head helplessly. I didn't know where to leave the flowers.

I took a deep breath and looked at Aisha, who was staring at her hands, knotted together in her lap. "Sorry. I didn't mean to go into all that," I said. "It's just . . . I'll do what I can to find your sister, but I don't want you to get your hopes up. I may not be able to find her. She may not want to be found. Or we may find out something you'd rather not know."

"I want to know," she said, so softly I could barely hear her words.

"You have my card?" She felt in the pocket of her windbreaker and nodded. "You better go see what your brothers are up to."

She nodded again and climbed out of the car, then turned, hugging her arms around her for warmth. "Thank you for lunch," she said, her tone remote and polite. "And for getting me that job."

"Aisha? I'm not going to call social services about your situation, but I'll be seriously pissed off if things go wrong and I wish I had. You have my number. If things get bad, you call me. Promise?"

She nodded. I watched her go into the house.

THIRTEEN

t was only a short drive to Olivia Jackson's place. She invited me into her kitchen, where the stove was crowded with pots and the table was full of foil-covered pans. "I got a family reunion to cater," she said, nodding at the food. "Just waiting for my nephew to bring his van around and load all this up. You hear from that woman?"

"Not yet."

"You might, might not. I did what I could. She don't want to deal with it. I told her she could trust you, but . . ."

"It's hard to trust anybody after what happened to her. But it looks like this guy has attacked at least half a dozen women. Maybe if some of the others are willing to come forward, she'll change her mind about talking to me."

"I hope so. 'Cause right now, *not* talking about it don't seem to be doing her any good. I'd tell you her name, but she made me promise not to."

"That's fine. I don't want to force anything on her. Listen, Aisha LeTorneau just told me her sister, Amira, was also beaten and raped not far from here."

"That's right. By that no-good jailbird, Lorcan Sills."

"Her boyfriend?"

"Boyfriend, shit. He calls himself a talent manager, thinks he's some kinda big-time businessman." She shook her head, disgusted.

"He's nothing but a pimp. His cousin is part owner of the K-Town Tap over on Pulaski. That's where his girls used to meet customers. Amira was doing that kind of work; she was one of his whores, is what she was. Only not anymore 'cause he's doing time over some guns the police found in his car. Good riddance to him."

"You sure he's the one who attacked Amira?"

"Everyone knows he used to beat on his girls if they displeased him. The police were trying to arrest him for it, but Amira wouldn't go along. You thinking it's this other man might have done it?"

"I don't know," I said. "I'd like to find Amira, though. Aisha told me she hasn't been around since July. Do you have any idea where she is?"

"I ain't seen her for . . . ooh, long time. She been working independent lately. It ain't great working for somebody like Lorcan Sills, but being on your own is worse. A pimp beat you up maybe once, twice a year, but at least they keep the johns in line. You work by yourself, you get beat up every week. Shame about that girl. She had so much potential."

"I hear she wants to be a nurse."

Olivia's eyes rolled to one side, as if watching that idea fly out the window. "Yeah, and I'm gonna get my own show on the Food Network any day now."

"Well, I still want to find her, so—"

Olivia burst out laughing. "That Aisha, she be all polite and sweet, but she knows what she's doing. She ask you to look for her sister, right? And she's paying you how much? Here I thought you was running a business."

"It's a lead that could help me put this case together. Besides, I like Aisha."

"She's good, taking care of her brothers like she does."

"What's going on with their mother?"

Olivia sighed. "I've known Ruby since she was little. We all thought she was set to go places. But after her first baby was born, she started having these spells. Gets so low she can't get out of bed. She been to a doctor for it, but her paperwork got all messed up and she couldn't get the pills no more. She had a city job, but she lost it. Then she had a position over at the Jewel for a while, but she missed a week and they let her go. I worry about them kids."

"Do you think there's a chance she'd harm them?"

"No, I don't believe she's ever so much as raised a hand to them. That Rashid? Now, somebody ought to tan *his* behind. I'll volunteer." She laughed, a warm, throaty sound, then grew serious. "Thing is, Ruby loves her kids, she really does, but she don't have the inner resources to take care of them all the time."

"Do they have any family around here?"

"She got a brother somewhere. Memphis, I think. But they ain't close. She don't belong to a church, and most of the friends she ever had are tired of dealing with her nonsense. I keep an eye on them kids, but there's only so much I can do. That's my nephew's van coming up the alley. You want me to call a few people, see if I can find out where Amira's at?"

"That would be great," I said, and made another contribution to her phone bill before helping load up the van with food.

was making a to-do list in my head as I unlocked my gate and headed down the gangway. I was so absorbed in my thoughts as I rounded the corner of the house, I almost collided with a man who was standing beside the wooden staircase leading up to my apartment. I stepped back, my hand moving automatically to the place on my right hip where I hadn't worn a gun for nearly two years. His hand moved in a mirror gesture.

"Old habits die hard, eh?" He grinned and held his jacket open to show he was unarmed. "Name's Kevin Casey. Sorry to startle you." He was a broad-shouldered man, with tousled dark hair flecked with gray. His smile was friendly, but his eyes were watchful.

"How did you get in here?" My heart had taken longer to respond to the threat than my hand. It was pounding now, and adrenaline was coursing through my bloodstream, making my scalp tingle.

"The gate was open."

"It was locked when I left."

"Wasn't when I got here. Well, I did have to jiggle it a little."

"Guess I need to get a better lock. What do you want?"

"We need to talk." He took my arm to escort me. I shook it off. He held his palms up in surrender. "Jeez, okay."

"Talk about what?"

"About Jerry Pozorski. My partner."

The name the man had given me finally clicked into place. It had been in Thea's files: Kevin Casey had worked with Pozorski on the Lincoln Park Rapist case. I wondered, with a sinking heart, how much Pozorski had told him. So far, I wasn't doing a very good job of keeping Jill McKenzie's involvement under wraps. "You'd better come in."

He followed me up the steps. I unlocked the door and waved him in. He looked around curiously. "Who did the conversion?"

"I did. My brother helped."

"You know, if you wanted more light, you could put a skylight . . ." He broke off and laughed at himself. "Sorry. I'm always remodeling other people's houses."

"Is that what you do in your retirement?"

"Who said I was retired? No, I dabble in real estate in my spare time, but I don't have time to do anything more than slap paint on walls between tenants."

"Have a seat. Would you like a cup of coffee?"

"Tea, if you've got it." He sat at the kitchen table.

I put the kettle on the stove, put tea bags in two mugs. "So, you were Jerry Pozorski's partner."

"Couldn't ask for a better one." He reached out to align the salt and pepper shakers, frowning absently as he thought over what he had to say. "Look, I went by his place this morning. He told me you're revisiting the Lincoln Park case. Who you working for?"

"I can't tell you that."

"Fine, but if Chase Taylor and his pals are offering you a percentage, you're wasting your time. The only way they'll win a compensation claim would be if someone else was proven good for the crime, and that ain't going to happen. Taylor did it."

"There was a judge who didn't think so," I said, relieved that he hadn't heard that it was Jill who had hired me.

He was shaking his head before I finished speaking. "All bullshit technicalities. It was a good investigation. We got the right guy."

"I was expecting resistance from the state's attorney's office. Didn't think a cop would be doing their bidding."

His jaw tightened. "I'm not doing anyone's *bidding*, I'm here out of solidarity with my partner. You might not understand that." He waited to be sure the barb had sunk in. "It was a tight case. It was tight because Jerry was good."

"I've heard nothing but praise for his work."

"Then you should give him a break." He ran a hand through his hair. "Look, when you talked to him, he was sloshed, right?"

"I smelled alcohol on his breath. I don't know if—"

"He's got a problem these days, okay? Nobody's denying it. But he was sober when he was on the job. He was a fine detective, best I ever worked with, and this case—it was a bastard. The press was all over it, the public was hysterical. And this poor woman, a girl, really. She was . . ."

He fell silent for a moment, staring into space, then sketched a circle around his face with a finger. "She hardly looked human after he was done with her. Her body was all tore up inside. He'd slashed her with a knife, too, just for fun. And the dog. I know, it's just an animal, but to see him laying there on the lawn, like a piece of trash . . ." He reached out and straightened the salt and pepper again, suppressing a sigh.

"So if the person who did it is still out there—"

"He is, thanks to a judge and some interfering lawyers."

The kettle started to whistle. I got up and filled our mugs. "Look, you may be right," I said. "Maybe Taylor did it. But if I'm going to understand this case, I need to talk to the detective who led the investigation."

"You can't."

"I don't think you're in a position—"

"He ain't there anymore." When I set the mugs down, Casey pulled his over and stared down into it before he spoke again. "Jerry started to leave us five years ago, and at this point, there's not much left of him. Maureen, his wife—she tried to get him help. We all been trying. I got him involved in my real estate business, tried to give him something he could . . . Didn't work. He was too far into the bottle, couldn't handle the responsibility. He's got two kids, lovely girls. I don't think either one of them talks to him anymore. Not that I blame them. Ain't easy watching your father turn into a drunk."

He took a sip of tea, winced at the heat of it, touched his lip. "When the case got thrown out, things really went to hell. Like, whatever was holding him up the past few years finally collapsed. I gave him a job managing one of our properties so he'd at least have a place to live. The tenants are always complaining, but what am I supposed to do? He was my partner. Can't turn my back on him now."

"I'm sorry for his troubles, but—"

"When I went there today, I thought I was going to have to call for an ambulance. Actually, I thought it might be too late. He was passed out, laying on the floor in his own shit and vomit. I suppose you didn't mean to set him off, but . . . You got any idea what it's like to see someone who taught you everything, who was your closest friend in the world—" His voice had started to break up, his cheeks flushing deep red. He closed his eyes and tapped a fist against his knee, his lips tight, trying to compose himself.

After a minute, he cleared his throat and glanced at me. It seemed to embarrass him further to see how moved I was. We finished our tea in silence.

"I'm sorry," I finally said when I had control of my voice. "I didn't know. I won't bother your partner again."

"Thank you," he said softly, looking up at the ceiling as if he were saying a prayer.

After he left, I drove to the Home Depot on North Avenue to buy a new lock, but couldn't figure out which one would fit my gate. I finally called Martin from the store and asked if he'd mind riding the train into town Sunday morning to give me a hand. He'd made the Sunday morning trip often enough that it fit easily into his routine.

It wasn't until I got home that I started thinking about Casey. It seemed odd that he was unarmed. Chicago police officers don't have to wear their guns when off duty, but they usually do because they're required to respond to trouble, whether on shift or off.

It only took a few minutes on the computer to learn that, after two decades with the CPD, Casey had taken a job as an investigator for the Cook County state's attorney.

FOURTEEN

started making phone calls to rape counselors I had worked with. I had to leave voice mail for most of them, but managed to talk to a few, including a former nun I'd worked with frequently in the past. She greeted me warmly and we spent a few minutes catching up. Then I told her a researcher had stumbled across police reports describing attacks that seemed to be the work of a serial rapist. I was trying to get in touch with the survivors to see if a case could be made that these were all, in fact, related and worthy of a more aggressive police investigation. I described the attacks, the locations, and gave a composite description of the perpetrator.

"How many attacks did you say?"

"Seven. Though I'm aware of at least one more that may be related."

"Seven," she repeated numbly. "And the police haven't seen a pattern?"

"Not so far as I know." I didn't mention that the state's attorney's office had already dismissed it.

"I know one of these women. At least, I think so. She'll be willing to talk to you."

"Great."

"She's tough. She's a fighter. But she's not as strong as she thinks."

"I won't push it."

"No, but she will. Just . . . go easy, okay?"

My last call of the evening was to the house where Chase Taylor lived with his aunt. A woman answered the phone sounding polite and crisp. When I asked to speak to her nephew she said, "If you don't mind my asking, are you with the press?"

"I'm an investigator."

Her voice cooled several degrees. "In that case, I'll give you the name of his lawyer."

"No, wait. I'm not working for the police. I'm a private investigator, and I'm looking into some attacks against women that occurred while Mr. Taylor was incarcerated. The man responsible for those attacks may be the real Lincoln Park Rapist."

She was silent for a moment. "Miss . . . I'm sorry, I don't know your name."

"Anni Koskinen."

"Miss Koskinen, as you can imagine, we've had a lot of calls since my nephew got out. If you spend twenty years in prison for a crime you didn't commit, most everybody on the outside having forgotten your existence, it can be overwhelming to speak to members of the media or with people who say they want to help but actually just want to help themselves to whatever they can get out of it. There's always someone ready to take advantage."

"I'm sure this has been an ordeal."

"You don't know the half of it. I don't mean to be difficult, but we've learned the hard way to be cautious. I wonder if you could provide me some way to check on your credentials?"

"The Illinois Division of Professional Regulation keeps a list of licensed investigators in good standing. I can give you their phone number. Or you could contact Thea Adelman, Chase's lawyer. We've worked together in the past."

"Oh. Well, if you don't mind waiting, I'll call you back shortly."

When the phone rang five minutes later, she sounded brisker. "Chase will be free to speak with you tomorrow. Say, four in the afternoon? Let me give you directions to my home."

When I disconnected I saw a voice mail message was waiting for me. A woman's voice, which sounded young and confident, told me she was Stacy Aldrich, that she had just heard from a friend that I wanted to talk to her about her rape. She was willing to help in any way she could. I dialed her number.

"This is Stacy."

"Hello, I'm Anni Koskinen. The woman who—"

"Right. The ex-cop. You're looking into a series of rapes. I'm glad somebody is."

"I know it must be difficult to talk to a stranger about your assault, but your case may be connected to the others. Anything you could share with me would really help."

"Okay. You free now?"

"That works for me. If you're sure you—"

"Absolutely." She gave me her address. I gathered up my notes and files, stuffed them in my bag, and headed out.

She lived on the North Side in a trendy part of Andersonville, on the third floor of a block of apartments inhabited by students and young singles, judging by the noise level. It was nearing

8:00 P.M. when I arrived, and there was a palpable buzz in the air as the residents were gearing up for the social events of a typical Saturday evening, clusters of them passing me on the stairs as they headed out to clubs or bars.

Stacy Aldrich fit right in. In her midtwenties, she came to the door wearing a short skirt that hugged her narrow hips, layered T-shirts that emphasized a waifish frame, and boots that laced up to her knees. Her hair was dyed red and was as short as Jill's, except for a single lock that fell in a curve beside her right cheek. "I was just having a glass of wine," she said. "You want one?"

"That sounds good, thanks."

She waved me into a tiny apartment with a nook of a kitchen, a living room crowded with piles of books, and an alcove for a bed and dresser. Clothes hung from nails driven into the wall and the air smelled of cigarettes, sweetened by a smoldering incense stick. It didn't have the spacious austerity of Jill McKenzie's farmhouse, but there was something about the place that reminded me of Jill. Maybe it was the protective way books were stacked around the desk, like a fortification. Or maybe it was just the four stout bolts on the door that Stacy fastened before stepping into the little kitchen to fill a glass for me.

"So, you're a private eye?" she said, seeming amused by the idea.

I traded my wallet, opened to my license, for the glass. She studied it curiously before handing it back. "No fedora? No trench coat? How disappointing. But my favorite former nun says you're all right, so . . ."

I settled into a sagging couch covered with a quilt, then shifted to avoid an errant spring that was jabbing me in the back. "You're a student?"

"Your keen deductive powers at work. I'm doing a PhD program in law and rhetoric at Northwestern. If I had settled for a JD, I would have been finished by now, but that would be way too practical."

Stacy took a nearby armchair, hooked a crate over and propped her boots on it, cradling her wineglass in her hands.

"I thought about going to law school," I told her.

"Why didn't you?"

"My friends talked me out of it."

"Here's to good friends," she said, making it into a toast. I noticed her fingernails, painted the same rusty red as her hair, were chipped and chewed to the quick. "So, you want to know about my rape."

"I'm trying to find out if there's a connection among several sexual assaults."

"So I heard. What's in it for you?"

That was a question the ex-nun hadn't asked. "I have a client who was attacked. The police didn't find the man who did it. It's beginning to look as if he has raped at least seven women in the past ten years. Your case may be connected. If I can find enough points of contact among the cases, it may help us find the man responsible. That's why I hoped you could tell me about what happened to you, though I know it's not easy to talk about."

"I don't mind. It pisses me off that women get the message they're supposed to shut up about it, like it's not supposed to happen to good girls. But it does, all the time. If my speaking out helps even one woman, I'll talk until my head falls off."

"That's a refreshingly open attitude."

"I just don't get why it should be a big secret. Am I supposed to be ashamed or something? Because I'm not. A man raped me and beat me up. Why should I pretend it never happened? Silence is complicity; that's why I talk about it to rape prevention groups and criminal justice classes and anyone else who will listen. Of course, my parents don't see it that way."

"They aren't supportive?"

"They tell me I need to put it behind me—mainly because it embarrasses them. Of course, they also think I should be working for a corporate law firm by now. We don't talk much, actually."

"When was the attack?"

"Three years ago. June twelfth. At approximately five-fifteen in the morning." Her words grew increasingly stilted, as if reading an official statement, mocking it. As she spoke, I mentally flipped through the records. The timing matched; she was one of the seven victims whose names had been blacked out.

"I was living in Wicker Park then," she went on. "I'd been up all night because my roommate was having a crisis, which later on seemed kind of funny. She was all worked up because she got a C-minus on a paper and her boyfriend was acting like an asshole. Deeply tragic stuff. Anyway, it had been a crazy, emotional night, and I needed to clear my head, so I went for a walk. I used to do that, sometimes, go out before anyone else was up and walk for miles. I grew up in a suburb where there aren't even any sidewalks. Living in the city was so different, so exciting."

She drank some wine. "I headed past the park, then turned up Kimball. I suppose that was dumb. At least, the detectives seemed to think so. It's kind of a rough area, there, but it didn't feel dangerous. It had rained during the night and everything smelled fresh. The birds were singing. It was a really nice, quiet morning, the kind where you feel as if the whole city belongs to you. I was walking under the railroad tracks through an underpass when he grabbed me."

"That underpass . . . is that, what, along Bloomington?"

"Right. The train line there runs on a high embankment. When you walk under it, there's a row of arched pillars between the sidewalk and the street, all decrepit and crumbly. Kind of looks like a crypt in a spooky movie. I was starting to feel a little nervous when—*bam*. Something hit me really hard on the side of my head." She touched her fingertips to her right cheekbone, her eyes staring blankly ahead.

"I wasn't sure what had happened. This man grabbed my shoulders and hustled me through to a vacant lot north of the tracks. I was really confused; I thought maybe a chunk of concrete had broken off the ceiling and he was trying to help. But he threw me down and got on top of me and grabbed my chin real tight. He showed me a knife and stuck the point of it here." Her fingers moved from her cheek to a spot along the lower lid of her left eye, her eyes still staring ahead as her fingertips brushed her skin, reading a message he'd left in Braille. "He said 'You keep fussing, I'll take your eyes out.'"

"Those were his exact words?"

"Yeah. Funny, he sounded almost reasonable. Like, just be cool and it'll all be over soon. It was weird. It felt like it was happening to someone else. Like I was floating a couple of feet above us, watching the whole thing, feeling sorry for that girl who was going to get raped. Because by then I knew that's what was going to happen."

She took another swallow of wine. "The weirdest thing . . ." She chuckled, an abrupt sound, almost like a cough. "He was all calm, right? Until after he raped me. Then he got really angry. I remember telling him I was sorry. How fucked up is that? This guy's furious, he's punching me in the face and I'm apologizing to him. By that time, he had totally lost it. I think he would have killed me if somebody hadn't scared him off."

"There was a witness?"

"Some guy called nine-one-one on a prepaid cell phone, but he didn't give a name, and he left before the police arrived. They never found him. This guy, whoever it was, checked to see if I was alive, said everything would be okay, just hang in there. His voice sounded like he was black. I couldn't tell you what he looked like. My face was all fucked up; I could hardly see. So, anyway, the ambulance came and I talked to the police, and they told me they'd let me know if they ever found the guy who did it. Which they didn't." She downed the rest of her wine. "That's it. That's my story."

"Is it okay if I ask you some questions?"

"Isn't that what you're here for?" She reached for a bag hanging on the back of a chair nearby. She fumbled through it for a pack of cigarettes, took one, then offered the pack to me.

"No, thanks. I quit."

"Good for you," she said dryly as she lit up.

"The man who attacked you—can you describe him?"

She took a contemplative puff on her cigarette and let the smoke leak out slowly. "Sure. I have this incredibly clear picture in my head: an African-American male with an oval face, a little flat on the top. Hair trimmed short, no sideburns. Eyes close together; a wide, flat nose. A mouth that turns down a little at the edges, a receding chin. His ears are all blurry, though, because of all the erasing. I couldn't get the ears right."

"That sounds like a drawing a police artist made."

"Right, that's what I see. Like it's a cartoon monster chasing me, or a man wearing a paper mask. At this point I don't remember what he really looked like at all. Just that drawing. There were signs up for a while, posted around the neighborhood. It was weird, seeing them in store windows months later."

"What about his clothes? Any idea what he was wearing?"

"Something dark blue." Her eyebrows drew together as she concentrated. "It might have been a uniform, the kind of coverall that mechanics wear."

"A one-piece thing?"

She stood abruptly and strode into the kitchen to get the bottle of wine, her boots thumping firmly as she crossed the room. "I'm not sure," she mumbled around her cigarette as she sat and refilled her glass. She offered me the bottle before setting it on the floor beside her chair. "Now that I think about it, I'm pretty sure his chest was bare when he, when . . ." She drew on her cigarette. "Which is weird. Wouldn't it be inconvenient to have to take your coveralls off just to get your dick out? Especially while holding a knife to somebody's face."

"Maybe it had snaps or a zipper, something he could open easily."

She winced when I said the word "zipper" and tapped her cigarette against an ashtray already overflowing with ashes and scrunched butts. "Funny, I hadn't thought about this before, but when he got ready to do it, I had the impression something had changed, that he'd come out of a . . . a husk. Like, hiding inside this normal, everyday man there was something different. Something evil." She drank her wine. "That's a very racist image, actually."

"What do you mean?"

"Under a thin veneer of civilization, there's a naked savage lurking, just waiting for the opportunity to take advantage of a white woman. So *Birth of a Nation*." She sucked on her cigarette and gulped more wine. "That's part of why people don't want to hear me talk about it. The race thing. It confuses them. They'd have less of a problem if he had been white."

"He attacked black and Latina women, too. Your race wasn't a factor."

"An equal-opportunity rapist. How about that." She refilled her glass and set the empty wine bottle on the floor.

"Did you notice anything else about him?"

"Like what?"

"Any blemishes or tattoos?"

She shook her head.

"Was he wearing any jewelry?"

"I don't think so. I'm pretty sure I would have noticed rings or a chain."

"What about body odor?"

"He was sweaty."

"Was it pretty rank? Like he'd been wearing the same clothes for a long time?"

"Not like the homeless people who get on the El and everybody moves to another car at the next stop. More like mown grass that's been sitting too long in the sun and started to rot."

"Like outdoors," I said, remembering what Jill had said.

"The great outdoors."

"When you took that walk, was it a route you followed routinely?"

"I used to walk in the area, the park, especially, but I don't think I'd ever been on that street before. I would have remembered going under the tracks. He might have been hiding behind one of the pillars. I couldn't believe he'd hit me at first. He didn't seem . . ." Her words trailed away.

"Seem what?"

"Uh, dangerous." She blinked, rubbed her eyes. "Sorry. I didn't sleep too well last night."

And she'd just polished off most of a bottle of wine in less than twenty minutes. "I won't take too much more of your time."

"No problem. Really, I want to help. But I have to go to the john." She stubbed out her cigarette and got out of her chair a little clumsily.

While she was in the bathroom, I opened my bag and flipped through the seven police reports, found hers and pulled it out. When I looked at it before, the victim had been an abstraction: a white woman, twenty-one years old, her name blacked out, no more real than the police artist mask that Stacy remembered as her attacker's face. I heard the toilet flush, water running in the sink.

When she came out, her cheeks had more color and her eyes were bright. "Okay," she said cheerfully. "What else can I tell you?"

"You said he didn't seem dangerous. Can you tell me more about that? What were your first impressions?"

"He wasn't very big. Kind of wiry, compact. He was old, like in his forties or fifties, and he didn't have any of that 'I'll fuck you up' attitude you sometimes get from black men. He just seemed quiet and safe. Until later."

"I don't know if you ever saw this report." I handed it to her.

She skimmed it and shook her head. "No."

"Anything in it that's inaccurate?"

"Nothing. Everything. I mean . . . it's freaky. This is so neat and tidy. It wasn't like that."

"The paperwork never captures the truth, just the barest of facts. How did things go with the police?"

She shrugged. She handed the report back and took out another cigarette, the flame of her match jittering as she lit it. "I'm not sure how they're supposed to go. I was taken to the hospital. They gave me a shot of morphine, so everything was pretty fuzzy. I remember a nurse doing the rape-kit thing. It seemed like she'd done it before, a million times. Routine. A couple of detectives came and asked questions after that. I talked to them several times. They seemed nice enough, but always a little . . ." She picked up her glass, then the bottle, saw both were empty and suppressed a sigh. "All sympathetic and shit, but they kept jumping on everything I said. Like, 'Really? Are you sure about that? Because the last time you said . . .' Like I was making things up."

"Cops always have to test their witnesses to make sure things hold together. People tell white lies to save embarrassment, or invent things, trying to be helpful. It can ruin a case. Unfortunately, when it's a rape, the victim is often the only witness. So you get the treatment, even though you're the one who got hurt."

"At least there wasn't any doubt there's been a crime committed. A lot of women get the runaround. You know, 'You sure you aren't just trying to get your boyfriend in trouble? What did you expect, wearing clothes like that, going out alone at that hour? Why didn't you lock your window before you went to bed?' Like, this only happens to people who weren't careful enough. Even when they don't say it out loud, that's the message. These guys took it seriously, anyway. They didn't have much choice. I was pretty messed up."

"Sounds like it."

"Whoa, I forgot. I have pictures." She jumped up, burrowed through a desk drawer. "These were taken the same day, at the hospital. They're pretty graphic, but you were a cop; you've probably seen worse."

I took the pictures from her and felt my stomach lurch. "Oh, jeez . . ."

"The police wanted to document my injuries while they were fresh. I asked for copies, which they obviously thought was weird." She sat beside me on the couch as I leafed through them, as if she were sharing vacation snapshots. "Look at that one. Who knew sex could do that much damage." As I looked at the close-up of her damaged vaginal area, I sensed her scrutinizing my face, as if it was some sort of test. "They had to take stitches inside," she said. "It hurt to pee for weeks."

I flipped to the next picture and flinched. It was a close head shot of what must have been her face, but it was unrecognizable, her eyes swollen shut, her lips split and leaking, her cheeks misshapen and pulpy.

"The first time I saw myself in the mirror, I thought someone else had snuck up behind me, someone really ugly. *Boo!* It was a long time before I didn't look like a freak show."

"I'm sorry you went through all this."

"I don't usually show those to people," she said, taking the photos back from me. "I mean, I don't want them getting the idea it's only serious if there's visible damage. A lot of times it doesn't show, but it still hurts. Is this what it was like for the other women? The cases you're looking at?"

"I haven't seen photos, but yes, they were all beaten severely, especially around the face. Do you have any other documentation of your case?"

"A three-inch stack of medical bills and insurance papers. I doubt that would be very useful." Something occurred to her, and for the first time she seemed hesitant. "There is one other thing. I wrote an essay about it for a creative nonfiction course a couple of years ago. It's not any good. I had to follow a dumb assignment, and the teacher was all about developing voice and crap like that, so it's basically pretentious bullshit."

"Still, I'd like to see it."

She seemed more embarrassed about exposing her writing than her naked, battered body in those photos, but she nodded. "It's somewhere on my computer. I could e-mail you a copy. Just don't expect . . ."

"I don't know anything about literature, so don't worry on that score. It's just that there may be some useful details there, things I didn't think to ask about. I may have to double-check with you about just how creative your nonfiction is."

She gave me a sour smile. "The details are true. It's just the rest of it that isn't."

"My e-mail's on this card. The detectives who worked the case—do you have their names?"

"Somewhere. Hang on." She went back to her desk, thrashed through a drawer, and finally produced two well-thumbed cards. I jotted the names down in my notebook.

"Did they locate any witnesses or have any suspects?" I asked Stacy, who was absently worrying the skin around her thumb with her teeth.

"Not that I know of. The woman kept in touch for a while. I haven't heard from either one of them in ages." She noticed a bead of blood welling up beside her thumb and sucked it off. "So what do you think? Any chance you'll find this guy?"

"I don't want to get your hopes up. The vast majority of rape victims know their assailant, and even so, only a third of investigations result in a conviction. But if I can establish a pattern and get the police to—"

A sudden blast of music interrupted me. Stacy reached for her bag and hunted for her cell phone and flipped it open. "What's up? Yup . . . yup . . . Is Sunil there? What about Laura? . . . Hah, that figures! . . . Okay, I have someone with me now, but I'll head over pretty soon." She folded her phone. "Sorry. Friends. We made plans to meet up tonight. What else can I do for you?"

She looked away, suddenly self-conscious. There was something all too familiar about the brightness of her eyes, her jitteriness. The wine-induced blurriness had changed to sharp gestures and speeded-up speech. "That's it for now," I said. "I'll keep you informed as this thing develops. Everything you told me is confidential, but—"

"Screw that. I don't care who knows."

She might, if one of the people who found out she was talking to me was the rapist. But I didn't see any reason to alarm her. "We need to keep this investigation quiet for now. I'm already getting flak from officials who don't want their work questioned."

"You're shitting me. The cops don't want you to do this?"

"I'm not talking about those two detectives who talked to you. They'd love to arrest this guy, I'm sure of it. But people higher up in the organization take it as a slight if an outsider starts connecting unsolved cases. It's bad publicity, and they already have plenty of that to deal with."

"No kidding. After that botched immigration raid. Bunch of fascists."

"It would be best if you didn't discuss this investigation with anyone else, not until I have enough to go on that they can't ignore it."

"That makes sense, I guess. But if you ever need me to testify or anything . . ."

"Thanks. Let's hope we get that far. Meanwhile, you've been a great help. My cell number's on that card. Feel free to call anytime." I got to my feet. "I know you've got friends to meet, but can I use your bathroom real quick?"

"No problem."

I went in and closed the door behind me. A yellow rubber duck sat on the edge of the tub. The vanity had damp streaks on it from having been wiped clean recently, but when I lifted a box of tissues I saw some white grains she had missed. I licked my finger and tasted it. As I suspected: cocaine.

I flushed the toilet and washed my hands for show, then I left. As I sat in my car, thinking about those photographs, thinking about that yellow rubber duck sitting beside the tub, she came through the front door of the apartment building, something joyous and resilient in her quick pace. She was strong; she wasn't afraid. Nothing that man had done would change who she was. But it took a combination of the mellowing effect of a bottle of wine and the fizzing brightness of a line of coke to keep it up. Sooner or later, those fine, invisible fissures left from the attack would deepen and things would start to crumble.

I called the ex-nun, thanked her for the contact, and suggested she check in with Stacy in a day or two. "She'd make a terrific witness. But . . ."

"There's a lot of shit she hasn't worked through yet," she said, sensing what I was thinking. "And she doesn't know it. She thinks she's fine."

"She's using coke, and she drinks a lot. I'm worried all the questions I was asking could set something off. It doesn't sound as if she can count on her family for support. I just want to be sure she has some kind of safety net."

"She does. Thanks for letting me know."

FIFTEEN

woke in the dark, out of a dream I didn't want to go back to. It was nearly 5:00 A.M. I dragged myself out of bed, put on a pot of coffee, and went outside to fill the cat's food dish. As I waited for the coffeepot to make its last sputtering gurgles, I wondered idly about the amount of time I'd put in on Jill McKenzie's case so far. I had probably worked through her initial deposit and then some, but I wasn't in the mood to do the math.

In many ways, this was the most satisfying work I'd done since turning in my star. It was what I'd always wanted to do—talk to victims, track down the evidence, nail the bad guys. I wanted this guy; I wanted him off the streets as badly as any criminal I'd ever hunted.

But I had to face facts. That wasn't my job anymore. I had been hired by a woman who was driven by a misplaced sense of guilt to personally fund an investigation into her own rape when the system failed. As an associate professor at a small, undistinguished Catholic college, she most likely earned a modest salary. It wouldn't take much to exhaust her savings. And I had a living to make, one that was a lot more precarious since I'd left the city's payroll. I couldn't afford to run a long, complex investigation pro bono. I'd take the case as far as I could without bankrupting Jill—or myself. That meant pulling together so many compelling leads that the police would have to take it seriously. And I'd have to do it soon, before I had to take on other work to pay the bills.

I drank my coffee, looking out the front windows. It was still and quiet outside, a soft gray light filtering into the street. The morning Stacy was attacked, it would have looked about the same: silvery half-light just beginning to show the outlines of a sleeping city.

Martin wouldn't arrive for another two hours. I had plenty of time for a run.

I pulled on my shoes and a hoodie and set out. As I passed St. Larry's, I waved at a protester sitting on the front steps, resting her back against one of the pillars, blowing on her hands to warm them, her breath rising like cigarette smoke in the chill air. There were two other humped forms beside her, sleepers burrowed deep into sleeping bags.

I followed my usual course into Humboldt Park, past the boathouse and the lagoon, then changed my route, heading toward the spot where Stacy had been attacked. As I turned onto Kimball and saw the tunnel under the railroad tracks ahead, the muscles of my shoulders and neck tightened. It felt as if I were running toward something evil just out of sight behind those shadowed pillars. My feet slowed for a moment, then anger flared up inside. I put on speed and raced toward the underpass where a murky, yellow light from sodium fixtures seemed to deepen the shadows between the rows of arched pillars.

On the other side I stopped to catch my breath, bending over and bracing my hands on my knees. Then I walked through the vacant lot beside the railway embankment. A plastic bag trapped in some weeds fluttered in the wind; broken glass glittered among the rubble. The stunted shrubs near the sidewalk would have been in full leaf in June, blocking the view from the street. A few windows in an apartment building to the north looked out over the lot. Someone might still be living there who could have seen something three years ago, but it was too early to be knocking on people's doors to ask.

I replayed the scene as Stacy had described it, the quiet man stepping out of the shadows to take her by the shoulders and lead her to this spot, but after that, my imagination stuttered to a stop. I'd been to seminars and in-services, I'd read studies and interrogated plenty of rapists, but I still could never grasp what made them do it. I didn't want to understand it; I just wanted to stop him, once and for all.

Walking back through the dark underpass, I sent my thoughts up into the darkness above the crumbling arches: *I'm here. I'm going to find you.*

Back at home, I checked to make sure I had the ingredients on hand for *migas,* Martin's favorite breakfast dish, then started a load of laundry, sorted out some bills, and prepared invoices. I looked at the clock, expecting Martin at any minute. By nine o'clock I was getting concerned. I tried the number of the cell phone I'd given Martin with my number entered as a contact in case of emergencies. No answer. By nine-fifteen I was beginning to panic.

I called the Safety and Security office at Stony Cliff College. The officer on duty said he'd swing by Martin's studio apartment in the science building. He called back ten minutes later. Nobody home.

Martin followed routines. He would catch the Metra commuter train headed southbound, get off at Clybourn, board a bus, then transfer to another one that dropped him four blocks from my house. He'd made the trip a hundred times; he wouldn't get lost. I pictured him standing on a corner, watching for a bus that had strayed off schedule, a common enough occurrence. Still, I couldn't bear to wait any longer. I reached for my jacket and keys and headed out, stopping first to ask my downstairs neighbor to keep an eye out in case Martin arrived while I was looking for him.

I drove to the bus stop on Division and Halstead where Martin caught his transfer. I pulled up in a no-parking zone, crossed the street, and talked to a woman waiting there. She hadn't seen Martin. She hadn't seen a bus in over half an hour, either. "They keep raising the fares, and the service goes to hell. What's the matter with this city?" She was still complaining as I hurried back across the street and climbed into my car, trying to control the fear that was flapping in my chest like something with leathery wings and sharp little claws. I had just turned up Halstead toward the train station when my phone rang.

"This is Pete Knowles with the Chicago police. You have a relative named Martin?"

"What happened?"

"He's not hurt," he said quickly, picking up on my anxiety. "Just got into a situation with Metra security a little while ago. We got him here at the Eighteenth. Any chance you could come by and help us straighten this out?"

"I'm in the neighborhood. I can be there in a few minutes."

I heard a short exhalation of relief. "Good. Just ask for me at the desk."

The boundaries of the Eighteenth District encompassed one of the wealthiest parts of the city, the Near North Side, home to Navy Pier, office towers, and upscale department stores. The station house was in the only part of the neighborhood that could be called rough; it was just around the corner from the decaying remnants of the Cabrini-Green public housing project, slated to be demolished. It wouldn't be long before the last of the tower blocks was torn down and the entire district would be filled with luxury lofts and athletic clubs.

I asked for Pete Knowles at the counter, and was led down a hall to an interview room. "Do I look like a social worker?" I heard a voice say on the other side of the door. "Besides, why should we do her any favors? She's the one—" As I opened the door, the two uniformed officers inside fell silent and looked at me. Martin was standing in the farthest corner, his face to the wall, rocking and humming to himself. Every time he rocked forward his forehead connected with the wall, a sharp little tap.

"Ms. Koskinen?" one of the officers asked. "Thanks for coming."

"Thanks for letting me know he was here. Hi, Martin," I said to him. He still hummed and rocked, *bump, bump, bump*. He wasn't hitting the wall hard enough to hurt himself, but the sensation soothed him. He usually touched his fingers to his thumbs in a repeating pattern to deal with tension, but he couldn't do that now; his hands were cuffed behind him. The side of one was scraped, and a little blood was smudged on the back of his shirt.

The other officer, whose shoulders were slumped against the wall, pushed himself upright. "All yours, Pete," he said, his words casual but his voice taut with annoyance. "Do whatever you want." He pushed out the door without giving me another glance.

"Pete Knowles," the other said, unperturbed, extending a hand.

"Anni. Is my brother under arrest?"

"We haven't done the paperwork yet, but . . ."

"What's the charge?"

"Resisting. Also, assaulting an officer. Hit him in the nose with his elbow, but I don't think it was on purpose. I'm inclined to let it go."

"Your partner isn't."

"Yeah, well, it was his nose."

"For what it's worth, I'm sure it wasn't intentional. And whatever beef your partner has with me, it's nothing to do with my brother." Knowles acknowledged my words with a noncommittal tilt of his head. Even though I'd never met either of these officers, they knew who I was: the detective who'd betrayed the badge by testifying in court against another cop.

"Can you take the cuffs off?" I asked.

"Not sure that's a good idea. When I had them off earlier, he, uh . . . he started biting his hands. Hard enough to draw blood."

"He won't do that now that I'm here."

Knowles shrugged. "You know him better than I do." He unlocked the cuffs and slipped them off. Martin tucked his hands under his arms, still rocking and tapping his forehead against the wall, his eyes tightly shut. Knowles watched for a minute, then clipped his cuffs back on his belt. "He do that much, bite his hands?"

"Hardly ever. What happened, anyway?"

"A Metra officer wanted to talk to him about pictures he was taking of the tracks up at Clybourn. Your brother got a little agitated, so we stopped to assist."

"Is taking pictures there illegal?"

"Technically, no, but since nine-eleven everybody's cautious about security. And the way he responded—"

"He was scared."

"That's what I figured. He's what, autistic?"

"Yeah. He's not a risk to anybody. He just has a hard time communicating when he's upset."

"You take care of him?"

"Other way around, usually. He was riding the train into town to help me with some work on my house."

Knowles looked at Martin, curious. "He gets around okay on his own?"

"Sure. He has a job, lives in his own apartment. He's fine, unless something throws him out of his routine. I gave him that camera for his birthday. Didn't think it would get him in trouble."

"Oh, right, the camera. It's up at the front desk." Knowles was still studying Martin, thinking. "You mind staying here with him for a few minutes? I need to check in with my boss."

"Sure. Take your time."

When the door closed behind him, the tension that had drawn

my muscles tight relaxed all at once. Feeling too tired to stand any longer, I pulled out one of the chairs at the scuffed table and sat, idly tracing a gouge mark in the surface with a fingertip. After a few minutes, Martin stopped rocking and leaned his forehead against the wall for a while. Then he came over and sat in the other chair.

"You okay?" I asked. He nodded. "How about your hands?" He looked at them. A scrape on the side of one, a scuffed knuckle, a reddened semicircle where his teeth had broken the skin. "Maybe you shouldn't take pictures of train tracks anymore," I suggested.

He started touching his fingers to his thumbs, concentrating on the simple, meditative motion. It made me feel calmer, watching him.

We'd sat for nearly ten minutes when I heard a crabby voice out in the hall. "Jesus, Knowles. You wear me out. Just get the retard out of here and get back to work, okay?"

Knowles came in and said to Martin, "Got tired of the wall, huh?" He set the camera on the table between us. "No charges. You're good to go."

"Thanks," I said. "Sorry for the trouble."

"No problem."

"No, really. I appreciate this. You could have jammed him up."

"And then I would've had a shitload of paperwork to do." As I gathered myself up, Knowles said, "My nephew just got diagnosed. Same thing, autism. He's four."

"How's he doing?"

"He's a funny little guy. Like, he learned how to set the table a while ago? Now he sets it five times a day, using all the flatware in the drawer."

"That sounds familiar."

"You don't want to mess with those place settings. You so much as touch a spoon, he's all over it." His grin faltered. "Doesn't take much to set him off. He screams a lot, bites his hands, like your brother did. He used to talk some, but not anymore. My sister's having a hard time with it, knowing he's never going to be normal."

"It can be really tough, figuring out how to cope. But the thing is, your nephew's normal—for him. It's just not the same as other people's normal."

"That's one way of looking at it." He laughed to himself. "This job, you gotta wonder if *any*body's normal."

He walked down the hall with us, preoccupied, as if his mind had moved on to other things. As I followed Martin past the front desk, Knowles coughed and leaned on the counter. "Uh, any chance you'd want to get together for a drink sometime?" Then he looked embarrassed at my reaction. "Sorry. Never mind."

"I'm involved with someone. Otherwise, I'd love to."

My cheeks were burning as we walked to my car. Involved with someone? Where did that come from?

Back at my house, we knocked on my downstairs neighbor's door to let him know I'd found Martin. "Excellent," Adam said vaguely. I had the impression he'd forgotten all about my asking him to keep an eye out. "Say, I'm supposed to pick up that girl, Aisha, in a little while, but I can't find the piece of paper where I wrote down her address. You have a phone number for her?"

"She doesn't have a phone, but I can tell you where she lives." I gave him directions and he jotted them down conscientiously, this time in pen on the inside of his arm where they wouldn't get lost.

"Maybe I should buy some mops and stuff."

"A good mop, a broom, sponges . . . here, have you got something I can write on?" I borrowed his pen and took an old envelope that he offered, making a list of basic cleaning products. "There. That should get you started." I made sure he tucked the list into his jeans pocket instead of setting it down on the cluttered kitchen table where it was bound to get mislaid. "Another thing. Aisha's probably going to bring her brothers with her."

"That's right. She said that."

"The younger one is kind of a handful. Maybe I can give him a job in the yard to keep him busy. Meanwhile, Martin's going to help me fix the gangway gate. I found a guy in the backyard yesterday. He just walked right in."

"Jeez. Was he trying to break into the house?"

"No. He's in law enforcement, just stopped by to talk to me about something. But it's been making me nervous. I'll make sure you get a copy of the key."

"Awesome. Hey, Martin, maybe we can play a game of chess later."

Martin was still too distracted to even register Adam's offer. "Good plan," I said for him, guessing that by the time we finished having a routine Sunday breakfast he'd be settled enough to welcome a game. They often played each other, being fairly evenly matched opponents. If Adam ever noticed anything odd about my brother, he didn't mention it. In turn, Martin did his best to put up with the discomfort of being in Adam's messy apartment.

Upstairs, I made a fresh pot of coffee as Martin started on our meal, lining up all the ingredients in a precise row and rearranging them a few times to make sure they were in the right order. He didn't have a kitchen of his own, but he enjoyed using mine when he came over. His signature dish was *migas*, eggs with sautéed onions, peppers, green chilli, and tortillas torn into pieces, all scrambled together and topped with *crema* from a local Mexican grocery, avocado chunks, and salsa. He took his time chopping the ingredients, making sure they were all exactly the right size. I had to cut up the avocado, though. He hated getting avocado goo on his hands.

We ate our fill, made a run to the hardware store where Martin studied the options before making his choice, and then spent a few hours installing a sturdy brass lock. As we were finishing up, Adam arrived, unstrapping baby Daniel from his car seat as three helpers climbed out of his car laden with bags full of cleaning supplies. Aisha gave my brother her shy smile as I introduced them. Omar stuck out his hand to shake. "How you doing?" Martin put his hands in his pockets and turned away. Omar looked puzzled, but got distracted when Rashid bumped his head with a mop handle that he was waving wildly, pretending it was a sword. "Rashid," Aisha hissed. "Behave."

Martin started to put away his tools while I followed the children inside. Adam looked a little overwhelmed as he snatched the mop from Rashid just before it smacked into his expensive television set. "Uh, guys . . ."

"They need something to eat. Phone in an order for a couple of pizzas," I told him as I passed through into the kitchen and found a bottle of apple juice in the fridge. I got the boys to sit down long enough to drink big tumblers of juice. Aisha looked around the chaotic kitchen, eyes wide. "This is gonna take a while," she murmured, shaking her head.

"That's why you're getting paid double this first time," I told her, glancing over at Adam to make sure he remembered.

Omar's lips parted in surprise. "That's a hundred dollars," he said, his voice high and squeaky. "Hot damn." His sister clouted him on the side of the head for cussing.

She emptied the kitchen sink of the crusted plates and baby bottles and scrubbed it clean before filling it with hot soapy water. I took the boys into the backyard, where Rashid seemed to find his calling in yanking up dead flowers and scattering dirt everywhere. Omar went over to Martin, who was sitting on the back steps wiping his tools clean and arranging them in his tool chest. "Whatcha doing?"

Martin didn't look at him and didn't respond. Omar tried again. "You fixed that gate?" He turned to me, perplexed.

"My brother's not much of a talker."

"What's wrong with him?"

"Nothing. He just doesn't like to talk."

"There's a boy at school who don't talk. He's weird. He's always doing this." Omar flapped his hands and bobbed from side to side. "His name is James. Everybody teases him, and then he cries."

"I hope you don't tease him."

"Naw, I don't do none of that," he said, but he looked uncomfortable. "You want me to help with that, too?" He pointed to his brother, who was gleefully shaking a dead plant, dirt flying off its roots.

"I think Rashid's got the garden covered. Why don't you go clear off the kitchen table so there will be a place to eat pizza. Find some clean plates and napkins for everyone, okay?"

"Got it."

With Rashid busy thrashing his way through the flower beds, Adam sidled up to me. "That place where these kids live?" he said, his voice lowered. "It's really crummy."

"That's a rough neighborhood."

"There were guys on the corner who looked like they were selling drugs. And their house—man, from the outside you wouldn't think anyone could possibly live there. There's broken windows and shit. Kids shouldn't live in a place like that."

"It's not a good situation for them. That's one reason I wanted Aisha to have an excuse to come over here regularly, so we can keep an eye on them, make sure things aren't getting worse."

Daniel toddled over and lifted his arms to be held. Adam picked him up and nuzzled his neck, looking uncharacteristically pensive.

The pizza came, and the kids fell on it. Daniel stared, fascinated, from his high chair, in between picking olives off his slice and eating them contemplatively. As the boys were squabbling over the last slice, too full to eat anymore but determined to lay claim, Adam took

Daniel into the bedroom to change his diaper. Aisha used the opportunity to draw me aside. She confided under her breath, "This is the dirtiest house I ever been in."

"Adam can be pretty clueless about practical stuff."

"I worry about a baby living here without any momma to watch after him. You think it's safe?"

I had to suppress a smile. "I've known Adam for over a year. He's really smart and he's a good dad. He just doesn't know how to keep a house tidy. That's why I'm glad you'll be coming over every week, make sure things are in order. We can both keep an eye on things, okay?"

She nodded gravely, used to having responsibilities.

Aisha was scrubbing fungus-festooned grout with an old toothbrush in the bathroom. Rashid was conked out on the leather couch, one of Daniel's stuffed toys wrapped in his arms and a thumb in his mouth. Omar was playing happily with Adam's Wii, dancing around as he battled aliens. Adam and Martin were setting up a chessboard. Calm had finally descended on the house.

Just in time. Because I had to go see the man whose face haunted Jill McKenzie's nightmares.

SIXTEEN

went upstairs to change out of my grubby jeans, gathered up a notepad and car keys, checked a map to make sure I knew how to get to the house on the South Side where Chase Taylor lived with his aunt, and headed out to my car. As I unlocked the Corolla, my cell phone rang. I didn't recognize the number on the readout.

"Change of plans, Ms. Koskinen." It was a silky voice, slow and soft, but authoritative.

"Who is this?"

"Across the street."

I glanced behind me. A late-model black SUV was parked across a driveway. The window powered down and the man inside looked at me over his dark glasses, a cell phone pressed to one ear, an ironic smile tilted to one side. That long face with a polished shaved head was familiar from the newspaper stories I'd found online: Raymond T. Ashe. One of the childhood friends who caroused with Chase Taylor the night Jill McKenzie was raped, testified against him, then became his public champion on his release from prison. I snapped my phone shut and crossed over to the car. Ashe tucked his phone into the inside pocket of his suit coat. He introduced himself and held out a hand for a shake; I ignored it.

"What's this about?" I asked.

"I understand you want to talk to Chase Taylor."

"I made an appointment to meet him at his aunt's house."

"His aunt, God bless her, doesn't understand what a young man goes through when he's been incarcerated for twenty years for a crime he didn't commit. I'm doing what I can to reconnect him to society. He's at my office. It's not far from here."

I looked at him for a moment, and then opened my cell and scrolled through contacts until I found the number for Chase Taylor's aunt. "Oh, I'm so glad you called," she answered, sounding frazzled. "I was just looking for your number. My nephew went out earlier today and he still hasn't returned. I'm so sorry if—"

"That's all right. It looks as if I'll have a chance to talk to him anyway. He's with Raymond Ashe."

She didn't speak for a moment. "I see."

"Mr. Ashe has offered to take me to his office so Chase and I can talk there. Is there anything you'd like me to pass on?"

"No. There's nothing." Her voice was flat, but she added in a more hesitant tone, "Just . . . ask him not to stay out too late, please. I worry when he's out late."

"I'll tell him." I dropped my phone back into my purse. "So, I have to go through you, is that the idea?"

Ashe gave me a pained look. "Just doing you a favor, is all. You want to drive all the way down to Avalon Park, fine by me, but be a waste of your time. You want to talk to him or not?" He decided my silence was assent. He climbed out and opened the passenger door for me with exaggerated politeness. He was an imposing man—not especially tall or stocky, but with an aura of confidence that made him seem bigger. His shoes were expensive and highly polished and his suit fit so well it had to have been tailored. He caught me looking him over and smoothed a hand over the fabric of his jacket. "Still dressed for church," he said with a bashful little-boy grin.

"Surprised you can afford a suit like that on a bus driver's salary."

His grin widened. "Once a cop, always a cop, huh? I got a cousin does tailoring." He picked a speck of imaginary dust off his sleeve. "Maybe you're also wondering how a lowly bus driver got a nice car like this, custom leather seats and all. I got a few investments here and there; always been good with money. Like to have nice things. Matter of pride." He glanced pointedly over at my battered Corolla.

"Where are we headed?" I asked after he climbed into the driver's seat and started the engine.

"Social club over on Kostner. Don't worry, I'll bring you home safe."

There was an ironic reverberation in that final word, a plucked string intended to make my pulse race, my blood run cold. As if, as a woman, I was programmed for fear. I saw Ashe glance at me, measuring my response.

I'm not afraid of you. I didn't say it out loud, but he seemed to pick it up, and smiled to himself as he spun the wheel and pulled onto the street. He jabbed a finger at the elaborate sound system. A rap track filled the car with an insistent beat as we drove, Ashe's fingers tapping the steering wheel in time with the words.

Ashe pulled up in front of a building on a desolate corner in North Lawndale. The club had no name over the door, just holes weeping red rust stains where metal signs from a former business had once been fixed to the walls. It looked as if it had been a corner grocery. Inside, there were a few racks holding packaged goods—Little Debbie cakes, bags of chips, and candy bars. A cooler held sodas, frozen pizza, ice cream treats, and burritos. There was a folding card table with mismatched chairs, a pool table where two men were racking up a game, and a shabby couch where kids clustered around a video game, the one holding the controller getting a chorus of advice from his friends.

"Sell a few snacks here, give kids a place to hang out," Ashe said, greeting the kids by name, bumping fists with the pool players. "Ain't much, but it's better than nothing, which is mostly what we got around here. Let me introduce you to my good friend Chase."

Taylor didn't look like the stuff of nightmares. His smooth, round face looked much younger than his thirty-eight years, and he was shorter than I expected, no more than five foot six, muscular but pudgy, as if he had never shed his baby fat. His head was shaved like Ashe's, and he was wearing the standard street uniform: a blindingly white T-shirt that hung halfway to his knees, oversized jeans, and white athletic shoes that looked as if they'd never touched pavement. Though he appeared relaxed, leaning forward with his elbows on his knees and his fists braced in front of him, knuckles pressed together, he had chosen a seat that put his back to the wall and gave him a full view of the room. His eyes had roamed around it regularly, alert for danger. But he had avoided looking at me, until Ashe introduced us.

Taylor looked at Ashe as if for cues, and got an encouraging nod. He rose from his stool and pulled his shirt straight before putting out a hand for a shake. His grip was strong, but somehow it felt hesitant, as if he was reluctant to make contact.

"Let's go into my office." Ashe pushed a door open into a smaller room furnished with a desk, a filing cabinet, and two armchairs. Campaign posters from his run for the city council were stacked against the wall. "Make yourselves at home. Can I offer you a cup of coffee?"

"No thanks."

"Water? A soda? What about you, Chase?"

Chase looked at him, a frown of anxiety creasing his forehead. "A Coke?" he said at last.

"Sure thing." Ashe ducked out of the office. Chase stared at the opposite wall. He sat up straight and was trying to look cool and in command of himself, but underneath his pretense of indifference I could tell he was rigid with tension. From my seat I could smell his sweat, a clean scent that mingled hard exercise and bleach.

"Thanks for being willing to meet with me."

"No problem," he said automatically.

Ashe returned, handing a can of pop to Chase, carrying a bottle of Fiji water for himself. "I understand you're looking into a series of assaults that might be related to that Lincoln Park rape, the one that got everybody so worked up they arrested the first black man they could snatch off the street. But you're not police anymore. Who you working for?"

"Why is that any of your business, Mr. Ashe?" I asked pleasantly.

"Please, call me Raymond. The reason I'm asking is that I'm Chase's friend. Quite a few people have taken an interest in his story, and given that I have some experience in the ways of the world, I'm looking out for his interests. I don't want some film producer or book writer or any other opportunist to take advantage of Chase's situation without at least some proper recognition that he should have a measure of recompense for what he's been through."

And you're looking for a cut? I wanted to ask, but I didn't. Chase Taylor was nervous enough about talking to me. If I antagonized the man he obviously looked to for instructions I wouldn't get anywhere. "I'm not working for anyone who stands to make money from Mr. Taylor's situation," I said, keeping my voice businesslike and reasonable. "But there's a standard ethical practice PIs follow. We don't disclose the names of our clients, not to anybody. I'm just here to ask a few questions, that's all."

"Without asking you to compromise your ethics, may I ask if this is likely in any way to harm Chase's interests?"

I had a feeling Ashe was only concerned about his own interests, but I remembered Thea's concerns when I told her what I was working on. I turned to Taylor. "Look, I'll be straight with you. I know the cops have been giving you a hard time, and if your name showed up in the paper again, it could make them turn up the pressure. But you have my word I'll do everything I can to keep this whole thing out of the news. Still, might be a good idea to check with your lawyer before you talk to me. She'll give you good advice."

Taylor looked at Ashe, who fiddled with the cap on his water bottle before he spoke. "The police certainly have been singling Chase out for harassment," he said. "Even more than most black folk, and that's saying something. They won't accept the fact they let a rapist go free while an innocent man was incarcerated. Figure it would help cover up their blunder if he went down on some trivial charge or other." He took a swig of his water. "But Chase, you don't need to talk to any lawyer. As a public figure, I've developed a lot of contacts in the media. We have the resources to manage public perceptions in a positive way. Far as the press is concerned, we're cool."

"There shouldn't be any call for managing anything," I said. "My goal is to keep this all as low-key as possible. As I already said, I treat my client's interests with confidentiality. Staying out of the news will benefit both Mr. Taylor and my client. I just need to ask a few questions—in private—and then I'll get out of everybody's way."

"Private, huh?" Ashe looked from Taylor to me, then shrugged. He screwed the top of his water on slowly and deliberately. "Feel free to use my office for as long as you like." He rose from behind his desk, and gave Taylor a clasp on his shoulder on his way out. "You go ahead and talk to this lady. I'll be right outside."

"Okay," Chase said.

"I'm there for you, brother. Always. Right?"

"Right," Chase echoed. Ashe closed the door behind him. Out in the other room we could hear his voice raised in a cheerful boast about his talents with a pool cue.

We sat for a moment, Chase Taylor staring at the wall over Raymond Ashe's desk. His posture was relaxed, and his head nodded slightly, as if keeping time with some music only he could hear, but his fists were clenched tightly in his lap. There was laughter from the other room, the clink of pool balls. Then someone put on some music, percussion pulsing like a heartbeat through the walls.

"I'm not sure how much your aunt told you," I said.

"Said you wanted to talk to me, is all. That you wasn't a cop or a reporter."

"I spoke to her on the phone a few minutes ago. She asked me to tell you something."

"Yeah? What?"

"Don't stay out too late." I said it with a hint of humor in my voice.

He snorted. "Acts like I'm still a kid."

"She said it nice, though. Not all bossy."

"She's all right. What you want to ask?"

"I'm investigating a series of sexual assaults that seem to be linked. They all have a lot in common with the Lincoln Park rape."

"I didn't do it," he said automatically.

"That's what I understand. I just want to find out how you got caught up in that mess. Figure out what the police missed when they decided to go after you instead of whoever actually did it."

"You ain't a cop, though, right?" he asked suspiciously.

"Nah, I'm a private investigator. Got m'own business." I was slipping into his speech patterns, the softer, slower pacing, the gentle slides between syllables that had traveled from the deep south in the Great Migration and took root in Chicago's black communities. With my mixed-race background, I was used to being a chameleon, adapting my identity and accent to fit the situation. "One of the women who was attacked hired me to check it out 'cause she thinks the police aren't doing enough to find the man who hurt her."

"When she get hurt?"

"Few years ago, now."

"I was in prison then. I couldn't a done it."

"I know that," I said patiently. Thea had been right; he wasn't bright, and his anxiety was making him even slower to grasp what I was saying. "The guy who attacked her might have also raped that woman in Lincoln Park, the crime you got nailed with. So, here's the thing: You help me understand where the cops went wrong when they arrested you, maybe I can figure out who the Lincoln Park Rapist really was."

"Instead of me."

"Exactly."

"So I could, like, clear my name."

"That's the idea."

He studied his fists, thinking it over. "A'ight. Go ahead. Ask your questions."

"You were sixteen when they picked you up, right?"

"Barely. Had my birthday two weeks before; didn't even have a chance to get my driver's license 'fore they put me in jail. Got my first driver's license when I was thirty-seven years old." He shook his head, marveling at the freakishness of it.

"The police seemed to zero in on you right away. Why you think they did that?"

"I 'own know. They wanted somebody, didn't care who. Might as well arrest some kid from the projects."

"You all shared a pipe that night. First time, right? One of your friends brought some rock."

He looked straight at me. "My friends didn't have nothing to do with what happened to that woman, neither."

"You sound sure about that."

"They my friends. I knew them. They ain't like that."

"But you were all looking for trouble, right? Acting wild that night."

"All's we did was take some money off people, throw a scare in 'em. Kind of folks look at you like 'man, what the fuck you doing in our part of town?' It was no big thing. We didn't hurt nobody. Beating on a woman like that, abusing her? That's different. We didn't do stuff like that, not ever."

"Your friends told the police the last time they saw you that night, you were heading toward the park. Made it sound like you were involved."

"No, see, they just made that shit up. They didn't have no choice." He ducked his head and rubbed a palm over it. "I don't blame them for what they said about me. Them cops were scary. *I* even said I did it, and I *knew* I didn't have nothing to do with it. We were just kids trying to get out of a bad situation. They all standing up for me now, 'cept for Terrance and Huggy; they dead. The other ones, though, you go ask any of 'em. They'll tell you I'm innocent. My man Raymond, 'specially. He been standing up for me, all this time."

"I've seen his picture in the papers."

"He been on TV, too," he said proudly. "Ran for Alderman in the Twenty-fourth Ward. Would have been good at it, too. Knows all the angles, gets stuff done."

"Nice break for you, a famous person taking your side. But that's kind of funny, 'cause back when the police were questioning him, he told them he thought you might have done it."

"That was coercion, plain and simple." His voice deepened, grew more adult, as if he were channeling Ashe himself. "Like when I gave them that confession. They was acting crazy, slamming the table and throwing chairs and shit. Screaming cuss words at me. I could've handled that, easy, but it just went on and on. They wouldn't let me rest. Kept hammering at me all night, all the next day. I was just a kid. I wanted to go home. By the end, I was so tired I would have said anything."

I took a picture of Jerry Pozorski out of my bag that I'd printed out from the *Tribune* archives, a pixilated image of a man with a square face, wavy dark hair, dressed in a suit and tie, confident and professional. He didn't look like the man I'd met two days earlier. "Is this the one who did those things?"

Taylor glanced at the picture. "He was there, some of the time. It was mostly the other one. Man, that fucker was insane."

"Other one? Kevin Casey?"

"I 'own know his name. Some white cop. Mean motherfucker. They was all white, all mean. I don't know how they sleep at night, the stuff they do."

"That night, you were out with your friends till late. What happened when you split up?"

"I went home."

"What did your friends do?"

"Went home, too. We all lived in the same place. Different buildings."

"Did they go into their buildings first, or did you?" He looked confused. "I mean, did you see them actually go inside?"

A spasm of anger twisted his mouth. "Why won't you listen to me? I already told you, they didn't do nothing to that girl."

"Okay, I get that, but—"

"Why you asking all these questions, anyway?"

"Like I said, I was hired—"

"That's the thing, see. *You* getting paid. How come you get to make money over this, and I don't get nothing?" His voice was louder, and he seemed bigger, suddenly, leaning toward me, his fists clenched so tightly the tendons stood out. "Me, I spent twenty years in prison. More'n half my life, I been locked up with bad people. You don't know what that's like. You don't want to know."

"I realize you—"

"Other guys get out? They got programs for them. They give ex-offenders jobs, apartments, training. Help them get on their feet. Not me, 'cause I ain't an offender. I was innocent, so I don't get nothing. You think that's fair?"

"No, I don't. It's not fair at all."

"There's a law says I should be compensated," he went on, his heated words tumbling together, a little foamy spit gathering at the corner of his mouth. "Over thirty thousand dollars supposed to be coming my way, *thirty thousand*, only they won't give it to me 'cause the prosecutor still says I did it." He looked both furious and confounded by the senselessness of it all. "That's fucked up. I'm innocent. The judge said so."

"The judge only said the prosecution screwed up. It's not the same as having firm proof that someone else committed the crime."

Taylor punched his fist against his thigh. "But I didn't *do* it." He was shaking with frustration, but there was also something baffled and childlike in his expression, as if he still couldn't believe that things could go so wrong.

"Listen to me, Chase." I tried to get him to focus on me, hold his eyes with mine, but I was losing him. His arms were tensed as if they longed to break something, bulging with muscle that was tightened like steel cable. A vein throbbed in his forehead like a purple worm twisting under his skin. His eyes kept darting around the room. They were full of fury and bafflement, and when they finally looked into mine, they were opaque with hopeless anger.

"This is bullshit. You only in this for yourself." Taylor stood up abruptly, his chair tipping backwards, hitting a shelf behind him, knocking over a stack of papers and a sports trophy. When it wobbled off its balance, he snatched at it, but he was too late and it toppled to the floor. He let out a low moan of despair and regret as he stumbled back into a corner of the room and shut his eyes tight, muttering "Fuck, oh fuck, oh *fuck* . . ." as he punched his temples with his clenched fists.

I wondered if Raymond Ashe would hear the commotion and intervene, but apparently the music in the next room was loud enough to cover it. I reached for the trophy. A gilt wing had broken off the figure that was holding a basketball aloft. "It's all right, Chase. No harm done," I said, scanning the rug and picking up the broken piece of plastic. "I'm going to put it in a safer place, okay?" I set it out of sight behind the desk, tucked the gilt plastic wing into my pocket, and picked up the papers, stacked them neatly on the table. "Everything's okay."

He still had his eyes closed, fists pressed to his temples. He was strong, and wound tight as a spring. It was hard to make myself step closer, within reach of those clenched fists. Holding my breath, I touched him on the arm. It was rock hard with muscle, but shivered under my fingertip. "Come sit down," I said gently.

He slowly lowered his arms and took a deep, shuddering breath. He reached blindly for the arm of the chair and jerked it toward him, sat heavily, and scrubbed his face with the tail of his T-shirt. "Man." He studied the sweat stain on his shirt, then shook his head. "Thought I busted it."

"It's all right." I waited for his dazed eyes to stop roaming the room, to settle on my face. The knot of alarm in my chest was still tight, making it hard to breathe, but I had to appear confident. "Here's the deal, okay? I'm going to do everything I can to find the guy who they should have arrested for raping that woman. If we tie that attack to the more recent rapes, ones he can go to prison for, the police will have to believe you're innocent. You with me?"

It took him a minute to focus on what I had just said and work it through. "They'll have to tell everybody they were wrong?"

"That's the idea."

"Is that gonna get me compensated?"

"I don't know. I'm not sure how the compensation thing works."

"Raymond knows all about it. I'll ask him."

"I guess Raymond knows a lot, huh?"

"He's real smart. You ask him a question, he always got an answer. Carries himself proud, too, doesn't take shit from nobody. Day I came out, there was television cameras, all these lights and everybody yelling at me. It was crazy. I couldn't handle it at all. But Raymond, he stood up there in a fine suit and he made this speech, all about justice, about what I been through. It was on the TV. He talks better than the best preacher you ever heard. And he's been my friend, all these years, through thick and thin."

"That's really something, sticking together since you were kids. He visit you in prison much?"

"Sometimes." Taylor looked away, not good at lying.

"He's been your advisor since you got out, huh?"

"Yeah. Kind of like my agent."

"Like you're a sports star?" I joked.

He chuckled. "I ain't no star. He's the star."

"Your aunt stood by you, too."

He rubbed a palm against his knee. "She been good to me."

"You got other family?"

"Nah. She's all I got."

"She gave you a place to live."

"Yeah," he said without enthusiasm.

"But you probably don't like having to take her charity."

He shook his head slowly, introspective. "I'm grateful and all, but my age, having to move in with family? A grown man shouldn't have to do that. I want to get my own place, only I don't have no money. I been trying to find work, but everywhere you go, they ask if you been in prison. Don't matter if you was in prison for something you didn't do."

"Her house is way out on the South Side, right? Avalon Park? Nice neighborhood, but there's probably not a lot to do around there. For fun, I mean."

"Ain't *nothing* to do. Most every day I take the train into town, hang with my friends."

I was still tense from his last outburst, but I had to probe to find out what his triggers were. "Probably can't meet a lot of women out that way, huh?"

"Got that right. My aunt, she always tells me I'm gonna meet a nice girl at church. Shit, them nice girls don't want nothing to do with me. Even the ugly ones. Other thing I want is a car. I hate riding the damn train all the time, waiting in the cold and the rain, watching other people drive by. Get my compensation, first thing I do is get me a nice car."

"You have any special girlfriend before you were arrested?"

"I made 'em all feel special." He smiled at the memory. "One I was with at the time, her name was Mattie. Mattie Polk. She was nice. We used to laugh a lot. I don't know what she thought about me after I got arrested."

"She never got in touch?"

"Nah. Can't blame her, though, given what they said I done. Wasn't nobody believed in me till Thea Adelman started working on it. For free, not like my other lawyer."

"I know Thea Adelman. I work for her sometimes."

"Yeah? That's one sharp woman."

"I think she's kind of scary."

He laughed. "*Real* scary. She scared that judge good. Scare me, too, but that's okay. She did right by me."

"The woman who was raped. She told the jury she recognized you."

"That was a mistake. She said so in a letter to the judge."

"How do you feel about that? I mean, it really messed your life up."

"Thea, that lawyer? She told me most every rape case that's thrown out, somebody made a mistake like that. That girl was hurt bad, she was scared, she just said what they wanted her to say. Naw, I ain't mad at her."

"There was another witness at the trial who said he heard you bragging about hurting that girl. I can't think of his name right now."

"Otis." He rolled his eyes. "Fucking Otis. He made that shit up."

"Did you know him?"

"Crazy old man. He was always yelling at us kids for making noise."

"You know if Otis is still around?"

Taylor shrugged. "He mighta died by now. No point in talking to him anyway; he just lie to you."

"You're probably right. Anyone else who you knew back then who might know anything?"

He shook his head. "Building I grew up in got tore down. Most everyone had to move away. It don't look nothing like it used to around there."

"They got a fancy new police station right around the corner now."

"That figures," he said, more amused than bitter. "Tear down the homes and give the police a nice place to work."

"I hear the cops are still giving you a hard time."

"They always hassling me. Back when they kept me up all night and day, asking all those questions? I figured, tired as I was, prison be an improvement; least I could sleep. I was wrong." He stared into space, seeing something I couldn't. "It's a bad place," he said softly. "I'd rather be dead than be back there."

"Well, let's hope I get somewhere with this. Thanks for talking to me." I gave him my card. "I might want to ask you more questions later. Would that be okay?"

"I don't mind." He tapped the card against his knee. "Meanwhile, I'm gonna talk to Raymond about how that compensation works. I want to be ready."

I took a breath, wondering if I should say anything, unsure how he'd respond. I'd already seen enough of his temper, but I didn't want to mislead him and have him get even angrier later. "It's going to take time, Chase. A lot of time. And even then, I'm not sure how this is going to work out."

He looked up at me with a sad little twist of a smile. "Nothing new about that. I done a whole lot of waiting, and so far nothing much has worked out right."

SEVENTEEN

Raymond T. Ashe was in a speechifying mood as we left the social club and got back into his car. "You look around this neighborhood, what do you see?" He swept a hand in front of him. "Trash. Weeds. Broken dreams?"

I pointed at one of a row of graystones. "Had a homicide there. Sixteen-year-old girl. Another girl stabbed her over a dress."

"A crime scene, of course that's what you'd see. The whole damn neighborhood's a crime scene. Crime against humanity. Richest, most powerful nation in the world, and look at this sorry state of affairs. Unemployment rate for men in this community is near sixty percent. Everybody has a father, brother, or son in prison or on parole. Got churches here, and bars, more'n enough bars, but no grocery stores, no banks, no pharmacies, no factories like there used to be. We can do better than this. We have to do better than this."

"Speaking of broken things . . ." I felt for the jagged piece of plastic in my pocket and handed it to him. "It came off that trophy on the table."

"Trophy?"

"For basketball, I think. It fell over."

He frowned at it, puzzled, before tucking it in his pocket. "Found it in a closet when I bought the building. How'd it get broke?"

"Chase stood up too suddenly, his chair bumped into it. He was so upset, I told him it wasn't broken, stuck it behind your desk. Shouldn't be hard to glue this part back on."

"He get mad about something?"

"He has plenty to be mad about."

"When you said you wanted to talk to him private, I wasn't sure that was such a great idea. Boy's got a temper on him. We're working on it, but all those years of abuse at Stateville, locked up with the worst of the worst, no wonder he can't always keep it together."

"He's not the only one with a temper. You shot your neighbor's dog."

He laughed, astonished. "What, you have one of your cop friends look me up? I thought that was illegal, using police records for civilian purposes."

"I read about it in the newspaper."

"Ought to know better than to believe everything you read in the papers."

"How did you avoid doing time on a weapons charge?"

"It wasn't my gun."

"I thought maybe you had friends in high places."

"Enemies, more like. People in high places don't want to hear what I have to say."

"I notice you don't waste any opportunity to get your name in print. Just don't use my investigation to do that. It'll piss me off, and Chase has nothing to gain being back in the news."

"People need to know the system failed."

"They already know. He's pretty tightly wound. He loses it on camera, in front of a reporter, it's not going to help."

"What do people expect? We lock up more of our citizens than any other country in the world, we don't provide any opportunities for rehabilitation, and then we go and punish them again for having been punished. Court says the state didn't make their case, but you think that man's ever going to find gainful employment?"

"You're using him."

He pulled up across the street from my two-flat. All the good-natured charm was gone from his expression. "You got the wrong idea about me."

"I sure hope so." I gathered up my bag and got out.

Aisha had earned her money; the apartment was spotless. Adam took the three kids back to their home, and I drove Martin back to Stony Cliff, where I ate dinner with him in the cafeteria. Then we went to his apartment to watch a documentary on the building of the Hoover Dam. He seemed to have forgotten all about his brush with the law that morning, except when he fingered the scabbed-over scrape on the side of his hand and frowned.

I stopped at the Tilquist's house, that strange magnet pull at work. I only planned to say hello before heading home to type up my notes on my interview with Chase Taylor, but Sophie had just seen a teaser for a news story on Esperanza Ruiz's sanctuary bid. She insisted that I stay long enough to watch the nine o'clock news with them. "I think it's so cool that Father Sikora is taking a stand," Sophie said, settling on the couch, her legs folded under her and a cushion clutched to her chest as we waited for the news to begin. Alice, a cynical fourteen-year-old, rolled her eyes. "What? It *is* cool," Sophie insisted.

"Maybe. But you always get so excited about everything."

Sophie stuck out her tongue at her sister before turning back to me. "Have you been to the church? Have you met Esperanza?"

"I saw her yesterday."

"What's she like?"

"Young. She's about your age."

"Wow. And she's defying the feds. That's so brave. I might go down myself to help out with the vigil." She glanced at her mother, checking her reaction.

Nancy was correcting papers, a stack of them beside her. "Don't get yourself arrested," she said, unperturbed, as she took the pencil from behind her ear and jotted a note in a margin.

"That wouldn't happen, would it?" Sophie asked me.

"I don't know. There were some arrests the night Father Sikora announced they were offering her sanctuary. Things got pretty violent."

Sophie glanced at her mother. Not too long ago, the allure of being arrested for a good cause would have only increased her excitement. Now she gave a little sigh and rested her chin on the cushion, only perking up when the news segment started.

It was anticlimactic, a brief piece that recapped the general outline of Esperanza Ruiz's sanctuary bid, with a shot of parishioners streaming into that morning's Spanish-language mass, and a brief clip replaying the disturbance of a few nights ago. So far, no word from federal authorities on how they planned to respond. Then, on to the weather.

When I got up to go, Sophie walked with me onto the porch. "If you're planning to join the vigil—" I started to say.

"I'm not going. I have a big project due for school." As I started down the steps, she blurted out, "Anni, how come you never come over anymore?"

It took me a moment to answer. "What do you mean? I'm here tonight."

"But it's the first time I've seen you in weeks. Is something wrong? I mean . . ." She gave a little shrug.

I felt a cold lump form in my chest. "No. I've just been really busy lately, that's all."

"It feels weird, not having you around. Everything feels weird anyway."

"I know. But it's not, it's just . . . work, you know?"

"Okay," she said. "Just checking." She gave me a little smile before slipping back indoors. But I could tell that she felt I hadn't really answered her question.

As soon as I got back to my apartment I powered up my laptop and checked my e-mail. Stacy had sent a message with an attachment:

Here's that essay I told you about. I'm not even going to reread it, 'cause I know it sucks. Let me know if there's anything else I can do to help.

I opened the file, a fifteen-page document.

It was an accomplished piece of writing. Though describing acts of almost unspeakable violence, her tone was cool and analytical, tinted with irony. Reading her essay, I felt chilled, as if I were watching the crime unfold on the other side of a clear layer of ice, but I could tell that some of the small, evocative details she'd included had lodged themselves like splinters of broken glass driven deep into my consciousness.

It was time to bring Jill McKenzie up to speed with the investigation. I composed a short e-mail. "I talked with one of the seven research subjects you identified," I typed, choosing my words with care. "I'm hoping to reach some of the others, and I've identified another possible subject to include in our analysis. Based on preliminary results, it seems quite possible that your hypothesis is correct. However, the initial funding for this project is just about used up. I'm willing to continue if you are; just let me know how you'd like me to proceed."

Late as it was, her answer came within a minute of my hitting the send button. "Please continue. I'll send a check for the same amount as before."

Though I was tired, I knew from experience I had to type up my notes while they were fresh. I did that, then updated my list of things to do. It was discouraging to see how long it was. I poured a glass of wine and stretched out on the couch with a book, reading the same page three times before I was able to focus. But after a few more pages, I must have drifted off to sleep because the book was lying open on my chest when the sound of my cell phone jerked me awake. It rang four times before I was able to dig it out of my bag.

"Anni? Sorry to call so late." It was Dugan.

"That's okay. I wasn't in bed yet." I blinked at the clock: 1:30 A.M. "What's up?"

"You didn't tell me you were working on the Lincoln Park case."

"Oh. You must have talked to Jerry Pozorski. I didn't like holding it back from you, but—"

Dugan cut me off. "He wants to talk to you."

"Okay."

"We're at Clarke's. The one on Lincoln."

Right now, apparently. I blinked at the clock again. "I can be there in fifteen minutes."

He clicked off without another word. I slipped my phone back into my bag, trying to guess from Dugan's tone just how sore he was at me.

ugan knew I'd have no trouble finding Clarke's. Cops know all the twenty-four-hour diners in town. The tables by the window were occupied by some tired nurses in scrubs, drinking coffee, and a pair of uniformed cops eating hamburgers. The restaurant wasn't crowded yet; when the bars closed, the place would fill up with

DePaul students operating on the theory that big platters of eggs and bacon prevented hangovers.

Dugan raised a hand from a booth across the room to catch my eye, then slid over to make room. Across the table, Jerry Pozorski nodded a greeting. He was dressed neatly this time, wearing a blue windbreaker over a polo shirt. His hair was combed, and he had shaved the grizzled stubble off his face, but he couldn't hide the spidery blotches of the heavy drinker on his cheeks and nose. There were plates on the table with the remains of scrambled eggs and fried potatoes congealing in their own grease. It looked as if neither of them had had much of an appetite.

Pozorski cleared his throat. "Sorry about the other day, shutting the door in your face." His voice sounded a little rusty, as if it hadn't been used much lately. "Caught me by surprise, hearing that you're working for Jill McKenzie."

"I don't usually disclose who my clients are, but she specifically said it was okay to tell you."

He looked confused by that. He drank the last of his coffee, set his mug down, and wiped his mouth. "How's she doing?"

"Pretty well. She teaches at a college in Iowa now." I glanced at Dugan, but I wasn't sure if he was listening; he was absently rubbing a finger across a chip in his mug, staring at nothing.

"So, what are you trying to do? I know you told me, but I . . . I didn't catch it all."

"She's doing a study on sexual assaults in Chicago in the past decade. That's not her usual research area, but after Taylor was released, she wanted to gain some kind of handle on what had happened to her by studying the data. She obtained thousands of incident reports from the CPD for the project. As she went through them, she found seven cases that seemed a lot like hers."

"What do you mean, 'like hers'?"

"Within the past ten years, seven women in their early twenties were raped and beaten early in the morning by a stranger who threatened them with a knife. All of the assaults were extremely violent. Jill's wondering if the guy who hurt her might still be at it."

"She talk to the police about this?" Dugan asked.

"She planned to, but when she found out the detective she trusted had retired, she decided to write to the prosecuting attorney instead, Peter Vogel. Her rape was his first high-profile case. She gave him the details, including the case numbers, told him what she suspected. A few weeks later, he wrote back to say they'd checked it out, there wasn't any connection to her case. But given he still insists that Taylor was guilty, I'm not sure how seriously they looked into it."

A waitress came by, and I asked for tea and an order of sweet potato fries. She wrote it down on her pad without looking at me. Working the night shift at a diner patronized by drunken college students probably wasn't conducive to developing a warm and cheery customer-service attitude.

"Could we get some more coffee, too?" Pozorski asked her.

Her pinched face smoothed into a fond smile. "Sure, Jerry."

"Wow," I said to him after she left. "She's not going to get the grumpiest employee of the month award if she keeps that up."

"I eat here a lot," he said with a faint smile that didn't last. "These cases . . . seven of them?"

"Within a five-mile radius on the West and Northwest side," I said.

"You know anything about this?" Pozorski asked Dugan, who shrugged. "Seven violent rapes, and nobody's—"

"I was working at headquarters until this year," Dugan said. "It never came across my desk."

"Still, you'd think . . ."

"Given the span of time involved, I wouldn't be surprised if nobody saw a pattern," I said. "Usually a serial rapist attacks repeatedly within a matter of weeks, all in the same area. You can't miss it. These attacks are all a year or more apart, in different neighborhoods. They would have been caught by detectives out of two different areas, Harrison and Grand Central. And the women involved came from different backgrounds. Only two of them were white."

"So, you're saying—" Dugan bristled.

"The fact they're from different racial and socio-economic backgrounds doesn't help you see connections, that's all," I said. "The incident reports Jill obtained had the victim's names blacked out, but I was able to locate one of the women. A college student in her twenties. From what she told me, her attack was similar to Jill's, except she wasn't slashed and the beating wasn't as severe, probably because he was interrupted. Someone saw the incident and called the police. The witness didn't stick around to talk to them, though. No record of who it might have been. I'm working on finding the other women. One of them was walking a dog in Garfield Park, by the way. Her attacker killed the dog. Slit its throat."

Pozorski stared down into his empty mug. "We thought we had the right guy."

"Maybe you did. Maybe these other cases are the work of a copycat, or just some other nut with a knife and a lot of anger. I've seen your case notes. You conducted a good investigation."

"Always kept my paperwork in good order," Pozorski said, then closed his eyes. His face, blotched and pale, drained of what little color it had. He picked up a paper napkin and wiped his mouth. "Excuse me for a minute." He climbed out of the booth and headed slowly and stiffly for the restrooms.

"Is he going to be all right?" I asked Dugan.

"No." He played with a spoon, his face rigid.

"Dugan, I'm sorry," I said after an awkward minute of silence.

"For what?" he snapped.

"Not telling you."

"Not telling me *what*?"

"Who my client is."

"I'm not going to spread it around, if that's what's bothering you."

"It's not that. I hated leaving you in the dark when we talked on the phone. But Jill doesn't want the news to get out. She lives in a constant state of alert. You should see this woman: twenty years later, and she still carries a gun every time she leaves the house, even to go into her own backyard. If the media gets involved, I don't know what it would do to her."

"Look what it's doing to him." Dugan jerked his head toward the restrooms. He set the spoon he'd been playing with down and swore softly when he realized the handle was bent. He picked it up and tried to straighten it before tossing it down again.

My stomach was knotted up. I'd never seen Dugan so angry, so cold. "I wish now I'd never gone to talk to him, that I'd left him out of this completely. But after reading those reports, talking to that girl . . . Dugan, I can't just walk away from this. And I don't—" I cut my words off, the knot in my stomach twisting painfully.

"What?" he said.

"I don't want you mad at me," I whispered, feeling small and stupid.

He looked at me directly for the first time since I'd sat down in the booth. "You think this is about *you*?"

I felt my cheeks burning with shame.

He picked up a paper napkin and twisted it into a wad. "I knew he was having a hard time. I knew he was all fucked up over that shooting, but did I bother to pick up a phone? Some friend, huh? Jesus Christ."

The waitress returned with my order and refilled Dugan's coffee mug as he tried to hide the mangled napkin under his plate. "I'll leave this for Jerry," she said, setting the plastic jug down. "You done with those?" She stacked up the platters, then paused and scooped up the tortured knot of napkin that was left exposed in plain sight.

"All those years of service he put in, and I couldn't find five minutes to check in," Dugan said when she had gone. "I'm such a dick. What's so funny?"

"It's not funny. It's just—I thought it was me you were mad at. And you did pick up the phone, remember? Pozorski's wife acted like everything was fine."

"That was two years ago; it doesn't count. Why would I be mad at you?"

"Because I held back from you. Because your friend's having a bad time, and I'm making it worse."

"You're just doing your job. Besides, he's not your friend. You don't owe him anything. I do." Dugan's eyes had wandered to my sweet potato fries.

"Help yourself."

"I'm not hungry," he said, but he reached out and took one anyway.

"Pozorski's old partner stopped by my place yesterday. He said he found him passed out drunk on the floor after I stopped by. He asked me to lay off. Thought bringing this up would be too much of a strain. Or maybe he just doesn't want me looking into it."

"Who is this?"

"Kevin Casey. He worked on the Lincoln Park case, too. He's an investigator for the SA now. Casey owns that apartment building, gave Pozorski the building manager job there."

"I've met him. They went into real estate together a few years ago. Maureen, Jerry's wife, was always worried about it. It used up all their savings, and she was never sure it was going to pay off."

"From what Casey said, I get the impression it didn't work out so great."

"Shit. They have two kids to send to college." Dugan reached for another strip of sweet potato. "These are good."

"Look, I don't want to cause Pozorski more problems. The papers weren't too sympathetic when he shot that nutcase. If the press started hounding him again over this—"

"He's coming back."

We both tried not to look around. Pozorski made his way back to the table, then braced his hands on it and lowered himself onto the bench, looking as if his joints hurt.

"The waitress brought coffee," Dugan said, pointing to the jug. Pozorski refilled his mug.

"Want one?" I asked, nudging my plate over.

"No, thanks. So, what did you want to ask me?"

"Uh, well . . . I've been able to go over your notes and case files. They're so thorough, I'm not sure I really need anything else."

"Why did you come to see me, then?"

"Jill suggested it. Look, I don't want to—"

"This was my case, dammit. I want to know what you got."

"Not much, yet. The seven rapes looked related, but I can't be positive they're tied to Jill's rape. Maybe you're right, you got the right guy."

"Were you listening? I said we *thought* we got the right guy. We had a group of kids who'd been smoking crack and raising hell that night. They all pointed the finger at Chase Taylor. We found a corroborating witness. Taylor confessed. It all fell into place, boom, boom, boom. Except—"

"Except?"

"It got thrown out. We must have messed up somewhere."

"Taylor told me his confession was coerced. He says he was kept up all night."

"He was."

"He was barely sixteen."

"He'd been arrested before. He knew what he was doing when he waived a lawyer."

"No family member was notified?"

"What family? His mother was hardly ever home, and she was never clear on who his father might be."

"Taylor told me he was roughed up."

"I didn't lay a finger on him."

"Not by you. Some other detective."

"If you saw what happened to that girl—" He shook his head, started over. "My guess, Taylor's lying. I made it clear to everyone working that case that we were doing it by the book. We couldn't risk screwing up that conviction by doing something dumb. But if it turns out one of our guys lost it at some point . . . Maybe you never so much as raised your voice during an interrogation, but—"

"I got suspended for two weeks once for hitting a suspect."

"Two weeks?" He was impressed. "Must have hit him pretty hard."

"Not hard enough. You didn't have any other viable suspects?"

"We questioned a lot of people, but no. Not even close. You don't usually get a case like this one, where everything snaps into place that fast. But it did this time."

"That witness, the one who said he overheard Chase bragging, Otis something . . ."

"Parchmann. Otis Parchmann."

"His testimony sounded kind of rehearsed."

"It had to be rehearsed, like a hundred times. That guy was practically brain dead. The attorneys had their work cut out, getting him ready for the courtroom."

"It wasn't just the way he said it. The stuff he claimed to have overheard, it just didn't sound like something a rapist would brag about."

Pozorski shrugged. "The jury had no trouble with it. Neither did the defense."

"One of the kids who you questioned, Raymond Ashe. He's been taking Taylor's side since he got out."

"So I saw in the papers."

"What was your impression of him?"

Pozorski rubbed his eyes wearily with a finger and thumb. "I don't know. He didn't stand out at the time. Now I guess he's a community activist, but back then he was just another punk from the projects."

"And Chase? What did you make of him?"

Pozorski drank the rest of his coffee before he answered. "He was pretty much what you'd expect from a kid growing up in a shithole without a responsible adult in his life. Barely literate, short a few bricks upstairs, chronically pissed off. He had an attitude, like you might expect. When we pulled him in this time, he tried to act cool, like always. But something was different."

He reached for the coffee jug, but apparently changed his mind, pushing his mug away. "Underneath the pose, you could tell he was scared, scared shitless. Like he knew he'd crossed the line for real this time. After he confessed, he was so relieved he broke down and cried like a little kid. I was sitting on the bench next to him. He laid his head against my shoulder, sobbing his heart out, so happy to have it off his chest, and then—" He snapped his fingers. "He fell asleep. It was like a light switching off. Innocent people don't do that. That's what I used to think, anyway."

"I talked to him today. He's got a pretty volatile temper."

"How'd you find that out?" Dugan asked.

"He was calmly answering questions until the subject of compensation came up. Then he just blew up. Ashe put it into his head that the state owes him thirty thousand for his wrongful conviction. I don't see that happening, given there's no DNA evidence available that might clear him."

"When you say he 'blew up' . . . How violent is this guy?" Dugan asked.

"Hard to say. He's like a kid with poor impulse control."

"You know, there's a reason cops usually go on the street in pairs," Dugan said.

"Really? That's funny. I got pretty used to working on my own that last year on the job."

"I'm just saying it's not a great idea for you to be questioning a man who just spent twenty years behind bars and is . . . what did you call him, Jerry? Chronically pissed off."

"You'd dealt with Chase Taylor before he was arrested for the rape," I said to Pozorski. "Had he ever been violent toward women?"

"He got in fights, but with guys, not with women."

"Any previous sex offenses?"

"Not that we knew about."

"He told me he had a girlfriend at the time he was arrested. Mattie Polk. Ring any bells?"

Pozorski mulled it over, then shook his head.

"When you first started looking at Taylor, were you surprised that he would be involved in something that violent? Or was it more like, 'it figures.' The kind of trouble he'd eventually get into?"

He didn't say anything for a while, his eyes distant. "I'm trying to remember. Everything kept pointing toward this kid. He had a record and he was acting squirrelly. So I guess . . ."

"You weren't all that surprised, then."

"I was surprised, all right. I didn't think anything could shake me up after all those years on the job. But seeing her . . . It's hard to figure that anyone could do that to another human being."

The waitress came back. "How're we doing here?" she asked brightly.

"We'll take the check," Pozorski said, sounding suddenly exhausted.

EIGHTEEN

He insisted on paying for all of us, painstakingly counting out bills and calculating a generous tip. As he led the way out, some raucous students shouldered into the restaurant, practically knocking him off his feet, leaving a wake of beer, cigarettes, and youthful arrogance behind them. Outside, the night air was nippy. Under the glare of a streetlamp, Pozorski looked drained and sick, his blotched face hollowed with shadows.

"Thanks for taking the time to talk to me," I said.

He didn't respond right away, looking as if he was thinking about something else, but after a moment he said, "Tell Jill I said hello."

"I'll do that."

"It's good to hear she's doing okay." He put out a hand to shake. His grip was stronger than I expected. "You were friends with Jim Tilquist, right? Shame, what happened. He was a good man."

"The best."

"Left a family behind, right?"

"Wife and three daughters. The youngest is six."

"Three kids." He stared off down the street, shaking his head. After a moment, he smiled to himself faintly. "There was this girl who was looking for her family way back when. Like, ten years old, living in some foster home. She turned up at Harrison asking the police to find her mother, ended up at Jim's desk. Nothing to go on, but she wouldn't quit looking, and neither would he. He talked about her all the time. I seem to remember she ended up on the job."

"That was me."

"Thought it might be." He nodded to himself, lost in thought. We stood there in an awkward group. Dugan rocked on his heels and blew on his hands to warm them. "Well . . ." Pozorski said, coming out of his trance.

"It's late. See you around," I said to Dugan and turned toward my car, parked in the next block.

"Hang on," Pozorski called out. He reached inside his windbreaker, fumbled a manila envelope out of an inside pocket, and handed it to me.

"What's this?"

"Might help," he said. "Let's keep in touch." Then he turned to climb into the Jeep. Dugan climbed in the driver's side. I watched as he executed an erratic U-turn out of his parking spot.

When I reached my car, I opened the envelope. There were two pocket-sized notebooks inside, their covers stained with coffee rings and wrinkled from rain, edges worn soft. I flipped one open and tilted it toward a nearby streetlamp to try and make out the scribbles inside. I recognized the handwriting, the same as the neat case notes that had been photocopied and handed over to Chase Taylor's defense, but on these pages it staggered sideways across the page, scraps recorded while on the move. Dates, times. Fragmentary sentences.

I flipped a few more pages and caught sight of a familiar name: Jill McKenzie, all by itself, underlined, in the center of a page. Below that, "DePaul ID. Blonde, 20 yrs. Shoulder broke—blood loss—face bad." I flipped back. "North pond, 20 yards west." Another note: "Clothes torn. Cuts to breasts, torso, pubic." And at the bottom of the page, boxed with penciled lines, drawn so hard the marks were scored deeply into the paper, "Raped?"

His case notes. Not the ones on record. The real ones.

stayed up far too late, leafing through the spiral notebooks. My thoughts were spinning as I tapped out comments and questions on my laptop, rubbing my eyes when they started to glaze from the effort of making out Pozorski's hasty scrawl. When I realized it was approaching 4:00 A.M. I shut my computer down and went to bed.

When I woke, the room was flooded with sunlight. I put on a pot of coffee and pulled on some clothes, then went outside to fill the cat's dish. The sun was pouring down, making the yellow leaves of my walnut tree bright against the deep blue sky. It was warm for October, so I took my coffee out onto the porch, sitting on the steps to enjoy the sun as I drank it. I could hear the voices of kids at the elementary school down the street, happy to be cut loose for morning recess, chattering like a flock of roosting birds.

I kept seeing Pozorski's scribbled observations angling sideways across blue, ruled lines. Detectives had to make their notes available to the defense as part of discovery. Though it was technically against the rules, a lot of cops kept two sets of books, one for themselves and another for the record. Sometimes they did it to fudge the facts or clean up mistakes, but that's not what Pozorski did. The on-record notes described the crime scene in detail, while the ones I'd read last night lacked the specifics, simply forming an off-the-cuff outline Pozorski could use to reconstruct things later. But unlike the official version, the raw notes conveyed the gut punch of seeing a young woman being loaded into an ambulance, her face so battered it seemed beyond repair. Flipping the pages, I felt his shock, felt the seeping realization that this case was a new kind of crime, one that would set off a firestorm of outrage.

One page had the date, time, and "vic stat NW Mem" at the top: a victim statement taken at Northwestern Memorial Hospital the afternoon of the attack. It read like a prose poem, short enough that I could remember it word for word:

> *black man*
> *young, thin, strong*
> *knife point to eye*
> *"stop fussing"*
> *Cut her breasts, pubic—*
> *rape*
> *then he got angry*

Below a stroke of pencil and another notation of the time, indicating the end of the interview, there was a looser, furious scrawl: *Christ she's just a kid.*

My phone rang. A woman's voice said, "I, uh . . . Is this . . ."

"I'm Anni."

"A friend gave me your number?"

"Okay." I kept my voice low-key, relaxed, trying not to scare her off.

"She, um . . . she said you're looking for a guy that's been attacking women."

"That's right. From what I can tell, he's hurt a lot of people."

"You're not with the police, though."

"No. I used to be, but now I'm a private investigator working for one of the people he attacked."

A child's voice asked something in Spanish in the background. My caller must have muffled the receiver with her hand because I couldn't hear anything but a mutter in response. Then she came back on the phone. "Thing is, I don't want to be involved in some court case."

"Whatever you choose to say to me will be confidential."

"She said I could trust you, this friend of mine. But . . . I'm not sure about this."

"It will be just between us, if that's how you want it."

"You swear?"

"I swear."

She exhaled a trembling breath. "You know the playground in Humboldt Park? By the pond? I'm taking my kids over there to play."

"Look for me by the fountain. I'll be wearing jeans and a gray, hooded sweatshirt."

t was only a few blocks' walk from my house. I found an empty bench near the fountain where children cooled off on hot summer days. Now it was just a wide space filled with dried leaves. I heard sirens howling somewhere in the neighborhood, but the park was an oasis of peace. A soft breeze wafting across the lagoon brought the scent of water and a whisper of cattails.

I wondered which of the women inside the fenced area might be my caller. I was putting my bets on a young Hispanic mother until a short, plump woman in her midtwenties came through the gate with two children clinging to the handles of a stroller. She caught my eye and nodded shyly, then crouched down to talk to the oldest child, who took the toddler's hand and hoisted him into a baby swing. The woman wheeled the stroller over to my bench. "You're Anni?"

"That's me."

"Sorry I'm late. We couldn't find my little boy's shoes. His room's a mess."

"No problem. It's such nice weather, it feels good to sit out here."

"That's why I wanted to make sure we got out to the park today. I hate winter. Takes forever to get them into their coats, and five minutes after you get there, you got to go back inside 'cause they get soaked from playing in the snow."

I leaned down to get a better look at the sleeping baby, barely visible among the blankets. "Six months old?"

"Four," her mother said proudly. "She's a big girl. Nine pounds when she was born. You got kids?"

"No. Not even married." She looked saddened by that, prompting me to add, "I was sort of engaged, once, but it didn't work out. Say, thanks for calling me. I know it's not easy to talk about this stuff."

"This woman you're working for, she got attacked, huh?"

"Raped and beaten so badly she almost died. This was several years ago, but it looks as if the same man has been doing it ever since."

She watched her children at the swings. "It was three years ago, for me," she said softly. "Back then, I had a job cleaning offices down-town. I had to go to work real early, five in the morning." Her words trailed away.

Three years ago; the same year as Stacy's attack. "Where did it happen?"

"Just over . . ." She looked over her shoulder, then turned back as if she didn't want to see the place. "I was just walking up the street to catch the bus downtown when a man snuck up behind me. He hit me so hard I almost blacked out. He showed me a knife, made me go into the alley with him. There was an old car parked back there. He pushed me down behind it and did his business. Then he got mad and beat me up pretty good."

As she spoke I was mentally reviewing the list of incident reports and the map I'd made. "What time of year was this?"

"Spring. Late April."

It wasn't among the reports Jill had given me. "Did you contact the police?"

"I didn't want to, but the people at the hospital called them. Wasn't much point. It was too dark to see anything, and after he hit me in the head, I wasn't seeing too good anyway. I still get headaches a lot. I don't know if it's from that or something else."

"The man who attacked you, could you tell if he was big? Medium-sized?"

She shrugged. "He seemed like a giant, but that's just 'cause I was scared."

"Did you get any impression of what kind of clothes he was wearing?"

"Work clothes. Coveralls, like you wear to fix cars, only that's not what he did. My husband's a mechanic. I know how his clothes get. It was that kind of coveralls, but they didn't smell like oil or grease."

"What did they smell like?"

"Like . . ." She frowned in concentration. "Like smoke. Like he'd been burning junk to keep warm, maybe. I'm glad, 'cause you know? If my husband came home smelling like that man, I wouldn't feel good about it."

"Were you in the hospital for long?"

"Just overnight. My jaw was broke. I couldn't eat nothing but milk shakes for a while. At least I didn't lose the baby."

"You mean—you were pregnant when this happened?"

"I wasn't showing yet, so I don't think he even knew. It was all I could think about though. Please, God, let the baby be okay. And he was." She nodded toward her son across the playground.

It took me a minute before I could speak. "I'm glad your baby was all right. Is there anything else you can tell me about the man who attacked you?"

"His hands were rough. And not to be racist or nothing, but he sounded African-American. His accent."

"What did he say to you?"

"Just that he would cut me if I made any noise. I was quiet, but he cut me, anyway." She gestured at her waist. "Down there. Not too deep, though. It doesn't hardly show. I told my husband it was stretch marks." She smiled faintly at that. Then she turned to me, her face serious. "I don't want him to know about this." She must have seen something in my eyes, because she added, urgently, "You promised you wouldn't tell. It would make him really mad."

I had to bite back the first words that came to me. I watched the kids playing for a moment. "You're not to blame for any of this."

"Blame?" She looked confused, then realized what I meant. "Oh, he wouldn't be mad at *me*. He's not like that. But he would be so angry at that man, it would just eat a big hole inside of him."

"Sorry, I misunderstood. How did you explain your injuries to him? Or did you meet after this happened?"

"No, we—" She broke off, watching her kids intently as the little one, getting restless, started to climb out of his swing. She waited until her daughter safely lifted him from the seat and they were set-tled beside the fence, poking sticks into the dirt in some secret game. "We got married right after we graduated high school. He had a good factory job for a while, but they laid everybody off, and he couldn't find nothing else so he joined the army. It wasn't just for the money. He believes in what America stands for, he wanted to do his part. He got deployed to Iraq just nine days before this thing happened to me."

"My God. You must have been worried sick about him, and then . . ."

"I couldn't tell him about it. I didn't want him stressing about stuff at home when he was over there, risking his life every day. Then they extended him for another year. Oh, man, that was hard. I thought I'd never be able to wait that long. But it was only a couple months later his truck flipped over. It messed his leg up, but at least he got to come home."

"Sounds like you have a good marriage."

"We do. He works real hard to take care of us. That's partly why he enlisted, the bonus money was so good. Sometimes he wonders if he should have done things different, but you can't go back and do it over."

"Do you ever think he might want to know? That he wouldn't want you to have to deal with this all by yourself?"

"Oh, that's what *he'd* think. But it would just make him go through all the stuff I did." She laughed ruefully. "Man, you wouldn't believe how angry I was. I just wanted to hurt that man, hurt him bad. The hardest thing I ever had to do was forgive him. I don't know if you're religious, but it's real important to me, my spiritual life. I'd go to the church every day and light a candle and pray about what was going on with me, what I was feeling. There's this little, what do you call it? An altar for the Virgin. That's where I go when I need to pray. She went through a lot worse; she had to forgive the men who killed her son. She gave me the strength to put it behind me." She looked at me. "You don't believe me?"

"I'm not sure you can put that kind of thing behind you, not really."

She shrugged. "I'm not so good at explaining things, I guess. All I can say is I'm not mad anymore, thanks to my faith. Also, my friend helped a lot, the one who told me about you. She talked to me at the hospital, explained the things they were doing. Stayed with me when the police came. After, I would call her when I was feeling down. That's the reason I'm talking to you. 'Cause I owe her. But, like I said before, I'm not testifying in court or nothing."

"I understand. The detectives who investigated this, do you remember their names?"

She shook her head, more of a refusal than an answer. "Look, I know you want to catch this guy, but even if you caught him and put him right in front of me, I couldn't say for sure it was him. So there's no point in me being involved. It would just make my husband feel bad that he was over there instead of here, protecting me, protecting our son. Mexican men, nothing's more important than family to them. He'd want to find that man and do something to him. He's got enough problems from the war, he doesn't need this."

"But . . . sorry, I'm not married, I don't know how these things work, but don't you think you should be honest with him?"

She shook her head. "It might make me feel better, but what good would it do him?" She reached down to tuck the blanket around the sleeping baby. "Since he got home from the war, he gets frustrated about things. Somebody cuts him off in traffic, or kids make too much noise outside the house at night, it's hard for him to keep his temper. It worries me, 'cause he's still waiting for his citizenship papers. If he got into something and ended up arrested they could deport him. When that happens, you can't never come back."

"But—he was in the service."

"Oh, he's legal. You can't enlist unless you have a green card."

"But I thought if he served . . ."

"Veterans are supposed to have priority, but it still takes a long time. I just wish it would come through so we wouldn't have to worry about it no more."

I watched the kids at play for a minute. "Look, I understand why you don't want to go public with this. But I'm going to keep looking for this man, and sooner or later the authorities will have to take it seriously. If the police start seeing connections, they may reopen your case, even if they don't hear about it from me. I'm just being honest, here."

She nodded. "I already thought about that. Guess it's something else I'll have to pray about, huh?"

NINETEEN

left her in the playground and walked around the lagoon. The light bouncing off the water dazzled my eyes and made them sting. I realized my cell phone was in my hand, that I'd automatically scrolled to a familiar number without even thinking about it. "What's up?" Dugan was asking as I put it to my ear. He sounded tense and harried. I heard urgent voices raised behind him.

"Sorry. You sound busy. I'll call you later."

"No, wait. Let me take this out into the hall." The voice faded out, as if the volume had been turned down. "What's wrong?"

"I found another one."

"Another . . ."

"Another victim. Same MO, same everything. Dammit, Dugan, she's not even on my list. How many women has he raped?"

"Jesus. Look, I—"

"She doesn't want anyone to know, wouldn't even give me her name. She told me she forgives him. *Forgives* him? I want to find this guy and rip his head off."

I could hear voices in the background again. "Can you hold on a sec?" I heard a confused mumble in the background before he came back on. "Look, something just happened. Things are crazy here. Can I call you back?"

"Don't worry about it. I'll just . . . I'm sorry, I shouldn't be bothering you at work." Someone called his name. "Forget it. You have things to do."

"Okay. But Anni?"

"Yeah?"

"I'll call you soon as I can."

I folded my phone and stuffed it into my pocket, feeling restless and angry and dangerously on the brink of tears. Then I remembered Father Sikora telling me I should stop by more often, that he was always available to talk. Fine: I'd see how he would explain a religion that made women think their most important task after being assaulted was to forgive their rapists.

By the time I approached the church, I was primed for an argument, as if a fuse had been lit and it was sizzling down to its last inches, but when I turned the corner I saw the street in front of the church blocked with fire trucks. "What's going on?" I asked a man standing on his porch.

"Somebody tried to burn down the church."

"There was smoke coming out the back door," the woman beside him chipped in.

"Is anyone hurt?" I asked.

She shrugged. They both stared at the scene vacantly, as if they were watching a television show.

I pushed past a knot of onlookers, realizing it couldn't be too serious or the firemen standing idly beside the trucks would be busier. They didn't even have their hoses out. Az Abkerian was talking to one of them, scribbling furiously in his reporter's notebook.

Three college-age kids sitting on the steps, with backpacks and bedrolls strewn around them, were eyeing the crowd nervously. "You okay?" I asked them.

"Yeah." The girl who spoke fingered one of the studs in her left ear. "We didn't even know there was a fire till the trucks pulled up."

"How long have you been here?"

"Since last night," one of them said. He sounded as if he had a cold.

"See anyone go inside?"

"Lots of people." He sneezed. "We're not keeping track or anything. We're just here to protest the way immigrants get treated in this country."

"It's getting scary, actually," a skinny boy with a scruffy beard and earnest eyes said. "People yell at us as they drive by. Sometimes they throw things." He turned around and showed me a dented can of refried beans. "Like this. That's so offensive. Besides, if this hit my head, I could have been seriously injured."

I saw Az tuck his notebook into a pocket, so I went over to talk to him. "Nothing but a little smoke damage," he said, waggling his pencil at the church behind him. "It was basically out before Chicago's Finest even got here."

"Was it deliberately set?"

"Kind of hard to imagine how someone could have accidentally poured lighter fluid over a box of church bulletins and dropped in a match. Nobody's saying anything on the record, but the bomb and arson unit is sending some officers to check it out. Looks like whoever it was slipped out the side door before anybody noticed they had a barbecue happening in the vestry."

"Was anyone even in the church at the time?"

"Just Esperanza Ruiz and her baby."

"Oh, shit. Of course, they can't leave."

"One of the church ladies took the baby next door, at least until the smoke clears. The firefighters wanted Esperanza out, too, but she refused. That gal can cuss like a sailor. I wanted to get a quote, but she wouldn't say anything fit to print."

"Her baby could have been hurt. No wonder she was upset."

"It was my impression she wasn't all that worried about the kid. She mostly wanted to find whoever did it so she could take his balls off with a pair of rusty pruning shears. Pissed her off that she can't leave the church to go after him. She's the one put the fire out, just filled a wastepaper basket with water from the baptismal font and dumped it over the fire a couple of times. To be honest, it looks to me more like a prank than a serious arson attempt. They been getting a lot of that."

"A lot of what?"

"The usual. Ugly messages spray-painted on the walls, couple of broken windows. Guy over there told me someone threw a can of beans at his head. He seemed to think the FBI should investigate it as a hate crime. Seriously, you should see some of the comments we've been getting on-line about this story. I had over a thousand postings on my last piece, ninety percent of them hostile, and that's not counting the comments we couldn't run. So long as Esperanza's holed up in the church—"

He broke off when his phone rang. He pulled it out of his pocket. "Yeah?" His bushy eyebrows went up as he listened. "No shit. How do I get there?" He trapped his phone against his shoulder as he pulled out his notebook and jotted directions. He glanced up at me as he tucked his notebook away, all of his mirth replaced by seriousness. "I gotta go. You know if Sikora's got any kind of security laid on for tonight?"

"No. Why?"

He had already turned away to hustle toward his car. "Just tell him he's going to need it."

I climbed the steps and went through the wide-open doors into the church vestibule where Father Sikora was talking to a fireman. Esperanza was glowering at them both, her hands cocked on her hips. "How are you doing?" I asked her.

"How you think? Some motherfucker just tried to kill us. Asshole."

"Sounds like he wasn't trying very hard."

"If I ever catch up with that son of a bitch, I'll teach him how to do it right. I got friends who could show him, too."

"Saying stuff like that isn't going to help."

"I know," she said gloomily. "But I'm getting sick of being stuck in here all the time. It's really boring. They don't even got cable."

"It's a church."

"Still." She leaned against the door frame, her arms crossed over her chest, looking disconsolately at the scene outside. "People are so mean. They drive by and yell things. Somebody busted a window right over the baby's bed. And all I can do is sit here and wait for immigration to come after me."

"Maybe they won't. Bad publicity for them to raid a church."

"And anyway, why bother? They already got me locked up. I hate this," she added softly. I didn't see any point in mentioning the alternative—a crowded cell in a detention center, maybe in another state. To go by the look in her eyes, she was already thinking about it.

A marked cruiser drew up and two officers got out, toting cases of equipment. One of them frowned at me. "This is a crime scene."

"The fire was back in the vestry." I pointed through the inner doors down the nave. "Other end of the church."

"And you are?"

I pulled out my wallet, opened it to show my license. His frown deepened as he recognized my name. "I'm here to discuss security precautions with Father Sikora. Do you know if the Wood District has scheduled any extra patrols of this area?"

"You'd have to ask them. We're bomb and arson."

The man from the Fire Department broke off his conversation with Father Sikora and beckoned to the officers. "I'll show you where it happened." The three of them set off.

Father Sikora shook his head. "I heard that. Telling lies in a church; you should be ashamed."

"Hey, at least I don't have a potty mouth like some people. Seriously, we do need to talk about security. Az Abkerian got a phone call a minute ago. He didn't tell me what was up, but something is. He says you need to be on guard."

"He's always so dramatic. But that's not why you came here."

"I was going to ask you something, but it's not important."

"Excuse us for a minute," he said to Esperanza, then put a big hand on my shoulder and steered me inside, down the far aisle of the nave. We sat in a pew near a side altar, where candles flickered in front of a statue of the Virgin. The usual scent of incense and candle wax had an acrid burnt-paper edge to it. "This isn't as private as my office, but it will have to do. What's the matter?"

"You can't afford to leave the church unlocked, not with all that's going on."

He waved a hand, as if he was erasing my words. "What's on your mind?"

"Is there some Catholic teaching that you're supposed to forgive people who hurt you and keep hurting other people? Because that doesn't make any sense to me."

"It sounds as if you're thinking about a specific situation."

"It's this thing I'm working on. A guy has assaulted a whole string of women over the past twenty years. I just talked to one of his victims. She said she couldn't help me out. All she cared about was praying really hard so that she could forgive him. What's up with that?"

"Do you think she's withholding information that could help you with this case?"

"No. At least that's what she says."

"You think she's lying?"

I sighed impatiently. "She's not lying. That's not the issue."

"You just don't think she should be so ready to forgive a man who isn't repentant."

"He doesn't deserve it. There's such a thing as right and wrong."

"Of course."

"She says this is all about her faith. Like she has to give him a pass so she can be in good standing with God. That's fucked up. Sorry."

"Who's the potty mouth now?"

"It slipped out; I apologize. But I don't get it. He did horrible things to her. Why shouldn't she be angry?"

"Because she doesn't want to be?" He looked up and tilted his head to one side, as if he was listening to some faint sound. "Maybe forgiveness is something she has to do for herself, so he doesn't have power over her anymore. A way to heal." He sat for a moment, his hands resting on his knees, gazing up at the shadowy ceiling. "How have you been lately?"

"Fine. Busy." I flashed on that long to-do list I'd made last night. It made me tired just thinking about it. And so far, all I seemed to do was make things worse. Jill had to worry about being identified and hounded by the press. It took a line of coke and a bottle of wine for Stacy to talk to me. Pozorski got so drunk he passed out on the floor in his own vomit. And now a rape victim had to worry her husband would get angry and get himself deported if my case brought hers to light.

"I see you running some mornings. You look very . . . intent."

"Just trying to stay in shape."

"You look like you're running for your life."

"I like to push it a little. Nothing wrong with that."

"Hmm. See much of the Tilquist family these days?"

"Not so much. Sophie's been doing okay lately."

"I didn't mean professionally. You were so close to the family."

"I've been busy."

"Is that really why you don't see them?"

"I don't know. It's not the same anymore."

"Because . . . ?"

I sighed. "Because when I go there, I can't help thinking about all the stuff they don't know. All the lies."

He mulled that over. "Are you still angry at Jim?"

"No. He had his reasons for keeping things from us. It's just awkward. I don't know what to say to them."

"Do you have to say anything?"

"Do you have to answer everything I say with a question?"

He laughed to himself. "I didn't notice I was doing that." We sat in silence for a few minutes, the ribs of the ceiling looming over us. "So, let me see if I have this right. When you're with his family, you see how much they miss him, and so do you. But you also miss the person you thought he was. It's like you lost him twice."

"Yeah, that's what it feels like. I just wish he'd never asked me to investigate that case."

We sat for a while. "Want to know what I think?" he asked, rousing himself.

"There you go again with the questions."

"I think it's time you forgave yourself."

I couldn't think how to respond to that. I stared at the candles in front of the statue glowing in their little glass holders. Even with the arson investigators talking to each other in the vestry and sounds of the firemen's radios coming through the open doors, the quiet of the church was soothing. I could see how a woman racked with bad memories would find comfort in a place like this, where in the silence she could find some still center deep inside herself, untouched by things beyond her control.

"How much does it cost?" I asked after a minute.

"What?"

"Lighting those candles."

"Nothing."

"Baloney. There's a money box right there."

"For donations. It's a tradition."

I felt for change in my pocket, got up and pushed two quarters through the slot. They fell with an echoing clank. As I took a stick and lit one of the candles, I wondered how many that woman had lit in the months after her rape.

"Hey, Sikora," a familiar voice called out. Simone Landry, Diggy Salazar's flamboyant defense lawyer, came waddling up the aisle, short and overweight, wrapped in a glittery Indian skirt topped by an aubergine tunic and a multicolored cardigan that smelled of wet sheep. "I heard someone tried to start a bonfire with some hymnals."

"Just old bulletins, fortunately." The priest got up and worked his way down the pew to meet her. "A couple of police officers are here to check into it."

Her frizzy hair was scooped into a bun, but half of it had escaped and fanned around her face, as if her manic energy was filling it with static. She set her shoulder bag down on the end of the pew, then had to disentangle her scarf from it before she noticed me. "I know you." Landry narrowed her eyes at me, trying to coax the memory out.

"I testified at Phil Maloney's trial."

"Oh my God, don't remind me." She put a palm to her forehead, then shook her finger at me, scolding, as she turned to Father Sikora. "This woman. She was a total pain in the ass. I tried six ways from Sunday to shake her story, but she wouldn't budge."

"She's very stubborn," he agreed.

"Want to come work for me? I could use a good investigator."

"Thanks, but I'm tied up with something right now."

"I don't have any money to pay you with, anyway. Though you could do it pro bono. Might be satisfying, sticking it to the boys who kicked you out of their clubhouse. You think?" She dismissed me with a wave. "Ah, she's still sore at me over that cross."

"You lost the case," I pointed out.

"So? He was guilty."

"You put up a good fight, though."

"It was a brilliant defense, if I may say so myself."

"Why not? You always do," Thea Adelman said, headed toward us. "What are you doing here?" she asked me.

"I saw the fire engines, wondered what was up."

"It's not the first time someone's caused trouble, but it seems to be escalating," Landry said. "Setting a fire—that's getting serious."

"I put it out, easy," Esperanza said dismissively.

"Next time it could be something worse. How's it going with you?" Thea asked me.

"Good. That case I told you about? It's getting interesting."

She frowned. "So there's something in it?"

"I'm sure there is."

"Keep us posted."

I nodded and started to leave, but turned to say "I wish you lawyers could talk this priest into taking security precautions. I was just talking to a reporter from the *Trib* a few minutes ago. He got a call and took off in a hurry. I don't know what's going on, but whatever it is—he said the church would need extra security tonight."

"Which reporter?" Landry asked me.

"Az Abkerian."

She started burrowing in her large leather bag.

"He's covering Diggy's case," Thea murmured to Esperanza, whose usual bravado slipped. For a moment, she looked anxious and lost before she crossed her arms across her chest and reassumed her air of scornful invincibility.

"Father, locking the church when it's not in use is an absolute necessity," Thea said, using her bossy voice. "We should also see if some parishioners would be willing to join the vigil outside. More presence would help, especially if we could get a few good-sized men to be on watch overnight."

Landry had found her cell phone. She punched at the keypad as she walked down the aisle toward the altar. "Hey. What's going on?" she asked someone in a low voice. She turned away to keep the call private. It made me wonder if she had an informant within the police department, or maybe the *Tribune*'s newsroom.

"We can get people to turn out," Father Sikora said. "But I like to keep the church open, for at least a few hours a day."

"Someone should contact the watch commander at the Wood District police station and see if they can lay on extra patrols," I suggested. "Not me."

"I'll make the call." Thea reached for her phone.

Landry snapped her phone shut and came back toward us. She looked unusually solemn. "What happened?" Esperanza asked, her voice tight.

She reached out and rested a hand on the girl's shoulder gently. "I'm afraid Diggy's case is about to shift into high gear. They just found Kathy Miller's body."

TWENTY

Russian immigrant had been hunting for late-season mushrooms in one of the forest preserves that ring the city. Rambling in the Cap Sauers Holdings, a nature preserve that had the distinction of being the most isolated spot in Cook County, he had left the footpath to scour the side of a ravine, but instead of mushrooms, he found badly decayed human remains tucked under a rocky overhang and hidden behind stones. Though the body was decomposed, what was left of her clothing was identifiable, as was the St. Christopher medal and ring that she had been wearing the night she disappeared. It would take time before they had positive proof of identification, but a police spokeswoman speaking to a CNN reporter left little doubt that the long-missing woman had been found. Coverage included a clip of family members comforting one another, and a firm statement from the state's attorney, Peter Vogel, that every effort would be made to ensure Kathy had justice at last.

After leaving the church, I went home and settled down to work, tracing the whereabouts of Chase Taylor's former girlfriend. But it was hard to avoid thinking about that body in the woods. The case had attracted the same kind of attention that Jill McKenzie's had, saturating the media for months, but Jill had been a nameless, abstract victim, an everywoman who could assume the appearance of any girl whose safety was at risk. Kathy Miller's face was well known. We'd seen her smiling on home video clips shown during television appeals and on faded posters taped to lightposts. Word of her death would be taken personally by Chicagoans. It felt as if there'd been a death in the family—a death so brutal that there would be a lot of fury mixed in with the grieving.

I tried to push it away and concentrate on my job. After two dozen phone calls, I had a lead on Mattie Polk. She had married and moved to Milwaukee, but nobody picked up the phone at what I hoped was her current residence. I left a message and looked over my list. I could try to get hold of Otis Parchmann, the prosecution witness so witless he had needed extra coaching for his stint on the stand, or the two friends who had been with Chase Taylor and Raymond Ashe the night Jill was attacked. But I was sick of making phone calls, sick of sitting at a desk. I'd hit the streets and see if I could find any traces of Aisha's sister instead. I printed off a flyer with the question "Have you seen this woman?" along with my phone number, and headed out.

My first stop was the club where Olivia had told me the girl had started to work as a hooker. I drove past blocks of vacant lots, boarded-up buildings, depressed-looking tenements, and a scattering of storefront churches, until I reached a corner where a handful of small businesses operated—a grocery, a grill that advertised "fast and soul food," and a currency exchange. The K-Town Tap was in an elegant if decrepit old building that had a round tower over the recessed front door. All of the ground-floor windows save one had been boarded up; the remaining window, alongside the door, had a metal grill over it, but the glass behind the grill was cracked. Looking more closely I saw the cracks radiated from a hole where a bullet had punched through it.

Nice place.

A couple of sleepy girls inside declined to talk to me, though I could tell from the way they glanced at each other that they recognized Amira from the photo I showed them. They referred me to a burly man in a back room who said the bar was under new ownership; he was fixing things up, planning to make the bar a nice gathering place. He took Amira's picture and scratched the side of his nose. "Yeah, I seen her before. Not in here—we don't have none of that stuff going on anymore. She was up by Roosevelt. There's a gas station up there with a car wash. She come up to me once when I was filling up my tank. Looked all skanky, though, not like in this picture." He shook his head. "Look how pretty she used to be."

I bought a catfish sandwich at the grill and chatted with the woman behind the counter as I ate. She knew Amira, but hadn't seen her in months. "Real shame. That girl could have made something of herself, but she wanted to get out of the house, live independent. Ended up dependent on a bad man. She got mixed up in something that brought the police around, so he cut her off. Maybe that's a blessing in disguise; I saw her more than once with a black eye, thanks to him."

"That's strange. I thought he was employing her. You know, entertaining other men."

"Whoring for him, you mean?"

"Right. How did he expect her to earn if he was putting bruises on her?"

"Exactly. That's why he never amounted to anything. Thought he was a businessman, but he didn't treat any of his girls right. He's in jail now."

"So I heard. Any idea where Amira is now?"

"She don't live around here anymore. You can leave one of her pictures if you want. Maybe somebody's seen her."

I stopped in at the corner grocery and bought a cold drink as an excuse to talk. The South Asian man working there didn't know anything as a matter of principle, but before I left, one of the girls from the K-Town Tap came in. Seeing me, she tipped her head to the rear of the store and I met her there as she scanned a cooler full of wilted produce and bruised fruit. "Why you looking for Amira?"

"It's a favor for her little sister, Aisha. She's concerned."

"You used to be a cop, right? I remember you asking about a shooting down the street."

"I don't work for the police anymore."

"Since that officer beat on a kid and you told everybody what happened. I know that family from church. You know that boy still can't feed himself?" She weighed a lemon in her hand. "You might find Amira up on Madison, around the forty-five, forty-six hundred block. I seen her there a few times. She didn't look too good. Using, you know. Used to help her family out, but now it all goes into her arm. Say, you got a few dollars you can spare? I got to pay the babysitter today and I'm short."

A s I returned to my car, I flipped through my notebook looking for the address of Amira's girlfriend, the one she stayed with after her pimp threw her out. Before I found it, my phone rang. "Yes?"

I heard someone clearing his throat. "This is Jerry. Uh, Jerry Pozorski? Wondered if you found anything in those notebooks."

"Thanks for letting me see them. They gave me a good feel for the case. I did have a few questions, though."

"Why don't you stop by tonight and I'll try to answer them."

"Tonight?"

"I thought we could get together at my place, if that works for you."

"Sure. I can come over."

"And bring what you got on those other cases. The ones that seem to be related. We can do some brainstorming."

I didn't say anything for a minute. "I'll have to give that some thought."

"I'm not trying to horn in. I just thought it might help you out to run it past someone else."

"It's a confidentiality issue. Some of the people I've talked to don't want to go on record."

"Fine. We'll leave them out of it, just take a look at the big picture." He paused before adding, a little desperately. "Look, I realize you don't got any reason to trust me, especially given the way I acted when you came by my place. But you're working for Jill, and she sent you to me. I thought she'd be angry about the way things turned out. When they threw that case out two years ago, it was like the one good thing I had to look back on was gone. Worthless."

"It wasn't anything you did."

"It was my case. I would really like another chance to get it right, okay?" He paused, but then rushed on before I could respond. "You like Indian food? There's a place around the corner that's pretty good. I thought we could have carryout. Or we could do something else if you want."

"I love Indian food. What time?"

"Six?"

"I'll be there."

"Okay, then." He seemed at a loss for what to say next.

"See you."

"Right. Bye." Before the phone clattered back into its cradle, I heard him heave a deep breath as if he'd just run a mile.

noticed there was a text message waiting for me from Dugan. "Still busy—talk later?" I thumbed a reply: "No rush."

I had a couple of hours before I had to set off for Jerry Pozorski's basement apartment in Lincoln Park, so I drove to Amira's last known address. It was an old brick three-flat that had been divided into a warren of small apartments. Among the faded tags beside doorbells was one with the name of Amira's girlfriend. But she wasn't in a friendly mood when she came to the door and glanced at the photo. "She ain't here. Moved out."

"I know. I was wondering if I could ask you a few questions about her. Her sister's worried. Amira hasn't been by to see the family since last July."

"Why you asking me? I don't know where she is." The woman stood in the half-opened door, blocking the way, arms crossed defensively.

"But this is the most recent address they could give me. When did she last live here?"

"She didn't *live* here. I let her sleep on my couch for a while, but I ain't got room for another person, and anyway, the landlord would charge more if he found out. Finally had to ask her to find her own place."

"Did she? Find a place?"

"I don't know. Ain't my business what she does. Just don't want her around here no more. She stole money from me. Used to be, she was a decent person. We were good friends in school, real tight. But after she hooked up with the wrong kind of people, she let herself go. I can't be doing with a thief living in my house. Barely got enough to get by as it is."

"Last April, she was attacked near Garfield Park. Got beaten up, sexually assaulted."

"She was in a bad relationship at the time."

"You think her boyfriend did it? Lorcan Sills?"

She gave a shrug. "She said it was some stranger. Why you asking about this, anyway? That was a long time ago."

"I'm just trying to figure out what's been going on with her since she left home."

The woman counted off on her fingers. "She took up with an evil man, got hooked on H, got the shit knocked out of her, got thrown out by her no-good boyfriend when the police hassled him about it, and then she came here to sleep on my couch and take money out of my purse when I wasn't looking. What happened after that, I have no idea—and you know something? I don't even care."

"Thanks for your time," I said. She just shook her head wearily and shut the door.

I spent the next hour and a half checking out the stretch of Madison between Garfield Park and Cicero. It looked too ordinary to be a red-light district—a strip of body shops, gas stations, and vacant lots—but I remembered that arrest reports for soliciting ran high in this beat, and not just on the night shift.

Most of the people I talked to were politely unhelpful. Two of them tried to sell me some crack. A man wiping tables in a Chinese restaurant recognized her, but she hadn't been in for a long time. He shook his head at the picture. "Not like that. Skinny." He sucked in his cheeks to demonstrate.

I left a dozen copies of her photo with my name and number on the counter of the Chinese restaurant, and handed more of them out to anyone who seemed slightly willing to help, before I headed back to my Corolla. As I crossed a street, a car slowed and its window powered down. "Hey, sugar. You busy?"

I flipped him the bird. He seemed to take the hint.

stopped at home to pick up my laptop and Pozorski's notebooks, then battled rush hour traffic across town until I reached the red brick building where Jerry Pozorski lived. Only ten miles separated West Garfield Park and the narrow, tree-shaded streets of Lincoln Park, but I felt as if I had just traveled from a third world country to a developed nation. It was much harder to find a parking place in Lincoln Park, though.

"Watch the cats," Pozorski said as he opened the door.

I grabbed the tabby kitten as she tried to escape into the hall and carried her inside with me. The air was fragrant with curry and coconut. "What's her name?" I asked as the kitten kneaded my chest with sharp little claws.

"I don't know. The other one's Francie. Says so on her tags."

"They're not yours?"

"People leave them behind when they move out. First time it happened I got a lady upstairs to take it, but nobody wanted these guys. I think two's my limit, though. It's a small apartment, and I don't even like cats."

"They seem to like you." Francie was winding around his legs.

"You're a nuisance," he said to the cat, who only butted his ankle and purred.

"Sorry I'm late. It took me a while to find a parking spot."

"No problem. Food's on the table. I picked it up just a little while ago. It should still be hot."

He'd been busy since Friday, when I last dropped by. The fast-food containers, glasses, and bottles that had been scattered on the coffee table and around his recliner had been cleared away, the rug swept, the furniture dusted. The room was brighter, curtains drawn back so the late afternoon sunlight filtered in through plants growing in the basement window wells. He had set out plates and napkins, a pitcher of water, and glasses filled with ice and lemon slices on the coffee table. "Hope you don't mind," he said, gesturing at the chair pulled up to the other side as he settled into the recliner. "Don't have room for a dining table."

I slipped my backpack off my shoulder and propped it beside the chair. "This looks . . ." My words trailed away. There was a large corkboard mounted on the opposite wall, one I hadn't seen until I turned to take my seat. One end of it was crowded with pictures and notes. The rest of it was empty except for a street map, trimmed to show a ten-square-mile portion of the West, Northwest, and North Sides.

"Oh, yeah," he said, following my gaze. "That bulletin board's been sitting in the storage room forever. A tenant must have left it behind. Thought I'd put it to use."

I walked over for a closer look. Notes written in a neat cursive hand on 3×5 index cards were pinned to the left side of the board: a header with the name JILL McKENZIE at the top. Under it, names, summaries of witness statements, sightings with dates and times. And there were photographs: a photocopy of a snapshot that showed Jill McKenzie with long hair and a mischievous smile as she sat cross-legged on a dormitory bed. Chase Taylor, looking very young, staring wide-eyed out of his mug shot. Pictures of five other kids were in a row below him, their expressions ranging from frightened to defiant.

I recognized Raymond Ashe, his face long and thin, his hair cut in a tall hi-top fade, cutting-edge fashion in the mid-1980s. He locked eyes with the camera as if challenging the lens to a staring competition. There was also a handful of pictures of the crime scene. The map had one colored pin stuck in it, marking the spot in the park where she had been found.

"I kept copies of some of my case files," Pozorski said from his recliner. "Brought it all with me when I moved for some reason; hadn't opened that box in years." His eyes tracked me apprehensively as I went back to my seat. "Not trying to step on any toes, here."

"As you said, it was your case."

"*Was.* It isn't anymore. I mean, you're the one Jill hired. I just . . ." He looked down at the back of his hands, something defeated in the set of his shoulders. "I thought maybe I could lend a hand, but if you want me to butt out, I will."

"I'd be grateful for your help."

He took a breath and coughed into his fist. "Okay. Good. Better eat before the food gets cold."

We ate seriously, in silence, for a while no more than "this is good" or "try some of that chutney" interrupting our concentration. He had bought far too much food. He finished before I did, his appetite no match for the feast, and sat back in his recliner. "Not bad, huh?" he said as I crammed a forkful of food into my mouth.

"Mmm. It's great," I mumbled.

"You and Dugan—how long have you known each other?"

"A little over a year. He took my place at Harrison when I resigned."

"So you never actually worked with him?"

"Not as a cop, but he helped fix up my backyard this past summer. He's quite the gardener."

"Is that right?"

"You should see his place in Hyde Park. It's amazing." I tore off a piece of garlic naan and used it to wipe up the last of my tadka dal. "He told me you worked together at Belmont."

"Yeah. Sharp detective, hard worker. Had a knack for getting the punks to do what he wanted without getting all Dirty Harry about it. Wasn't surprised when they tapped him for headquarters. I always thought he could go all the way to the top. Turns out he prefers actually working for a living."

"I gather his mom was not happy about him transferring to Harrison."

He chuckled. "I'll bet she wasn't. Kid has backbone, standing up to Annemarie Dugan. She's a formidable woman. Whole family bleeds blue, you know. Got, let's see . . ." He counted off. "A son who's head of patrol in the Naperville PD. One's a lieutenant working in the Twenty-third. One works OC here in the city. Another works for the ATF. Got a daughter went to law school; working for the Northern District last I heard. And Dugan, he's the baby of the family. He was going to be a priest."

I had been drinking water as he spoke and had to reach for a napkin to wipe up the mess. "A priest? You're kidding."

"This is a good Catholic family, you know. One of them was supposed to join the priesthood, and he was the only one who wasn't always getting into fights. Only it turned out he wanted to be a cop, just like the rest of them. Are you two . . ." He made a vague gesture.

"Just friends."

"Don't mean to pry. It's just kind of funny. All these years, he's never settled down. Bit of a scandal in the family."

"Why? They think he's gay?"

"Bite your tongue. No, he was engaged two-and-a-half times, but—"

"Two and a *half*? How do you do that?"

"She said they were engaged; he said he had no recollection of proposing, and there wasn't any ring in evidence. But, whatever, always the same thing: before they'd even get close to setting a date, he always backed out. Almost forty years old, and still a bachelor. Annemarie has so many grandkids already she doesn't have anything to complain about. Not that that stops her."

"Are those your girls?" I nodded at the framed photos on top of the television set.

"Yeah. Don't see much of them these days. I screwed that up pretty good." He leaned forward and poured himself a glass of water, topped off mine. "You got family?"

"A brother. He lives in Stony Cliff."

"Whoa. Must be earning good money to live up there."

"Not really. He's a lab tech at the college. He could never afford to live in that town, but they give him an apartment in exchange for being a caretaker for the science building."

"He wasn't ever tempted to join the force, like you?"

"Martin doesn't like a lot of excitement in his life."

"What about you? You miss it?"

"Being a cop is all ever I wanted to do. It hasn't been easy, leaving it behind. Working on this case . . . I realized the other day it was the closest I've come since I resigned."

He nodded thoughtfully, then glanced around the room as if he was measuring how much his world had shrunk. "Bring your notes with you?"

"Yup," I said, patting my backpack. "Let's clear this stuff away."

He stacked our plates and wiped off the table while I packaged up the leftovers and bundled the trash into a bag. He carried it all into the kitchenette as I pulled out my laptop and switched it on.

"It's all in that little thing?" He looked at me from the doorway, skeptical.

"Everything so far. I scanned the reports Jill gave me, and the files I got from Thea Adelman are in digital format. I can burn a copy for you if you want." He looked at me blankly. "Put it on a CD."

"Ah. That's okay. I don't have a computer anymore."

"I have to type all my notes; my handwriting's terrible. Yours, on the other hand—how do you do that?"

"I was taught by nuns. They used rulers on our knuckles in those days."

"Hey, one of your tenants has unprotected wireless. Sweet. We can get on the Internet."

"What for? You're going to ask Google who our suspect is?"

"No, but if we need to look something up, it's handy. I like what you did, putting everything up on the board."

"I used to do that, sometimes, make a big diagram of the case, add new stuff as it came in. Good way to make sure everyone was working with the same information."

"Oh, that reminds me. I brought your notebooks back." I put them on the table. "I have a few questions about your investigation—little details, nothing major—but I think I'll start by going over the incident reports Jill obtained from the CPD. That's what kicked this all off. After we get those up on your board, I'll fill in what I've learned so far."

He brought out a stack of index cards. I used colored pins to mark the locations of the seven attacks on the map. Then I read out the reports from the computer, as he filled out cards with basic descriptions of the victims and their circumstances in his neat script. When he finished taking down the details of a particular assault, he pinned up the cards, arranging them in chronological order.

"I've spoken with her," I said as he pinned up a card headed STACY ALDRICH. "She was very forthcoming, provided a thorough rundown of what happened, and later she sent me a detailed written description of events. She gave me the names of the detectives who worked it, but I haven't tried to talk to them yet. Frankly, I doubt they'll be interested in sharing anything with me. I haven't been too popular since that lawsuit."

He nodded, familiar with the reason for my resignation. "You have their names?"

I scrolled through my notes and found them. "Anthony Rizzo and Judy Bogdonovich."

"I know Tony pretty well. We worked on a homicide together not too long before I retired."

"Want to talk to him?"

"I don't know. I've been on the sidelines for so long, and you know how people feel about civilians going after information. I'm not . . ." He wiped his mouth with the back of his hand, looking a little shaky. "Not sure what he'll say."

"Don't worry about it. Stacy didn't think they'd gotten anywhere with it."

"Hell, I'll call him. Worst-case scenario, it'll embarrass the both of us." He jotted a note to himself. "Did you identify any of the others yet?"

"I know this woman doesn't want to talk to me." I pointed to the card headed UNKOWN NO. 3, containing details about the woman who was attacked with her dog in Garfield Park. "The others—it's early days. I only put the word out on Saturday. Even if they hear about it, they may have to think it over for a while. It's hard to take that step if you've been trying to put it behind you."

"Like Jill. Bet that was tough, having this all raked up again."

"That's one of the reasons I want to be sure to keep this all under wraps. So when you talk to that detective, Tony Rizzo—"

"I'll make sure he doesn't know where this is coming from."

"Jill's prepared to deal with it if it lands in the news, but it would be better if it didn't."

"Just as soon avoid reporters myself. They find out this guy's been attacking women ever since we arrested the wrong man, they'll crucify me." I started to speak, but he cut me off with a wave of the hand. "I'm used to it. Jill isn't. She doesn't deserve being put through that kind of shit."

"In addition to these cases that she uncovered, I came across two other rapes that might be related."

"You're kidding. *Two more?*"

"One I can't say much about; she's very concerned about confidentiality. But I can say it happened within the same geographic area as the others, not far from a city park, and it proceeded in exactly the same way. He came up from behind and hit her in the side of the head, threatened her with a knife, dragged her to a private place, and told her to be quiet. He slashed her as a warm-up, like he did with Jill. Then the rape, followed by the beating. It was pretty bad. He broke her jaw."

"The police knew about this?"

"It was reported by hospital staff. The detectives, whoever they were—she wouldn't give me names—didn't have much to work with. She couldn't identify her attacker. But all three of them—Jill, Stacy, and this woman—said that apart from the first blow, the one that gave him control, he didn't hit them again until after the rape. That's when his anger boiled over."

He wrote a header on a card—UNKNOWN No. 8—and filled in the details I'd given him.

"There's another thing that ties these three together. All of them said he was wearing something dark, either blue or black. Jill couldn't be sure of the details but said it wasn't jeans or a T-shirt. Stacy and the other woman both said he wore some kind of one-piece coverall, like a mechanic's uniform. Something he could wash or dispose of easily, which implies advance planning."

"So does the fact he chose women who had a routine, out walking early in the morning. He picked them out ahead of time."

I waited as he finished filling out the note card. "Another thing. Two of the victims couldn't describe their attacker when the reports were taken—well, three, counting this last woman—but all of the rest said he was a light-skinned black, medium build, around one-seventy. Lot of consistency there. And Jill and Stacy both said he had rough hands."

He reached for another index card. "You say you identified another rape?"

"Happened here." I took a drawing pin and got up to push it into the map. "Amira LeTorneau."

"Spell it?" he asked. I did, then added, "That's just my best guess. I've never seen it written down."

He made an asterisk and noted my caveat at the bottom of the card in a tidy footnote. I flashed on him at Clarke's, saying he always kept his paperwork in order—right before he headed for the bathroom, looking sick. Then I realized he was looking up at me, waiting.

"Hard to say if this one's related or not. I don't have any details of the attack, other than that she was raped and beaten last April as she was walking home from a party. That would put it late at night or in the early hours of morning. The beating was severe enough that she was found unconscious on a railway embankment. The police thought it was a domestic battery; her boyfriend—her pimp, really—had hit her before, more than once. Amira insisted it was a stranger attack, but they seemed to believe she was just covering up for her pimp, who got pissed off at her anyway and threw her out. He's currently in prison for an unrelated offense."

"Have you talked to her?"

"Not yet. A family member told me about it; they don't know

where she's staying these days. I just started looking for her today. The last sighting I heard about put her on Madison, working the street. Sounds like she's not doing well. Hooked on skag."

"That part of town, she's black, I assume?"

"Right."

"Age?"

"Seventeen. Sixteen when it happened."

"Jesus," he muttered under his breath, pausing before he finished filling out the card and handed it to me. I remembered I had copies of her photo in my bag, so I pulled one out and pinned it up. We both looked at the board.

"Okay," he said at last. "What else you got?"

TWENTY-TWO

We spent a couple of hours combing through my notes. Every now and then Pozorski would uncap his pen and some tidbit would go up on the board. The sections of the board surrounding Jill and Stacy's names were crowded, some of the notes so close they overlapped. The rest made for a sparse map of possible connections.

"This guy, Raymond Ashe." Pozorski picked up one of his old notebooks, leafed through it. "The one with goofy hair. I don't even remember what I said about him."

"There's nothing much in your notes. He was quick to finger his friend, though."

He paged until he found a few lines. "Yup. First one to say Chase was headed toward the park when they decided to call it a night. Guess he had twenty-twenty vision when it came to reading the writing on the wall." He went back a few pages, frowning, then looked up at me. "He was just giving us what we asked for."

"There was a lot hanging over him, with those muggings. He wanted out of the crack."

"But at this point, they didn't even know we were looking at a rape. He up and volunteered this thing about Chase taking off in the opposite direction, like he had some radar telling us what we wanted. That's what started us looking hard at Chase."

"Let's say Ashe made it up. Why would he pick on Chase?"

"Because he was the one most likely to crack? I should check the notes in the files. They're more detailed."

"I have them here." I started to scroll the directory.

"So do I." He went into the adjoining bedroom and came out carrying a file box.

"I'll find it before you do."

"Wanna bet?" He took off the lid, flipped through binders, pulled one out and started leafing through it.

"Here we go. Dated May third."

He held up his open binder. "Snap." He set it down on the table in front of him and read through it, leaning forward and massaging his forehead with two fingers.

"Looks straightforward to me," I said. "You asked the obvious questions, he answered them."

"Right here." He jabbed a finger at the page. "Hardly five minutes into the interview, talking about where they'd been that night. He realized we were after something more important than a few muggings. One of them was going down for it, whatever it was, and he decided which one it would be. He played us."

"But the others said the same thing later." I skimmed through the notes of their interviews while Pozorski hunched over his binder, a finger trailing down the pages as he read, frowning. "That Chase had turned back toward the park when they were on their way home. They volunteered it. There's no indication here that anybody fed it to them."

"Not while I was in the room."

"Did you tape the interviews?"

"You kidding? We didn't even tape confessions in those days."

"You're thinking someone else might have let it slip, that Ashe had pointed the finger at Taylor?" He didn't answer, still frowning at the official record, studying it carefully. "That other witness, Otis . . ."

"Parchmann," he said absently, still reading.

"One thing that surprised me, looking over your notes. You gave his age as around thirty. Chase told me he was an old man. I thought he must be, like, in his sixties."

"To a teenager, thirty's pretty ancient. And given the way Parchmann looked, the way he carried himself—he was so timid, he just about curled up into a ball and cried if you so much as raised your voice. Somebody must have dropped him on his head when he was an infant. Seriously, the guy was mentally challenged."

"I couldn't tell who actually found out he witnessed Chase bragging about the attack."

"Casey, I think. At least, he was the first detective to talk to him. Might have been a uniform who actually brought it to his attention. We were canvassing everywhere."

"Kevin Casey. You guys were partners, right?"

"For a couple years. Real estate."

"I mean before you retired, when you were both working at Belmont."

"Partners? Well, we worked a lot of cases together. When this one broke, he was new at the shop, pretty excited to be working on something big so soon after his promotion. Threw himself into it, but he was pretty green when it came to detective work. He was more used to dealing with punks on the street. His first assignment out of the academy was in The Deuce."

The Deuce—District Two—had been home to the city's largest and most lawless public housing complex, a legendary training ground for rookie officers back in the day. "Baptism by fire."

"Full immersion. Casey came to us with a confrontational style, as you can imagine. It got results, but he racked up some complaints and had to tone it down. Belmont's not the South Side. Ended up being a pretty solid detective."

"What about Jill's case? Do you think he might have cut a few corners?"

"No way," he bristled. "I mean—okay, it's possible, but I seriously doubt it. We were doing it by the book. It was too important a case to screw it up over technicalities."

"Taylor said one of the cops threw chairs around and cussed a lot."

"So long as you're not throwing furniture at somebody's head, that's not brutality. Casey might have put on a show, but he wouldn't have done anything to put a conviction at risk."

"He thinks very highly of you."

Pozorski was suddenly wary. "Where'd you hear that?"

"He came to see me, right after he talked to you on Saturday. Asked me to leave you alone, actually."

"I was, uh . . ." He looked away. He opened his mouth and closed it, taking a minute to find words. "I was still kind of shook up when he came by that morning. Might have given the impression that I didn't want any part of it."

"He was just worried it might cause problems for you, digging all this up. I know this case meant a lot to you. I wouldn't want to do anything that would . . ." I wasn't sure how to finish the sentence, but I could tell from his expression I didn't have to spell it out.

He straightened the stack of note cards in front of him carefully, his lips tight. "Look, I've made a mess of things—my marriage, my relationship with my daughters. Our finances. I have a problem with alcohol. A bad problem. It runs in the family. My parents both were alcoholics, and so was my brother, big-time. It finally killed him, few weeks after he turned forty. I mostly stayed away from it, except in social situations, and even then I was careful. It was all under control until, until . . . until I wasn't careful anymore. And it ruined everything."

He took a strained breath, then continued doggedly. "I'm not proud of it. I'm not sure I can get back on my feet. But I'm trying." He looked down at his hands. They were shaking. He clenched them into fists, willing the trembling to stop. "I realize you're taking a risk, letting me in on this. But I promise you, I'm not . . . I won't . . ." He closed his eyes and leaned forward as if he had a sudden pain in his gut. "Shit," he muttered after a minute. "Forget it. Maybe we should just—"

"Jerry, this is still your case so far as I'm concerned."

He sat hunched, resting his fists against his mouth, before he took a long breath. "Thanks for saying that."

"I mean it. When Casey came to me, he didn't know I was working for Jill. He thought I might be trying to cash in on some compensation scheme. He was just trying to look out for you."

"That's Kevin Casey for you. He's seen me at my worst, and he's put up with things from me that—well, let's just say I haven't made it easy." He rubbed his hands together, as if trying to massage away the shakes. "Thing is, I've made a lot of promises in the last few years. Haven't kept any of them. You need to know that."

"All right. No promises. We'll just see how it goes."

He nodded, cleared his throat. "Okay, then. You want some coffee?"

"Sure."

"It'll just take a minute." He pushed himself out of his chair and shuffled stiffly into the kitchen.

I rubbed my temples, feeling drained. He was in the kitchen so long, I began to wonder if he had a bottle stashed in there. But he came back with two mugs in his hands, the liquid trembling as he lowered them to the table. There wasn't any smell of alcohol on his breath. "So, where were we?" he said.

"I'm still thinking about Otis Parchmann. Do you think there's any chance someone might have fed him that story, just to put one more nail in the case, make sure it was tight?"

Pozorski considered it, then shook his head decisively. "Doesn't make any sense. If I was setting up a false witness, Parchmann would be my last choice. He sounded like an idiot whenever he opened his mouth, he got confused easily. He wasn't physically impressive. If Taylor's lawyer had been even slightly on the ball, he would of made mincemeat out of that testimony. Anyone who wanted to pull a stunt like that would choose somebody more reliable."

"Though Parchmann was submissive, right? Might go over well with a jury, a black guy from the same projects as the accused, but with a nonthreatening demeanor. I mean, let's face it. Race was a big issue in the case."

"With the public, maybe. Didn't make any difference in the way we handled it."

"But the prosecution wasn't so evenhanded. Reading those trial transcripts—Peter Vogel played it up, every chance he got."

"That's different. Prosecutors don't have to figure out who's responsible, they just have to make a conviction stick. Parchmann may have lied—he had beef with those kids, said they caused trouble around the buildings—but I don't think anyone primed him." Cradling his mug in both hands, Pozorski walked over to the board, now covered with notes. I scrolled back through my files, looking for anything we'd missed.

He gave a grunt of surprise and I looked up. He pointed at the map. "Bus routes."

"Sorry?"

He sketched perpendicular lines with one finger. "Where do the bus routes run in this part of town?"

"Raymond Ashe is a bus driver."

"Exactly. It's kind of far-fetched, but we're dealing with someone who knows where these women are, who knows their routines. Somebody who drove an early morning bus route might see someone walking a dog or crossing a street every day. . . ." He scratched the crown of his head thoughtfully, uncovering a bald spot that had been combed over. "I wonder if I have a route map somewhere."

"Here you go." I pulled up a map of CTA routes and carried the computer over to compare them to the pins stuck in the map on the wall. "That's interesting. The eighty-two runs within a couple of blocks of three of the most recent attacks. The fifty-two is close to . . . wow, four of them."

He took his pen and traced the three routes onto the map on the wall. "Couple of outliers, here."

"Those ones . . . Both are two or three blocks off the sixty-six route."

"Wonder how long Ashe has been driving for the CTA?"

"More than ten years. There was a story in the paper about him shooting his neighbor's dog back in 1996. It mentioned he was a CTA employee."

"He shot a dog?"

"Weird, huh?" My phone started to trill as I spoke. I dug it out of my bag.

"Anni? Sorry it took me so long to call you back. It's been nuts at work."

"It's Dugan," I told Pozorski. "I'll bet you've been busy."

"You heard the news."

"Yeah. I was at St. Larry's when it came out. I was trying to talk Sikora into taking more precautions. I suppose now there'll be even more hostility over Esperanza and her baby taking sanctuary there."

"There's hostility everywhere. People are upset, and no wonder. But that's not why I called. I hated having to cut you off this morning. You sounded like you needed to talk. I know it's awful late, but do you want to get together?"

"Sure. You want to come over here?" I glanced at Pozorski, who nodded. "I'm at Jerry's place."

"What are you doing there?"

"We're going over Jill's case and the ones that seem related."

Dugan dropped his voice. "Are you sure this is a good idea?"

"It wasn't mine, actually," I said, keeping my tone neutral. "And no, I'm not totally sure."

"How is he doing?"

"I think we've made some progress, but it's really too early to tell."

"I'd better come by. I have to stop and pick up something to eat, though. Haven't had a chance to eat all day."

"You like Indian, don't you?"

TWENTY-THREE

Dugan looked wrung out when he arrived. "Long day," he said, slipping off his leather jacket. "And damned if I could find a place to park. I finally had to—" He broke off and stared at the wall covered with notes.

"We've been trying to get a look at the big picture," I said.

"We used to do this at Belmont." He glanced at Pozorski, who was carrying a chair in from the kitchen.

"Guess it's old hat now, thumbtacks and index cards. Anni's high tech. Show him what you've been up to."

I'd been trying something out while we waited for Dugan to arrive. "My downstairs neighbor showed me this program a while back." I turned my laptop so Dugan could see it. "You upload documents and it creates a relational tag cloud out of them." The screen was jumbled with text of various sizes. "Rape" and "beating" and "unknown" dominated. Somewhat smaller were the words "dog," "coveralls," and "outdoors." All of it was webbed together with connecting lines. "Cool, huh?"

"Looks like it was made by a spider on crack."

"It was an experiment, okay? Sheesh."

Dugan turned back to look at the wall, his eyes moving across it slowly, any hint of good humor fading from his face until he just looked tired and grim. "That's a lot of violence."

"The seven rapes Jill uncovered, plus two more that have turned up since."

"All the work of the same guy."

"Looks like it, though we still don't have IDs from six of the victims, and this recent one, Amira LeTorneau—the police considered it a domestic. Still, the pattern of violence is virtually identical in all of them."

"Take a seat." Pozorski gestured at the chair he'd set by the coffee table. "I'll go nuke the food."

Dugan stood in front of the wall for another minute before turning and groping blindly for the chair. He sat heavily. "When you spread them out like that . . ." He blinked, tried to collect himself. "What are those lines on the map about?"

"Bus routes that run close to several of the incidents. We were just playing with the possibility that a bus driver might have seen these women going about their routines."

"Or someone who rides the bus."

I studied the wall. "Jill's Freedom of Information Act request was for records within a ten-year period, 1997 to 2007. She got thousands of reports, but pulled out these seven because they were obviously similar to her case. Took me only a matter of days to add two more. But if you think about it . . ." I felt my stomach lurch with the sickening realization. "She asked for records of crimes identified in the initial report as criminal sexual assaults. What if it was written up differently? What if it was called a battery, and only later they discovered the woman had been raped? We could be talking a much higher number."

I turned back to Dugan and saw that he wasn't listening. His face had drained of color. He leaned forward to rest his forehead against the heel of his hands.

"You okay?" I asked. He nodded, but he didn't lift his head. I went into the kitchen and filled a glass at the tap. "There's ice in the—" Pozorski was saying as I hurried back to the living room. Concerned, he followed me out.

"Here."

Dugan sat up slowly, rubbed his face with both palms, hard, then took the glass and drank. "Sorry. Been putting in some long days."

"I thought you were going to pass out for a minute, there."

"Things just caught up with me all at once. I haven't had much sleep this week."

"When did you last eat?"

"Must have been . . . actually, I don't remember."

Pozorski went back into the kitchen and brought out a plate full of steaming food. "You need to eat." He frowned as Dugan picked up his fork halfheartedly. "What the hell are you thinking? You used to have more sense than that."

"He's working on the Kathy Miller homicide," I explained.

"So you're on a heater case. All the more reason to take care of yourself."

"You worked crazy hours when you had a big case going," Dugan said. "Way I remember it, taking care of yourself wasn't especially high on your agenda."

"Yeah, well, I'm not much of an example to follow, am I?" Pozorski took the pitcher and headed to the kitchen to refill it. "How'd you get involved in that case anyway?" he called from the other room. "It was on the North Side. Belmont should have caught it."

"I'm on a team that's collating information coming in from different directions. We have three detectives who've been part of it since it was a missing persons case, two of us from Harrison; we've been running down Diggy's neighborhood connections. And there's a couple of guys from the gang investigations section. They're sorting out all the crap that comes in from people with a grudge against the LKs."

"Diggy's with the Latin Kings?" Pozorski asked, setting the full pitcher down. "What a charmer."

"A kid like him is going to be in a gang; it's just a matter of which one. Unfortunately, that means members of the Maniac Latin Disciples suddenly want to do their civic duty and assist the police. All of it's garbage, but we have to evaluate it anyway. Of course, ever since the news broke today, all kinds of shit has been pouring in, but it's mostly angry people looking for a way to lynch the guy."

Pozorski was looking lost. "Today?"

"Kathy Miller's body was found this morning," I told him.

"Oh, jeez. Where'd they find her?"

"In one of the forest preserves, southwest of the city," Dugan said, picking up his fork and stirring his food with it before setting it down again. "A technician from ET South briefed us. The body had been wrapped in a tarp and wedged into a crevice in the rocks. Looks like he carried some flat stones up from the creek to cover up the opening. I suppose he did it to prevent discovery, but it actually did us a favor; kept animals out. As it is, decomposition was advanced, but enough of her clothes were preserved that—" He stopped, pinched the skin at the top of his nose. "I can't say much, but there's no question it's her."

"That poor family," Pozorski muttered.

"Yeah." Dugan said it dully, as if all the emotion had been drained out of him, along with his energy.

"Should make the case go easier, though, right?" Pozorski seemed determined to cheer Dugan up. "Lot harder to convict someone when you don't have a body."

"I suppose." His mind was elsewhere, in some dark place.

Pozorski gave way to impatience. "Eat, would you?"

Startled out of his pensiveness, Dugan gave him a fleeting grin and dutifully went to work.

———

hat was good," he said when all the leftovers were gone. He'd put away at least two helpings of everything and looked less haggard. "So, what do we do with this?" He waved at the board.

"I've asked more than a dozen rape crisis counselors and victim advocates to put the word out. They might have talked to some of our unknowns by now. If I get more details, we can build a stronger case for this being a serial offender. Meanwhile, Jerry was going to talk to one of the cops involved and I'll follow up on the bus-route idea."

"Wait, hold it. Look at the scale of this. The CPD needs to investigate."

"Once we have more information, but I'm not sure they'll take it seriously right now. The state's attorney's staff already dismissed any connection among these cases."

"They're full of shit. Give me the case numbers. I'll get the ball rolling."

"But if we move too fast, if they blow it off again, they may never take it seriously. I need more time to—"

"*No.* You can't do this by yourself. It's too big."

I was taken aback by the sharpness of his tone. He saw my reaction and backtracked. "Sorry. I didn't mean . . . Let's go over it, okay? Fill me in with everything you've got."

I exchanged glances with Pozorski. "Why don't you run him through it?" I suggested. "I'll take notes. That way we'll all have the same basic facts in writing."

Pozorski seemed rattled by my suggestion. "I'm not sure . . ." But he rubbed his chin and started over. "Okay. Let's take them in order." He pointed at Jill McKenzie's picture, the one of her sitting cross-legged in a college dorm, laughing at whomever was holding the camera. His hand was visibly shaking, but he moved through the salient facts of each case clearly and thoroughly, sometimes pausing to organize his thoughts, then picking the story up again, his words accompanied by the tapping of my keyboard.

hirty minutes later he finished, summing up by listing the points in common and the points that were still unclear. I was impressed. He had managed to reduce the large and cluttered board to three pages of succinct information. It brought to mind the detective I'd envisioned when I read the neatly organized case notes from Thea's files: a man who was smart, focused, and professional. He was still in there, under those sagging, alcohol-blotched cheeks.

I skimmed over my notes and filled out the places where I'd taken cryptic shortcuts. Then I sent a copy to Dugan's e-mail address, promising to print a copy out for Pozorski.

"I'll get on this tomorrow," Dugan said.

"You can't just start pulling up a bunch of cases from the system with no good reason," I said. "And you can't let anyone know it's related to Jill's FOIA request. We need to keep her name out of it. Mine, too. If your bosses learn that you're helping me out—"

"I'm not doing this to help *you* out. We're looking at serious crimes, here."

"I know, but for a lot of people there, whatever I touch is tainted. It could discredit the whole thing."

"I'll think of something."

"How will you find time for this? You're swamped."

"I'll just have to fit it in somehow. Speaking of which—" He looked at his watch. "Got a seven A.M. meeting scheduled. I need to get some sleep." He stood up and reached for his leather jacket. "You've done good work." He looked from me to Pozorski. "Really good work."

I started to pack up my laptop. "Want some help with the dishes?" I asked Pozorski.

"Don't worry about it," he said. "But there is one thing I wanted to ask you, if you don't mind waiting . . ."

Dugan gave us a little salute and left. Pozorski lowered himself into his recliner. The calico cat jumped into his lap and he petted it absently.

"What's up?"

"This is kind of . . . I shouldn't be asking this."

"No. Go ahead." I could see his hands were shaking badly now, and sweat was starting to glue wisps of his hair to his forehead.

"Would you mind sticking around for a little while? I know it's late, and you hardly know me, but I don't have much in the way of friends these days and the thing is—the thing is, the liquor store, the one I always go to? It closes pretty soon. If I can hold off for the next forty minutes . . ."

"Sure," I said. "I'll stay."

TWENTY-FOUR

t wasn't until I read the paper the next morning that I learned that the outrage over Kathy Miller's body being found had led to a near-riot outside St. Larry's church. A crowd began to gather in the street after the ten o'clock news, riled up that Diggy Salazar's woman was inside, violating a deportation order. Police had to separate angry people from the phalanx of parishioners who were trying to protect the building. Windows were broken, a dozen arrests were made, and four people, one of them an officer, were treated for minor injuries. I noticed on my run that morning that someone with a paintball gun must have returned during the night; the front doors and pillars were spattered with dripping gouts of red paint.

Similar confrontations recurred throughout the week. Talk show hosts called for the authorities to show some backbone and execute their deportation order. A delegation of concerned Catholics presented the archbishop with a petition asking that Father Sikora be relieved of his pastoral duties. Even parishioners at St. Larry's were divided. One of the men taking a turn guarding the church said to a Fox News reporter that he wasn't sure why they weren't helping one of the deserving immigrant families in the community instead of a woman with a drug conviction and a criminal for a boyfriend.

Father Sikora gave a brief public statement, saying that he thought it would be unethical to cherry-pick candidates for sanctuary based on popular opinion. Jesus had welcomed a thief into heaven with him; he didn't take a poll first. Esperanza came to the church for help, and they offered her sanctuary with no strings attached. That was all he had to say about it. Snippets of his statement played on the news with numbing frequency, along with photos of Kathy Miller's smiling face, film of the grieving family, and shots of the rocky outcropping where the decayed remains of her body had been found.

The weather had turned frosty. Clouds lowered over the city all week, giving a hint of winter on its way. I rose before dawn every day and ran a regular three-mile route, my lungs aching with the cold. Occasionally specks of early snow stung my face, or pellets of freezing rain. But I needed the physical exercise to push everything out of my mind, let it go fallow before the day's work.

I threw myself into the case, working every angle I could. I talked with the two witnesses who had recanted their testimony twenty years after the night they shared a crack pipe and went on a mugging spree with Chase Taylor. Their memories were too inexact to be useful, and I could see why Thea had her doubts about their accuracy.

It took longer to track down Otis Parchmann. He worked for the city through a contract with a nonprofit organization that helped the otherwise unemployable find jobs. According to the woman who managed the program, he'd worked for them for years. Unlike most of their clients, he didn't have any problems with drink or drugs, and he didn't waste time gabbing with the others. He wasn't much brighter than the average second-grader, but he always arrived on time, regular as clockwork. She checked a schedule and told me he'd be at work in a public playground.

When I got there, a fine, cold drizzle was coming down. He was the only one there, a stooped man in a Bears windbreaker, a big trash bag slung over his shoulder as he rooted for blown trash in a hedge with a stick. When I went up to introduce myself, he didn't pause in his work, and barely gave me a glance, but he answered my questions politely as he scooped newspapers and crumpled wrappers into his bag, and when I asked if I could snap a picture of him with my phone, planning to add it to Pozorski's board, he posed proudly for it.

He liked his job, he told me. It was better in the summer when it was warm, but he didn't mind the weather too much. He lived on the near North Side, naming one of the mixed-income developments that were replacing the city's public housing projects. He got along with everyone there. Used to be he lived down the road in Cabrini-Green, but that was crowded and noisy, kids always acting up. He liked it better where he was now.

When I asked him about the testimony he gave in the Lincoln Park Rapist case, it took him a few minutes to grasp what I was talking about, but when he finally got it, he recited what was in the trial transcript, almost word for word. They put his name in the paper, he told me with pride. He'd cut out the article, but it got lost when he moved. When I asked questions about the conversation he had supposedly overheard he got frustrated and said he couldn't remember that far back. Besides, he had to get on with his work. I left him batting his stick at a plastic bag caught up in a bush.

Chase Taylor's former girlfriend, Mattie Polk, returned my call. She now preferred to be called by her full married name, Matilda Johnson. She had a responsible job as a middle school teacher now, and a husband and three children; she didn't want them to be dragged into anything.

She was surprised to learn that Chase remembered her after all these years, and was even more astonished that he had referred to her as his girlfriend. "We knew each other, sure," she said. "Used to study together at the kitchen table. Well, that's not entirely true. He would hang out and talk while I did my homework. He hardly ever went to school, never did a lick of schoolwork."

"How did you know each other?"

"Our apartments were across the hall from each other. His mother was always out partying, didn't come home most nights. Boy was lonely, that's all. Hungry, too. He'd wait till I came home from school and show up just in time for an after-school snack. My parents weren't happy about him coming by so much. Once he started getting in trouble, they put their foot down, told him to stay away. I thought they were being too strict, but it turned out they were right about him."

People in the building had been shocked when they heard he was responsible for that terrible crime in the park, but Chase had been running with a bad crowd for months. His group had been escalating the mayhem, from shoplifting and vandalism to outright robbery, egging each other on just to see how far they could go. It wasn't hard for her to imagine an encounter with a woman in the park starting out as a dare and everything going horribly wrong. Chase didn't have a lot of self control when he got angry.

"Did he ever lose his temper with you?"

"No, but I saw it when he was with other kids. He got in fights a lot. Something would just snap inside."

"What about the crowd he was running with? It sounds as if you believe they could be involved in the assault."

"The police didn't seem to think so, but I always figured . . ." She seemed reluctant to go on.

"What?"

"You have to understand. When Chase used to come over, he was sweet. He was looking for a family, that's what I think now. But my parents had their hands full with us, so he had to find some other place to belong. And he ended up in a group of bad kids. He didn't feel good about himself, given the way his mother neglected him, so it was easy for him to lose his cool, and then it was like something evil inside just took over. I always thought those boys liked calling that out of him, see what he would do."

"Can you give me an example?"

"Chase was kind of shy around girls. He didn't have the right clothes, the right moves. The other boys teased him about it, said he was gay, which was about the worst insult you could throw at someone in those days. That's what I figured happened that night. He tried to prove something, and when he realized what he'd done, he just went crazy on that poor girl."

"What did you think when the case was thrown out?"

"First thing that came into my head—how does *she* feel about this? Lord, that must hurt, watching the man you identified walk free. But if you're asking about Chase, I don't know. From what I read, it sounded like he got off on technicalities. Oh, there was a lot of racism in the way people talked about that crime; I know the police sometimes do bad things to get confessions and innocent men end up in prison. But he was running wild that night, in the very place where a woman was raped and nearly killed."

"You still think Chase was responsible."

"Want to know the honest truth? I think they're all responsible, all those kids, even if he's the one who did it."

"How well did you know the guys Chase was running with?"

"Not well. They didn't go to my school, or if they were enrolled there, they didn't ever show up. But everyone knew they were trouble. There was one with hair that was in fashion back then, short on the sides and tall on top, trimmed flat. Hope that never comes back in style. Anyway, I don't recall his name, but he was the leader, a smooth-talking fellow. Girls went all mushy over him, but I always figured he'd end up in jail. Either that or in a pulpit, making money with that golden tongue of his."

"Pretty close. He's in politics now."

She laughed. "Doesn't that just go to show."

On Tuesday morning a woman called shortly after I finished my run and told me she had gotten word I wanted to talk to her about her experience. Her rape, she rephrased it after a pause. I met with her and took a detailed statement. By the end of the week, I had two more calls. What they told me filled my uneasy sleep with images of sudden violence and paralyzing fear, but the case was coming together. Note cards were filling Pozorski's corkboard.

We took turns buying carryout meals and sharing them at his apartment every evening, poring over the case together. Pozorski had taken the plunge and called Tony Rizzo, the detective who had worked on Stacy Aldrich's rape. They'd met for coffee at Clarke's. "Kind of like old times," he said. "We must have spent three hours shooting the bull. I thought he might be . . . I don't know. He retired last year himself after a triple bypass, but he remembers Stacy. Liked her a lot. A brave kid, and a dream witness, not that it helped. He said he was pretty sure there hadn't been any movement on the case since he retired. Someone would have called him."

"Did you tell him there were other cases that could be related?"

"He brought it up. Said it reminded him of the Lincoln Park case, except there wasn't the media coverage. Then he got all flustered because he remembered my case got thrown out."

"But he thought they were related?"

"No. He just meant that we each had a case that was hard to forget. I didn't press it after that, figured it was just looking for trouble, pulling Jill into the picture. He said it drove him crazy that they had absolutely nothing on this guy except a witness who wouldn't come forward."

I made a note to myself to go back to that apartment building that overlooked the site of Stacy's rape and ask around.

———

The next day, when I canvassed the block where Stacy had been attacked, I thought I was in luck. A woman studied my card as I told her that I was hoping to talk to a man who had chased a rapist off three years ago, and she nodded. "You looking for Kenneth."

"You know him?"

"Used to live across the street from me. You won't get nothing out of him, though."

"I'm not with the police. He doesn't have to go on record."

"He got shot dead last year."

"Oh. I'm sorry."

"What for? He was a gangbanger, always bringing violence into the neighborhood. You reap what you sow."

"But he told you he saw this attack?"

"Said he chased off some guy who was beating on a woman. Told me to watch out for some skinny black dude in a blue overall, 'cause he was a crazy man. That's all I know about it." As it turned out, that was more than anyone else knew. A dead end.

On Wednesday night, when I showed up at Pozorski's apartment, he smelled strongly of cinnamon breath mints; he was lucid, but it was obvious from his clumsy movements and slowed thoughts that he'd been drinking. He pinned up the picture of Otis Parchmann, the one I took with my cell phone and printed out; earlier, we'd added one of Stacy that I found on-line. Pozorski slowly wrote out the details of an interview I'd held earlier in the day, sometimes having to crumple a card and start over. He pointed out some connections I hadn't considered, and made some good suggestions, but he was easily distracted and kept glancing at his watch. I stayed late that night, finding excuses to linger until his local liquor store closed.

The next day, I took a break from work to check on him. After calling several times and getting no answer, I drove to the apartment building. A tenant let me into the lobby and pointed up the stairs, where Pozorski was replacing a broken toilet in one of the apartments. He was embarrassed that I had assumed the worst, and saw right through the excuse I made up on the spot for stopping over, and I did my clumsy best to apologize.

But when I arrived with dinner that night he was so drunk he could barely open the door.

He stood unsteadily, blinking at me as if he wasn't sure who I was. I shooed the cats inside. They wound themselves around my legs, complaining. I took the dinner I'd brought with me into the kitchen and saw that their food dish was empty, the water bowl dry. As I filled their bowls, I heard a heavy thud from the other room. My heart seized up when I saw him sprawled, half on, half off his recliner, and reached for my phone, ready to dial 911 and start CPR. But he mumbled a curse, made a halfhearted attempt to shift himself before he gave up, an arm slipping onto the floor limply.

With some effort, I was able to straighten him out and pull him upright into the recliner as he muttered unintelligibly, his breath sour and reeking of whiskey. I felt furious with him, and furious with myself, as I carried an empty fifth of Jim Beam to the recycling bin. I searched through the kitchen and bedroom to see if he had any other bottles stashed away, but he didn't. Just some worn clothes, a few dishes, a picture of his daughters, and a carton of case files. Not much to show for a life.

I tried calling Dugan again. We'd barely spoken in the past three days. I'd left him messages throughout the week, and managed to catch him in person twice, but both times he was heading into meetings and couldn't talk. He sent apologetic text messages. He was busy. He'd call soon. He wasn't sure when he'd be free. This time his phone rang five times before his voice invited me to leave a message. I snapped my phone shut, feeling furious with him, too.

I threw a blanket over Pozorski and left.

That night, I got a call from Kevin Casey. He was so angry he could hardly speak coherently. "You said you'd leave him alone."

"I know I did, but—"

"I just got a call from a tenant saying can I send somebody over to fix the stove tomorrow, 'cause the building manager's hammered again, and by the way, given how much rent he pays, when am I going to hire somebody competent? And then he tells me some lady came by looking for him earlier today, that Jerry's been on a bender ever since. That was you, wasn't it?"

"I didn't mean—"

Jesus fucking Christ! I thought we had an understanding."

"He called me. He wanted to talk."

"Sure, why not? Out of the blue, you ask him about the biggest case in his life, the one some goddamn judge overturned—you don't think that's been eating at him? It's going to kill him, you know. Not that you care, you selfish bitch."

"I'm going to hang up now."

"No, wait. That was uncalled for. I'm sorry." He took a big gasping breath. "But I thought I explained this to you. He's got a lot of problems. What did you say to him, anyway?"

"I don't think it's any of your business what we talked about."

"Fine. Just—think about this, okay? He served this city with honor. Please, I'm begging you. He's hanging on by a thread. Don't harass him anymore, all right?"

"I won't harass him." If anything, Pozorski would harass me if I shut him out now, and I didn't want to do that. The thread he was hanging onto was the chance to solve Jill's case.

F inding out which bus routes Raymond Ashe drove absorbed a lot of my time that week. The ruses I had prepared, asking about items lost on the bus on certain key dates, were defeated by automated telephone messages and indifferent bureaucrats. I made a point of riding both the 82 and the 52 for three mornings in a row, but Raymond Ashe wasn't behind the wheel, and the drivers who were weren't open to conversation.

Then I remembered there was a café not far from the big bus garage on Kedzie. It was usually full of drivers grabbing a meal before their shift. I became a regular that week, drinking gallons of coffee until I was familiar enough that I was able to join the table of a trio of female drivers on Thursday morning. They assumed that I was angling for a CTA job, and took my questions in good part. They explained how the routes were assigned by seniority, so when you finished your training you usually got the worst routes. In a roundabout way I brought up Raymond Ashe, and they hooted with laughter. He'd been there forever. He not only had seniority to get the pick of the routes, he had the juice, being high up in the union and having friends in City Hall. They bickered for a while about which was the best route in the system and whether he'd chosen well. It didn't matter to me, though; they were talking about express buses running on Lakeshore.

"Don't guess he'd be driving any of the routes around here, then," I said.

"Naw. These are terrible. They got too many stops, and people waste your time trying to use expired passes and shit."

"It's dangerous, too. Sometimes kids get on and see kids from another gang and all hell breaks loose."

"Crazy people, they're the worst," one of them murmured. "Had a guy the other day start to take his pants off. Had to stop the bus and kick him off."

One of the women held up a finger. "Wait. He did that for a while."

"Who?"

"Raymond Ashe."

"Took his pants off?"

"No, stupid. Drove the Kimball-Homan when he was fixing to run for city council." The woman dropped her voice into a deep, suave tone. "Want to get to know my constituents." They all howled with laughter.

"That's the eighty-two?" I asked.

"Right. Raymond T. Ashe, esquire, took the earliest shift so he could spend the afternoons kissing babies."

"Kissing butts, more like."

"The earliest shift starts . . ." I said.

"Four-thirty in the morning. Think he drove that route for almost two years. Must have backfired, though. He lost the election."

"Shit," one of her friends said. "How many people who ever waited on a late bus gonna vote for their bus driver?"

"Hell, I'll vote for him if he'll give me that express route of his."

They headed off for work, still joking among themselves. I headed home to see how the attacks coincided with the timing of Raymond T. Ashe's campaign.

t fit.

All three of the attacks near the 82 route occurred during the two years before he ran for the city council. Even better, I looked at the news story about him shooting his neighbor's dog. I hadn't paid attention to the address given in the story when I last looked at the brief news item. Now I realized he had lived only two blocks from the 52. CTA employees flashing their ID could ride free. Chances were good that even if he didn't drive that route, he rode it.

Got you, I thought.

But it wasn't proof. It wasn't anything but the beginning of a theory.

TWENTY-FIVE

Saturday morning, I was making my usual run, pressing hard, ignoring the chilly fog and my aching muscles. But I couldn't ignore the signals that tickled the back of my neck. I scanned doorways and alleys and the shadowy gaps between buildings. Nothing obvious. Just a sense that something was off.

It wasn't until I reached the park, still shrouded in darkness, that I saw the car, a late-model black SUV cruising slowly along the street, its headlights fuzzy in the damp haze. It turned onto Luis Muñoz Drive, ambling slowly through the park as I ran along my usual path, keeping pace with me. I couldn't make out the face behind the wheel, but the car looked like the one that Raymond Ashe drove. I ignored him at first, not deviating from my customary course, but when my footpath came within a few yards of the road, I swerved, put on a burst of extra speed, and intercepted the SUV, slamming a fist on the hood of his car. "Hey, asshole."

The car stopped. Raymond Ashe powered his window down. "Well, look who it is. Anni Koskinen."

"Why are you following me?"

He laughed. "Following you? You're under a misapprehension. Here I am, driving along, wondering if that woman who runs in the park every morning realizes just how dangerous it is. All by herself when it's still dark and nobody's around."

"Don't fuck with me, Ashe."

He acted as if I hadn't spoken. "So I'm thinking to myself, *maybe I should have a word with that lady, tell her she's putting herself in harm's way.* And then what happens? You start beating on my car. That's my reward for being a good Samaritan."

"It's not going to work."

"I'm sorry. What's not—?"

"I'm not easily intimidated."

He nodded knowingly. "That's the problem. You think you're safe, 'cause you're so tough and all. Ain't nobody messes with a cop, even one that's five foot two and weighs next to nothing. Got a badge and a gun, people respect that. Better yet, you got thirteen thousand fellow officers ready to get even if anything happens to you. But you don't got a gun anymore, you don't got that badge. And look around. There's nobody watching your back."

He abruptly grabbed my wrist and yanked me toward him. "You're just a little bitty woman," he said through his clenched teeth. It sounded flirtatious, something caressing and intimate in his tone. "A little bitty woman out here all by yourself."

I jabbed at his eyes with my other hand but he anticipated it, ducking back out of the way and trapping my other wrist before I knew it. His hands were strong, his grip bruisingly tight. He jerked me forward, my head banging against the door frame as he yanked me off my feet and half into his car, where I couldn't help seeing the bulge of an erection straining against the cloth of his trousers. I stopped struggling and gave a mew of pain. Though he didn't release me, he relaxed his guard just enough that I was able to cock my right elbow and jam it into his throat. He grunted as I ground the point of my elbow as hard as I could against his larynx. My shoulder set off his car horn, blaring, but he held my wrists tighter than ever, his arms shaking with the effort, teeth gritted in a snarl. He didn't release me until I was gasping with pain.

"See how easy that was?" His words came in a hoarse whisper, and he fingered his throat briefly before dropping his hand into his lap. "And I wasn't even trying."

I sucked air into my lungs. "Don't you *ever* touch me again."

"Just giving you a little hands-on lesson in personal safety. Women been hurt around here before."

"I'm not scared of you." My wrists burned, as if I'd dipped them in acid.

"I'm giving you good advice." He pointed a finger at me, and looked amused when I took an involuntary step back. "You need to be more careful, girl."

I finished my run, all of my warning signals thrown out of whack, unable to disentangle real threats from imaginary ones. When I got home, I looked in the mirror and saw a reddened lump where my head had cracked against the car frame. As I reached up to touch the spot, I saw five circles pressed into my wrist, four red finger marks turning purple on one side, another on the inside where his thumb had pressed deep. I could feel his touch throbbing with my pulse and I had to fight down a sudden wave of nausea.

I showered and pulled on a sweater with sleeves that swamped my hands, but whenever they slipped back and I saw those bruises, a feeling of claustrophobic panic swept over me.

It pissed me off.

I picked up the phone and started to make calls.

Pozorski looked rocky that night, the spidery blotches of broken blood vessels on his cheeks more prominent than usual against his grayish skin. His hair was clean and carefully combed and his clothes were freshly laundered, but they hung loose on his frame as if he'd shrunk. "Uh, last night—" he started to say.

"No promises," I said. "You made that clear."

"I don't know what happened. I just—"

"You're a drunk, Pozorski." I tried to lower my voice to a normal level. "You fell off the wagon right onto your ass, that's what happened. I don't have time to listen to excuses. Let's eat and get to work."

He wiped his mouth and nodded. Then he hesitated and tapped his head, at the place that matched the spot on my forehead where a bruise had blossomed. I thought it was hidden by my hair, but it hadn't escaped his notice. "What happened?"

"Nothing." I sat down and thumped a sack of food on the table. My sleeve rode up. His eyes widened as he saw my wrist. "Anni—"

I jerked my sleeves down over my palms. "Get some plates."

He started to say something else, but after a glare from me, he turned and obediently went into the kitchen. I unpacked a box of Popeyes' chicken and biscuits from the bag, then pushed the tabby kitten away when he started nosing at the box.

Pozorski returned with a bowl stacked on plates. "I made us a salad."

"I brought dinner."

"It's not your turn."

"Shut up and eat."

He shut up. I ate. He crumbled a biscuit and pushed lettuce around his plate.

"I had a run-in with Ashe this morning," I finally said. "He's getting squirrelly."

"He's the one who put those bruises on your wrists?"

I lifted my arms and let the sleeves fall back so I could inspect the finger-shaped blotches. "He was following me around the park this morning in his car, trying to throw a scare into me. I confronted him about it. Big man that he is, he decided to prove that he's stronger than I am."

"Anni, Christ."

"He was just showing off."

"He must be insane to attack you in a public place."

"It was early. Nobody else was around. And it wasn't much of an attack. All he did was grab me to make a point. I gave him something to think about." I hoped his syrupy-smooth voice still sounded as if he were gargling gravel.

"What were you doing in a park that early?"

"Running. I run there every morning."

"Which park is this?"

"The one near my house, what do you think?" I picked up a fork and jabbed at some salad. "Don't give me a hard time. I'm sick and tired of being told I can't go here, I can't do that, just because I'm a woman."

"That's not what I . . . Hell, I wouldn't feel safe there."

"That's your problem. I live in that neighborhood. I'm not going to let some bully with an attitude keep me from doing what I want." I ate some more salad, fed a tidbit of chicken to the kitten. "You know something interesting? It turned him on."

"Pardon?"

"Ashe. When he grabbed my arms and pulled me halfway into his car, it gave him a hard-on. He gets a charge out of hurting women."

Pozorski pushed his plate away. "Anni, look . . . I'm not going to tell you what to do."

"Good."

"But I don't feel right about this."

"I don't feel right about that." I pointed at the board. "And if Ashe has anything to do with it, he's going to be sorry he ever messed with me. I checked up on him today. Called his boss at the CTA. Called the chairman of the Transit Authority. Called a few politicians. Called the bank that holds his mortgage."

"What did you find out?"

"Nothing, but the people I called found out that a private investigator is doing a deep background check on their golden boy."

"You're baiting him."

"Just letting him know that he can't scare me off." Pozorski opened his mouth to say something and I pointed my fork at him. "Don't start."

He held up his hands in surrender.

I finished eating before saying anything more. "Okay, maybe it wasn't smart. It just made me feel good to mess with him."

"He knows we're looking at him now."

"He already knew. I was talking to drivers near the bus garage he works out of; it got back to him. That's why he decided to try and intimidate me." I felt the bruises twinge, as if he still had me in his grip. "One thing I found out today. I called Chase Taylor's house, spoke to his aunt. She was careful not to say too much. I get the feeling she's scared of Ashe, worried that if she says anything she might antagonize him and make things worse. But it's obvious she doesn't trust that guy, never did. And she's worried sick about Chase."

"Why?"

"He's been staying out all hours, acting cagey when he does come home. Someone gave him a cell phone. She thinks he's involved in something."

"Something to do with Ashe?"

"Something illegal, anyway. She's convinced that if the police pick him up again, he'll do something crazy. The times they've stopped him on the street for no reason, it left him so shaken up he couldn't eat, flew off the handle at the drop of a hat, had terrible nightmares. He never talks about what it was like in prison, but it's not too hard to imagine. He once told me he'd rather die than go back inside."

The cats were vying to be my new best friend, looking for tidbits from my plate. "You're spoiling those animals," Pozorski said, then tempted the calico away with a morsel of chicken.

"Say, last night . . ."

"I'm really sorry about that."

"No, I was going to say—did Kevin Casey talk to you?"

"No."

"I guess somebody called him about a problem with a stove." Pozorski winced with humiliation. "I fixed it today."

"He heard I'd been over here. He thought I might be causing you problems."

"God." He scratched the back of his head, looking away from me. "It's nothing you did."

"I thought maybe coming over here to check up on you yesterday . . . I hate it when people hover over me. I didn't mean—"

"It just happens, Anni. Something comes over me, and . . . I fall on my ass, like you said. All I can do is get up and try again. I'm sorry to disappoint you."

"It's not that, I just . . ." I didn't know what to say next. We were both relieved when my phone rang. "Dugan! About time we heard from you. Especially since you were supposed to have everything all wrapped up by now. Isn't that why you took those case numbers?"

"That hasn't exactly worked out." His voice was so dry it grated.

"I'm just yanking your chain. I know you've been busy. Look, we've made a lot of progress. I located three more of the victims. Their attacks all conform to the pattern. We've even got a theory. It's pretty slim right now, but I think we may have enough to get a real investigation launched. Any chance you could swing by sometime?"

"You're at Jerry's place?"

"Yeah, we're just—"

"Thought you'd be there. I'm about half a block away. Can you let me in the front entrance?"

"Sure." I lifted the kitten out of my lap and started for the door. "How much time can you spare? We have a fair amount to cover."

"You think three working days will do it?"

"What do you . . ."

"I just got a reprimand and three days without pay."

"What the hell?"

"Better yet, when I get back, I'm on administrative duty pending an investigation, thanks to a complaint some guy I barely remember filed with the Office of Professional Standards. I questioned him over a shooting months ago. Now he's in jail waiting to be arraigned on a burglary and he makes this shit up about how I cuffed him to a railing and kicked the crap out of him. It never happened."

"But—I don't get it. It usually takes ages for the OPS to investigate a claim like that. When did he file this complaint?"

"Two days ago. It's my own fault. I got called in by my boss a couple of hours ago. He told me the OPS was going to be looking into this allegation and maybe I should step away from the Kathy Miller case. I wasn't too happy about that. Words were exchanged. He told me I was being put on administrative duty, at which point I really lost my temper."

I'd reached the door by this time. He was standing on the other side, his face a little warped through the glass. I pocketed my phone and pulled the door open. "What does your union rep say?"

"That I should have gone to him before I opened my big fat mouth." He gave an abrupt laugh that sounded like a painful cough. "Don't tell Jerry this, but I sure could do with a stiff drink right now."

———

oesn't make any sense." Pozorski looked flummoxed. "This all stemmed from some low-life jailbird making an accusation? Why are they taking such a hard line? Do you even have a single sustained complaint on your record?"

I'd given Dugan the easy chair I usually sat in. He was slumped in it, practically recumbent, his long legs bent in front of him, the picture of dejection. "Not until now."

"Whatever happened to due process? What does the union say?"

"Nothing. Under the contract, the boss can hand out up to three days' summary punishment whenever he wants."

"Forget the union. What does your mother say?"

"I haven't told her yet." Dugan was massaging his forehead, staring blankly in front of him as the cats mewed around the table.

"Want something to eat?" I asked. He shook his head and I started to gather up the leftovers. "I'm putting on coffee," I said, feeling an urge to have a stiff drink myself.

"If I know Annemarie, she already knows about it, and she'll be hopping mad," Pozorski told him. "You must have really pissed somebody off."

"That's something I've gotten pretty good at lately." Dugan seemed to doze off until I brought out mugs of coffee. He struggled to sit up, reached for a mug, and froze for a moment. He set the mug on the table, then took my hand in his and gently slid up my sleeve. "Anni." It sounded as if he was the one who was hurt.

"Had a little run-in with Raymond Ashe this morning."

He studied the marks for a moment, then let my hand go. "Want to tell me about it?"

"I'd rather hear what you've learned about our unknowns."

He looked reluctant to let it go, but finally took a gulp of coffee and set the mug to one side, pulled out a notebook and a pen, and set them in front of him, thinking for a moment before he started to speak, all business.

"On Tuesday I talked to a detective who worked on two of the rapes. Number six and seven up there." He nodded at the board. "They're linked by DNA evidence. No match to a suspect on file, but the women were raped by the same man. This guy also raped at least three other women, according to CODIS: our number three— the woman who was walking her dog in Garfield Park—as well as a rape that happened twelve years ago, and another from 1992, both here in Chicago."

I felt a bubble of acidic fury rising in my chest. "All this time, they've known there's a serial rapist at work?"

"No. Evidence from number seven was submitted to the state lab two years ago. Took about three months to get the results. They had a hit, so that's when they joined the two cases, but it didn't help; they still didn't get anywhere with either of them. The older ones just came in. They were stuck in the backlog."

"Shit." Due to lack of funding, rape kits had accumulated on the CPD's evidence room shelves by the thousands as more pressing cases took priority. It wasn't until a newspaper exposé and a public outcry that the state legislature funded an effort to clear up the backlog. They'd only recently completed the task, finishing up with a final group of a thousand kits, some of which dated back into the 1990s.

"Where did these older rapes happen?" Pozorski asked.

Dugan found the page in his notebook, then took the box of drawing pins, rose from his chair and pushed two of them in. One was on Goose Island, half a block south of Division Street. "A twenty-two-year-old woman who worked at an industrial laundry nearby, raped and battered. Her description of her assailant is consistent with the others."

He pushed the other pin in less than a mile to the east. "That's Cabrini-Green," I said.

"A fourteen-year-old girl, found in the basement stairwell of one of the high-rises in 1992," Dugan said. "Head injury was so severe she never could tell anyone what had happened." He stood there for a moment, scanning the rest of the board, taking in the information we'd added since he'd last seen it.

"I'm not supposed to tell anyone this," he said at last, still looking at the board. "Kathy Miller was most likely raped."

It took a minute to process that. "You think . . ."

"She was attacked outdoors, in the early hours of the morning, in an alley not far from a city park." He made a compass of two fingers, measured the short distance between the alley and Oz Park. "And within a block of an all-night bus route. All the news reports said she was leaving a bar when it closed for the night. She wasn't, she'd left with a friend and went to his apartment nearby. We didn't make that public because the jerk happened to be married to someone else, a nurse who worked nights; the family didn't want Kathy's reputation to suffer, and we wanted something to hold back. She had been going there most Friday nights for a couple of months, always left his place shortly before dawn. When she headed to her car that morning, somebody forced her into an alley and raped her, then battered her severely. The only thing that's different than these other women is that she died, and the guy who killed her hid the body."

"No chance of a DNA match."

"After six months? Even after six days the decomp would be too advanced."

"How do they know she was raped?"

"The state of her clothing. There were buttons from her blouse found at the scene, which I didn't know until a few days ago even though I was supposedly working the case. They found the tab of a zipper, too, from her jeans. The blouse was pretty well gone when they found the body, but her panties were made out of some synthetic fabric that hadn't decayed. They were torn in the front, and there was enough left of her jeans to see that the zipper had been broken, wrenched open.

The buttons, that could have been something that happened in a struggle. But not the pants. She was raped."

"How does this scenario fit with Diggy's movements? Wasn't he filmed robbing a liquor store?"

"Almost three hours before the attack."

"So the timing is all wrong."

"Everything hinges on an eyewitness who placed him in the neighborhood at the right time. Diggy could have been hiding somewhere, hoping for the alarm to die down before jacking a car. It's possible. Except . . ."

"The rape doesn't fit."

"He belongs to a gang. He held up a liquor store. He's suspected in two armed robberies and he might have shot a rival gang member in the leg last year. He's a scumbag, but he has absolutely no history of violence against women and no sex offenses on his sheet. The whole case was built on the premise that it was a carjacking."

"Though Diggy could have raped her. You can't rule it out."

"Of *course* you can't. But it changes things." Dugan rubbed his eyes. "Sorry. I've been arguing about this all week."

"You knew." I remembered turning around to see the blood draining from his face, looking as if he was about to pass out. "When you were here last Monday, you already knew she'd been raped and what it might mean."

"I didn't put it together until you said that Jill's records might not include crimes that weren't an exact match for what she put on her FOIA request. But I couldn't say anything. We were holding it back out of respect for the family. That's what I was told, anyway. Now I think it's being suppressed because it doesn't fit the case they're building against Diggy Salazar."

"That's a pretty serious charge," Pozorski said.

"I know. I don't like to think this way. But when I put everything together and took it to the top, pointed out that the rape totally changed our theory of the crime, nobody wanted to hear it. They wouldn't even listen. We have a suspect. Don't do anything to screw it up."

"Who knows about this?" I asked.

"Hardly anyone. I didn't want to start a bunch of rumors, and I wanted to be careful that the press didn't link it to Jill. As much publicity as Kathy Miller's murder is getting, can you imagine what would happen if the Lincoln Park Rapist got mixed into it?"

"So, this is the real reason you're on administrative duty," I said.

"It's a little too fucking convenient that a guy awaiting arraignment, who still has a chance to cut a deal with the state's attorney, suddenly remembers me doing something I would never do in my life right about the time I'm proposing an alternate theory for a major case."

"So where do we go from here?" Pozorski asked.

Dugan just shook his head, still dazed by the day's events.

"What about the detectives you talked to?" Pozorski said. "Think they could combine what we've got with their cases and run with it? Wouldn't have to bring Kathy Miller into it. Not yet."

"I already talked to one of them. I wasn't in a very good mood at the time. I think I burned that bridge."

"I could talk to Tony Rizzo again," Pozorski said, but without much conviction. "Or what about Kevin Casey? He works for the SA's office. I know they didn't take this seriously at first, but now that we have so much more . . ." But he sounded doubtful even as he spoke.

"He's convinced that Chase Taylor was the Lincoln Park Rapist," I said. "He'd just dig in his heels, especially if another major case was put in jeopardy."

"Anni's right," Dugan said. "He works for Peter Vogel, and Vogel doesn't want his political career derailed by admitting that he blew two high-profile cases."

"This is about politics?" Pozorski sputtered, his face flushed. He jabbed a finger at the board. "What about them?"

"As far as the police are concerned, it's not politics. They honestly think they arrested the right guy. I'm bringing in a complication that might give ammunition to the defense, and when this complaint surfaced it was a convenient way to take me off the case. I wish I hadn't lost my temper. If I'd handled this differently—"

"Knock it off, Dugan. We just have a situation where we can't rely on the CPD taking it over, not yet anyway." I took a drawing pin, searched for the right spot on the map and pushed it in for Kathy Miller. Then I took down three of the cards labeled Unknown. "Let's get some names for these women."

TWENTY-SIX

We stayed up past 2:00 A.M., adding what Dugan had learned about the five cases that were linked by DNA evidence to our crowded chronology of violence. Then we added a summary of the attack on Kathy Miller. As we worked, I reorganized my notes and prepared a more complete synopsis of the case. From time to time, Dugan's phone rang and he had to step into the kitchen to talk to a family member, all of them checking in to see how he was doing and vent their spleen. Before long he was telling them he was looking forward to the time off, that he needed a few days' vacation, just to calm them down.

"Glad I'm not the guy who gave him that reprimand," Pozorski murmured to me as Dugan paced in the next room, phone pressed to his ear. "I wouldn't want the Dugan clan after me. They're armed and Irish."

When we'd finished pooling our knowledge, I read the summary out loud, making sure nothing important had been left out, that I had all the details right. The three-page document based on Pozorski's summation last Monday had turned into a fifteen-page report. After I read out the final paragraph, recapping the connections among the dozen rapes we had uncovered, the room fell silent.

"So, what now?" Pozorski asked at last.

"I'd better talk to my client," I said. "It's her case, too."

composed an e-mail to Jill McKenzie early the next morning, suggesting that I make a trip to Iowa for a meeting. The research had proceeded as far I could take it; we had some decisions to make. I hit SEND, then I set out on my run. Heading out, I saw that I had neglected the pots of chrysanthemums that Dugan had brought over; they were shriveled, the blossoms hanging limp on their stalks.

I'd slept badly, my dreams full of violence and vulnerability, and some residual anxiety was still pulsing through my bloodstream. My instincts were working overtime that morning, quivering and alert for danger. After deliberately stirring up a hornet's nest of trouble for Raymond Ashe, I had considered changing my route, but I hated the idea that he might think he'd won. So I ran my usual course, passing by the church where now a counterprotest had taken up a vigil on the corner, two cold and sullen groups drinking coffee out of thermoses. Both sides held up signs when a lone car drove by. The driver honked, but it wasn't clear which side he supported.

I reached the park and started onto a winding path. The lawns were shrouded in shadow, and mist rising off the lagoon smudged the playground and pavilion in soft gray fog. As I reached the northern leg of my circuit, I saw Ashe's black SUV parked on the drive, in the spot where we'd had our confrontation the day before. It was a little harder to breathe as I grew close to it, and my wrists tingled, but I didn't let my rhythm change, nor did I look in his direction. I just ran as if he didn't exist, though my heart was pounding faster than usual.

The SUV began to prowl behind me until my path deviated from the roadway. When I glanced back, I saw it heading out of the park. I felt ridiculously triumphant, though I was still alert, scanning the trees and bushes near the path, keeping a wary eye on passing cars.

That's why I noted a familiar Jeep parked at the perimeter of the park. I changed my course to head toward it.

"What are you doing here?" I asked when Dugan powered down his window. Pozorski was in the passenger seat. There was a pair of binoculars on the dash.

"Jerry never had a guava pastry before, so we came over here to hit up a Puerto Rican bakery," Dugan said. "There's one in here for you." He reached for the paper bag sitting between their seats.

"I don't need babysitters."

"No harm in having friends watch your back. And given you made an extra-special effort to shit all over Raymond Ashe yesterday—"

"Don't patronize me."

"That's not—"

"I don't want to see you here again, all right?"

Dugan's chin came up. "Yeah? Well maybe I don't want you to act like an idiot. He was right over there, watching you."

"You think I didn't know that? I have every right to run in a public park. I'm not going to be intimidated by Raymond Ashe or anybody else."

"Jesus, Anni. You had a run-in with him just yesterday, right here, and it didn't take much for him to get the upper hand. I know it pisses you off, but baiting him like this—you're acting like some ditzy blonde in a slasher movie."

"You know something?" I gripped his window frame so tightly my hands ached. "Nobody tells *men* they should stay indoors. That if they go anywhere alone they're just asking for trouble. Or that if they don't live in constant fear, they're stupid and irresponsible."

Dugan rubbed his forehead with his thumb. "Anni, look . . ."

"No, *you* look. I don't want you hovering over me. I'll take care of myself. I always have. So fuck you."

When I got home, I wondered how I could apologize to Dugan and explain, without losing my temper, why his attitude filled me with rage. Ever since I let myself get lost in a book just long enough for a boy to gain control over me, I knew I had to be careful. I couldn't afford to let my guard down, ever, no matter how unfair it was. But having a man protect me was like stepping into a very small cell and hearing the door clang shut. And accepting that imprisonment to accommodate men who were aroused by exerting power over women was something I refused to do.

I brought up my e-mail and saw that Jill had replied. "Would today work? Or tomorrow? I'm available anytime either day. I'm eager to hear what you learned, though I understand if you prefer not to make the trip on a weekend." I e-mailed her back and said I would leave right away and should be there by noon.

As I went down the back stairs, Aisha was at the sink, scrubbing dishes. She dropped her sponge and came to the back door, wiping her hands on a dishrag. "How you doing?" she said, giving me a brief glimpse of her big, crooked teeth.

"Fine. Yourself?"

"We're good. Boys are inside, playing with the baby while I clean the place."

"I hope it's not as bad as last time."

"No, it's not too nasty." She stood in the open doorway, her slanted eyes fixed on me, asking a question.

"I talked to some people who know Amira," I said reluctantly, and then felt guilty about the hope that lit up her face. "Haven't found her yet, but I put out some flyers."

She kept her upper lip tight over her teeth as she smiled. It made her look as if she had a well-kept but happy secret.

"Your sister—" I started to say, but bit my words off. She's hooking. She's shooting up. She's never going to be a nurse. She'll just be one more burden for your little shoulders to carry. "Don't get your hopes up," I said instead.

"I won't." But I could tell that she couldn't help herself. That was one thing that kept those shoulders so straight, so stubborn. Hope in spite of everything.

She went back inside, and I went through the gangway and slung my backpack and bag into the Corolla, double-checking to make sure I had brought a printed copy of the report for Jill. Then I set out.

TWENTY-SEVEN

Jill was standing on the front porch with her two massive dogs on either side as I pulled up in her gravel drive. She was dressed in a black turtleneck, jeans, and short boots, and she looked strong and confident as she welcomed me in. But when we sat across from one another at the kitchen table, her pale face seemed suddenly as delicate as fine porcelain, the barely visible scar along her jaw a reminder she had once been broken and pieced back together.

"I have a report for you." I pulled it out of my bag. "It won't be easy to read."

"I know."

"I worked on it with Jerry Pozorski and with a police officer we both know. It makes a case that the man who raped you has attacked at least a dozen women, and that in the most recent assault, the woman died. We have a possible suspect, but the evidence is circumstantial and so slight, it's really nonexistent. The best way to go forward would be for the police to launch a major investigation, but we've run into a barrier. We're proposing an alternative theory for a high-profile homicide case, and they don't want to go there. In fact, the police officer who worked with us has been reprimanded and put on desk duty."

"Is Peter Vogel involved in this major case?"

"Yes, he is."

She covered her mouth for a moment. "Kathy Miller," she whispered.

"When they found her body last Monday, there was evidence that suggests she'd been raped. They're holding it back for the family's sake."

Her eyes had filled with tears. "When I read about her going missing, that they'd found blood in an alley I thought . . ." She rubbed away tears and cleared her throat, back in charge of her emotions. "I guess I feel a kind of kinship whenever I read about a woman who's been attacked. But this was so close to where it happened to me, and she was about the same age. Even the hair. When I saw her picture I thought 'this is me.' But then they arrested someone, said it was a carjacking."

"To be fair to the police, they believe they have the right guy. They aren't trying to cover up the truth, they're just afraid their case isn't strong enough and they'll lose him."

"But they'll have to tell the defense about this, right? That Kathy was raped?"

"Yes, and it will give the lawyer leading the defense enormous leverage with the jury when it comes to reasonable doubt."

"Maybe he's the one who should get this report."

"It's a she. And she doesn't have the resources to find your attacker."

"But if she proposes this alternate theory at trial . . ." I let her think it through on her own. "The media will get it."

"It would be the kind of publicity that surrounded your case to the power of ten. And you'd be right in the middle of it."

"What about approaching other law enforcement agencies? Could you take this to the FBI?"

"They don't interfere with local authorities for crimes that have nothing to do with their mandate."

"So what other options do we have?"

"I could keep going. See if there's some way to get solid proof against a suspect. I think the odds of being able to do that are slim, and in the end, the police would still have to buy into it. I don't think it would be successful."

"You always say that. Remember how you told me you wouldn't get anywhere?"

"I got about a mile and half past nowhere, but we're a long way from a solution. And I don't see how you could even afford an investigation like that."

"My parents have some land. They would sell it if—"

"It wouldn't be fair." I laid my palm on the report. "I have twelve clients in here. Why should you foot the bill for all of them?"

"Because they can't. Because I want to."

"Then I'd strongly recommend hiring a firm that has more resources than I do. I'm not sure they'd succeed, but they'd have a better chance than I would."

"I want you to do it."

I sighed. "I want this guy, Jill. I want him as badly as I've ever wanted anything. But it's incredibly frustrating to realize how much I can't do. This needs a big push, not just a single investigator."

"Two investigators. You've got Jerry. How is he, anyway?"

"He's . . . he's had his ups and downs. He was touched to hear that you still respected him after the case was thrown out. That meant a lot."

"But I'm the one who identified the wrong man. Having that case thrown out must have been a terrible disappointment for him."

"He's had a lot of disappointments. Right before he retired he was involved in a shooting. He had to kill a guy, and it messed him up. It cost him his marriage. It cost him a lot of things. But he wanted in on this. It was like . . . I don't know, a chance to redeem himself. The truth is, I couldn't have done it without him."

"I should be paying him, too."

"He wouldn't want you to do that. He just wanted a second chance to get this case right. That's why deciding our next step is so hard. We both want to see this guy in custody. We'd keep working on it till we dropped. But getting results is what matters."

"I suppose I should read your report before we decide anything." She looked at it, lying on the table in front of her, apprehensively, as if it might give her an electrical shock. I still had my hand on it. She nodded and I slid it across the table. Her eyes widened as she saw the bruises on my wrist. "What's that?"

I felt an urge to simply pull my sleeve back over the marks, but instead I held up my wrist to show her. "This is a thumbprint. These are from his fingers." I pointed them out on both sides of my wrist. "I was shaking this guy's tree and he tried to shake back."

"Because of this case?"

"Because he thought I was a threat to him, and that maybe I'd stop if I got scared."

"I'm sorry."

"Part of the job."

Jill lifted the cover sheet of the report, then let it drop. "What am I thinking? I haven't offered you anything, and you had that long drive. Would you like something to drink? Have you had lunch?"

She took her time fixing me an elaborate sandwich. The precise way that she went about it reminded me of Martin, soothing himself with order. "How about a beer with that?"

"A beer sounds wonderful." She popped the cap off a local microbrew. I took the bottle and plate. I sensed she needed privacy to go over the document I'd given her. "I think I'll eat out on the front porch. That view is amazing."

"I'll, um . . ." She made a funny little gesture. "I'll just read through this."

"Take your time. I'll try to answer any questions you have when you've finished."

One of the dogs started to follow me out, tempted by the possibility that I'd drop some food on the floor, but he turned back after a few steps. They surrounded Jill as she sat at the kitchen table, one of them sprawled on his side, the other leaning against her, his head in her lap.

woke to find myself under a plaid blanket. The setting sun cast long shadows and lit up the bluffs on the Illinois side of the river, making the autumn colors glow like a gigantic bank of hot embers. "How long did I sleep?" I sat up and rubbed my nose. It felt half frozen.

"About . . ." Jill glanced at her watch. "Five hours." She was sitting in a chair near mine, her feet propped on the railing, a stack of papers in her lap. Her only concession to the nippy air was a sweater and scarf.

"Sorry. That beer put me right out."

"You barely touched it."

The nearly full bottle was on the floor beside me. The plate was clean. I had a vague memory of taking a bite of the sandwich. Maybe one of the dogs finished it for me. "That was the best sleep I've had in months."

"You must have needed it. When I came out here, you were so deeply asleep I didn't want to disturb you. Though at first I wasn't sure what to think. It seemed so odd."

"That I'd lay all that on you and then go take a snooze? I'd say that's odd."

"No, that you could relax out here. I would never be able to doze off in an exposed place like this. Want to go in? There's coffee on. Tom's making venison stew."

The kitchen was fragrant with garlic and red wine and something rich and gamey. "Venison? Is that, like, Bambi?"

"Last year's Bambi." He grinned up at me from a cutting board. "I'm cleaning out my freezer, making room. Deer opener's only a few weeks away."

"Deer opener. Sounds like a handy kitchen gadget."

"I can tell you're not from around here." Tom picked up the wine bottle with an inquiring look.

I shook my head. "I heard rumors of coffee."

"In the pot. Help yourself. You get those papers graded?" he asked Jill.

"Most of them." Jill handed me a mug, got a wineglass for herself. "I asked Tom to come over while you were asleep. We've talked it through. There's really only one approach that makes sense." She filled her glass and took a sip. "I'm going to go public with this. I'm taking it to the media."

"But that's—"

"You said yourself the important thing is to get results. I'm more optimistic than you are that you could get there, eventually, but it would take time, and it sounds as if the police may actively oppose it. The Kathy Miller case is huge news right now. If I go to a news organization with this, they'll run with it, and the police will be forced to respond. Now, not months from now."

"What about the cost to you?"

"Much higher if he had a chance to attack another woman. Besides, I've already helped to send one innocent man to prison; I don't need two on my conscience."

"But you realize . . ."

"This is what I need to do."

I looked at Tom. He was chopping shallots so intently it looked as if he had forgotten about his stew and was trying to pulverize them to a molecular state. "I don't like it," he said. "But it's her call."

"I'll need advice," Jill said to me. "I was hoping Thea Adelman would be willing to walk me through this. I don't know anything about how this works. I'd like to get the story to someone who will do it justice and is in a position to give it credibility."

"I know the lead crime reporter for the *Trib*."

"Is he good?"

"Depends on what you mean by 'good.' He'd sell his mother for a story, but it would be a great story."

"Could you introduce us?"

"Sure. He's a good guy. But he's not the only reporter you'll have to talk to. They're not all good guys."

"I realize that."

"It's like being in a firestorm. You have all these fires burning, and they're hot and destructive, but it's the combination that takes it to a whole different level. It'll take over your life, Jill. It'll change everything."

"I know. I already talked to my department chair, told him I needed an emergency leave. We've worked out ways to cover my courses for the next two weeks. I'll contact the college's public relations department before it breaks so they won't be caught totally off guard. I still have to finish grading those papers." For a moment she looked overwhelmed, as if one mundane task put the enormity of it all in focus, but she quickly regained control. "Do you think this reporter could meet with me tomorrow? I'd like to get on it right away."

"I can call him right now. He'll meet you whenever you like. But the thing is . . ." I set my mug down and rubbed my temples. "Jill, you only read this report a few hours ago. Maybe you should—"

"I know what I'm doing. Call him."

I glanced at Tom again. "Don't take too long. Supper will be ready in twenty minutes."

I pulled my phone out of my bag, and went out onto the porch where the reception was stronger. The sun had set, but its slanting rays still touched the trees at the top of the bluff, making a rim of fire dance along them. I punched in Az's number.

He picked it up after a few rings and belched. "'Scuse me. Just had a dog with the works. Oh, and three beers. Maybe that's what's causing all the gas."

"How drunk are you?"

I heard rustling paper, pictured him finding a fresh page in his notebook. "Stone sober. What you got?"

"Maybe another Pulitzer nomination."

B y the time I left, we had an appointment with Thea and Harvey Adelman scheduled for 11:00 A.M. and an interview with Az in the early afternoon. I e-mailed both of them the report, edited so all of the victims, apart from Jill McKenzie and Kathy Miller, were given numbers for the sake of their privacy. I also stripped out all mention of bus routes and our suspicions about Raymond Ashe in the copy that went to Az; it was too speculative a theory, and revealing it now would make it harder to pursue. I called Dugan and Pozorski to break the news that their lives would soon be invaded by a marauding army of reporters. We decided to meet at Pozorski's for breakfast before heading to the Adelmans' office.

I drove home through the dark, sensing endless cornfields stretching out around me. From time to time I saw lights in the fields, combines working late into the night to finish the harvest. As a ruddy bruise of city lights began to glow on the horizon like a false dawn, I groped for my phone and worked a familiar pattern of numbers with my thumb.

"Hullo?" Nancy sounded groggy.

"Sorry. Did I wake you?"

"No. Well, sort of. I was just having a glass of wine. Must have drifted off. What's up?"

"I need a favor. You know that colleague of yours who asked about me? The one who wanted my contact information?"

"Jill McKenzie."

"She asked me to do some work for her. I couldn't tell you about it until now, but the whole thing will hit the news, soon." I gave her a quick rundown of the case.

"I had no idea," she said when I finished. "I've known Jill for years, but . . . good God. What a dreadful thing. How is she dealing with it?"

"She's determined to go public, but it's going to be hard on her. The media will go nuts. You know what that's like."

"God, yes. I remember how they camped outside the hospital when Jim was shot. Couldn't set foot outside without some idiot with a microphone rushing up. Poor Jill."

"Thing is, I'll be right in the thick of it. I was wondering if you could check in on Martin for me until this is over, keep an eye on him. I wouldn't ask, but I don't know who else—"

"Jesus, Anni!" She was suddenly furious. "For a clever woman you can be incredibly dim. Do you really think—" I heard something crash. "Oh, bugger."

"Are you okay?"

"Hang on." I waited for a minute, then two. "Sorry. Knocked the wine bottle over."

"Oops. Did it make a mess?"

"It was nearly empty. Guess I'd drunk more than I realized. Where were we?"

"You were telling me how stupid I am."

"Oh, right. Look, there's something I've been needing to tell you, and I might as well do it while I'm slightly pissed." She took a breath. "I'm not sure what's been going on with you lately, but you and Martin, you'll always be part of us, no matter what."

"Okay," I said, hesitant.

"I know you've been going through a bad time. Something's eating you, and you can't tell me what it is, but it doesn't matter. We're none of us perfect. Even Jim. I know, I was with him when he woke up in a cold sweat from his nightmares night after night. There were things he didn't want me to know, lots of things, but I loved him anyway. I'll always love him."

"Me, too," I whispered.

"It's the same with you and Martin. Whatever this, this *thing* is, it doesn't change anything. You're stuck with us, mate, like it or not. Go do what you need to do, and for Christ's sake, don't worry about your brother. Of course we'll look after him."

It felt as if something was melting inside, shifting and breaking apart. "Thanks," I said, my voice husky.

"Don't thank me, you idiot. Just come tell us all about it soon as you can. Otherwise, I'll have to rely on the bloody newspapers, and they never get anything right."

TWENTY-EIGHT

We sat in the same conference room where Father Sikora had asked for legal advice. Pozorski was wearing a good suit that looked as if he'd borrowed it from someone a size larger in the shoulders and several belt-notches trimmer in the waist. Dugan kept checking his tie to make sure he'd brushed off all signs of the powdered sugar he'd spilled all over it at breakfast. Tom Farrell paced by the window, peering out at the city, looking as if he'd rather be anywhere else. Jill looked tough and determined. I'd caught Thea Adelman appraising her with a sidelong glance, assessing how she'd look on camera.

We had gone over the report and the police response. Thea laid out what to expect from the media. Someone in her office would field all requests for interviews. She emphasized to Jill and Tom that they would not have private lives for a long time. There would be cameramen waiting outside their door. Reporters flooding their Iowa town. Phone calls and e-mails and photographers ambushing them whenever they stepped outdoors. Jill nodded, still resolute. Tom stared out the window and picked at something between his teeth.

"This goes for the rest of you, too," Thea said. "Anni, you know what it's like." I nodded.

"Guess I'll get a lot of practice saying 'no comment,'" Dugan said.

"You're in a difficult position," Thea acknowledged. "But it's important for people to know that you raised these issues and were not only ignored but punished for it."

Dugan bristled. "That's not what happened. The complaint—crap like that happens all the time; comes with the job. But getting docked three days, that was because I mouthed off to my superior. He had every right to reprimand me."

"I see. You don't want to be seen as a whistle-blower."

"I work with these guys." Dugan shifted in his seat, trying to keep his temper. "They're not covering anything up; they're busting their butts to get a conviction. I don't want to hear them insulted."

Thea jotted something on her legal pad. "So noted. Though the fact that Kathy Miller was raped will become public knowledge."

Dugan already knew that, but he winced.

"Az will have heard it from four or five sources by now," I said to Dugan, under my breath. "It doesn't have to get back to you."

"It will, though. They'll know I shot my mouth off."

"Yeah, well, if they'd listened to you in the first place—"

Thea cleared her throat and gave us the kind of look teachers use on disruptive students. She glanced at her watch. "We don't have a lot of time. Let's talk about the press conference."

"I've been thinking about that," Jill said. "I'd like to try something different. I'll give a public lecture tomorrow evening. The press can cover it if they want, but I'll be talking to real people, and I'll be able to answer real questions, not some bullshit about how I feel."

"A lecture." Thea frowned, thinking it through.

"I'm used to speaking publicly. I would feel more comfortable doing it without a million microphones in my face."

"You want to prepare your own remarks?" Thea asked.

"Of course." Jill seemed startled by the question.

"I like it," Harvey pronounced. "More authentic. I wonder what kind of venue we can find on short notice?"

"We need one that works for people who wouldn't feel comfortable going to a university or a concert hall," Jill said. "I was thinking of a church."

"How about the Chicago Temple?" Harvey murmured to Thea. "It's right across from City Hall, close to the major media outlets."

"Across the street from City Hall is not what I have in mind," Jill said dryly. "I want to speak for all of the women he's raped, not just me, not just Kathy Miller. It should be closer to where those other women were attacked, so people realize this isn't something that only matters when it happens to young white women who live in wealthy neighborhoods."

She reached for one of the printouts spread across the table. That morning, I'd taken a series of photos of Pozorski's board and used a printer at the law office. They were now assembled like a big puzzle in the middle of the conference table. "If you look at where these crimes occurred, there's a church that's fairly central to them all." She studied the sheet that showed the city map studded with pins for a moment, then tapped an intersection. "St. Lawrence Catholic Church."

"That's where Esperanza Ruiz has taken sanctuary," Thea said.

"Ho, boy," Harvey said. "That would open a can of worms."

Jill tilted her head, as if she were puzzling over how to deal with an unusually dense student. "Isn't that exactly what we're trying to do?"

All the arguments against it—that implicitly endorsing a controversial act of protest would dilute their focus, that a lot of people would assume that this was a politically motivated stunt—failed to dissuade Jill from her plan. St. Larry's was in the right location, it could accommodate a sizeable audience, and it served a multiethnic congregation. Besides, Esperanza's bid for sanctuary was already part of the story. "She was targeted in the raids two weeks ago because she's close to a man who's been falsely accused in the most recent of these crimes. It makes perfect sense to me."

"It won't to anyone else," Thea said. "It muddles everything up. You're going public because you want people to know that the authorities have failed to stop a rapist. You're mixing it up with a completely different issue."

Jill's gray eyes took on the sharpness of flint. "Peter Vogel dismissed my concerns because they threatened his political future. He's the one who mixed it up."

"It seems to me—" Thea started to say, when a knock on the door interrupted her.

"Hey, I was hoping you guys—" Simone Landry poked her head around the door. This time she was wearing a red dress with a high-buttoned collar and a garishly colored Russian shawl. Given her short, pear-shaped body, it made her look as if she contained a vast family of nesting dolls. "Whoops! Didn't realize you were having a meeting."

"Liar. You walked right past our receptionist," Thea said, half amused, half irritated. "You always do that."

"She's always on the goddamn phone." Landry had come up to the table, her eyes drawn to the pages spread out there as Harvey started to scoop them up. "Hey." She snatched at one before he could grab it. "Why are you talking about my case?" She waved the paper with KATHY MILLER written on it in Pozorski's neat script.

"We're talking about a lot of things," Harvey said. "Private things. Confidential things. You know, lawyer stuff."

"Bite me." She started to read the page; Thea snapped it out of her hand. "What's going on, here?"

"Can you wait in the lobby, please? We'll be finished shortly."

"She'll read about it in the papers tomorrow," Jill said. "We might as well let her know now."

"And you are—"

"Jill McKenzie. I'm the woman who misidentified her attacker in the Lincoln Park Rapist case. I hired Anni Koskinen to find out who was really responsible."

Landry's mouth gaped open for a moment. "You're . . . oh, wow. This is getting weird."

Dugan put his palms on the table and started to rise. "I don't think I should be here."

"Detectives Dugan and Pozorski have been contributing their own time to help her," Jill went on. "They believe the man who raped me also raped and battered a dozen women over the years, including Kathy Miller."

"But she wasn't raped," Landry said.

"The state of her clothing when she was found suggests she was."

Dugan had reached the door, was pulling it open.

"Please." Jill looked at him. Something made him come back to the table, as if he didn't even realize he was doing it. "You might as well see this." She reached over and took the printouts from Harvey and laid them out on the table again, assembling them in order. Thea put the last one in place—the page she'd snatched out of Landry's hands. "These are photos of a chart that Detective Pozorski created. It lays out the connections."

Landry bent over it, fascinated. "This changes everything," she whispered to herself.

"We don't have proof of any of it," I said. "And we don't want the victims' names made public. But Az Abkerian will be running a story about this in tomorrow morning's *Trib*. Dugan tried to take it through the channels and got a reprimand for it; this is the only way we could get the authorities' attention."

"It'll do that. But this is in the wrong place," she said, pointing at the photo I'd taken of Otis Parchmann.

"What do you mean?" I asked.

"Should be over here." She tapped the sheet that detailed Kathy

Miller's case. "Where'd you get that picture, anyway? They wouldn't even tell me his name."

"I don't understand. What are you saying?"

"You put this guy's picture with the wrong case. He's a key witness for the prosecution." She saw I was still lost and spelled it out patiently. "He's the one who saw Diggy near the alley that night."

TWENTY-NINE

That's twice in the past few days that I thought you were going to pass out," I said to Dugan.

"I was not."

"You practically fell out of your chair."

Simone Landry had been at least as surprised as Dugan had been, learning that Otis Parchmann had also been a key witness for the Lincoln Park case, but she was the first to grasp its significance. "Maybe he's our guy," she said almost immediately. "What are the odds you'd just happen to be a witness in two cases like that? Who is he, anyway?"

I told her what we knew about him. Then I used the Adelmans' Internet connection to do a little more digging. No criminal history. He had a driver's license, which surprised me; I had formed the impression his intelligence was so limited he wouldn't be able to pass the written exam. And apart from his testimony in the Lincoln Park case, he was mentioned twice in the archives of the *Tribune*: as a witness to an officer-involved shooting which helped clear a narcotics cop of any wrongdoing, and testifying in a hit-and-run case that led to a conviction. All that coaching he'd gotten before testifying against Chase Taylor must have paid off; he'd gotten good at it. Thea, Harvey, and Simone Landry all got on the phone, tapping their contacts among current and former prosecutors to see if the name Otis Parchmann rang a bell.

Dugan and I were headed to the office of the nonprofit organization that placed him in a job, picking up trash for the city. "Tell you one thing," he said. "I thought being pulled off the case was a big deal. Turns out I was never really *on* the case."

"Turn right up here," I said, and grabbed the door handle as Dugan took the corner too sharply. "I can see why they kept Parchmann's identity on a need-to-know basis. When you're working with witnesses in gang-related cases, they tend to get killed. It's in the next block."

"Frustrating, though. I feel as if I've been working this case with a blindfold on."

The manager remembered me from the previous week. I explained that we wanted to see where Otis Parchmann had been working, for as far back as they had records. When she balked, Dugan discreetly opened his badge case. She glanced around to make sure that nobody else in the room had seen it, then invited us back into a room where there were a couple of desks, an ancient computer, and three battered filing cabinets. "I didn't know this was official. Is he in some kind of trouble?"

"That's what we're trying to find out."

"Aren't you supposed to have a subpoena or something?"

"I told you," Dugan said to me, playing Bad Cop. He would have to put in more practice to advance beyond Slightly Grumpy Cop. "We're wasting our time here."

"Why put the man's name into the system if we don't have to? Besides, you probably don't even keep those kinds of records," I said to the woman.

"Sure we do. You wouldn't believe how much information some foundations ask for just to give you a few dollars. We don't throw anything out." She took the handle of a filing cabinet drawer, still undecided.

"Forget it," Dugan said. "We'll send some uniforms over with a warrant."

"No, don't. It'll make our clients nervous." She yanked the drawer open, flipping through files and pulling out a chunk of several manila folders. "I don't suppose it matters. Just bring them back whenever you're done with them. You probably won't find anything." She hesitated.

"Probably not," I said. "Like you said before, he's a good worker, always shows up on time. Doesn't cause any problems." I kept looking at her, inviting her to say whatever was on her mind.

"I shouldn't say this," she said finally. "We have people here who did time for bad things. Armed robbery, home invasion, even murder. Otis has a clean record and he's meek as a mouse. But something about him . . . I don't know what it is. He just gives me the creeps."

We went to a café, got mugs of coffee, and worked backwards through the files, going through page after page of scribbled paperwork detailing where employees had been assigned to work on a contract with the city over the past fifteen years, focusing on the dates of the assaults.

When we finished, Dugan looked up at me. "He was working in a park near every one of these assaults. He left DNA evidence in what, five of the cases? He wasn't even trying to cover his tracks. How in the hell did we miss him all these years?"

I thought back to the day I'd talked to him in the public playground. "He doesn't seem smart enough to get away with anything. But he must have some instincts. When they were canvassing in Jill's case, he produced exactly what they needed."

"Same with Kathy Miller. A witness like that appears just when your case is on shaky ground . . . Somebody should have checked into him."

"They probably did. He has a long history of being reliable on the stand."

"All the time we put in, trying to make a case against Salazar, and this guy was right under our noses." Dugan scrubbed his face with his hands, then turned on his cell phone and checked for messages. "Guess Abkerian has been busy. I have . . . looks like eleven messages from my boss. No, twelve."

"Are you going to try 'no comment' on him?"

"Wouldn't that be sweet. No, if he lets me get a word in edgewise, I'm going to tell him we have a suspect."

made photocopies of all of the files and returned the originals. By the time I got back to the Adelmans' law office, Jill had been in the conference room with Az for nearly three hours. According to the receptionist, Tom had grown restless and had gone out for a walk. Thea was on the phone with a client, but when she was free I told her what we had learned. "We can't make it public, of course. But he's our guy. I'm sure of it."

"Want to know something else? He's been a witness in at least eight criminal prosecutions, and one of them was a criminal sexual assault. I don't have the details, but it's no wonder he's been able to literally get away with murder. He's practically on the staff of the state's attorney's office."

"Harvey must be pleased. This could torpedo Peter Vogel's political career."

"And once questions are raised about Vogel, it might draw the focus away from Jill. I'm still strongly opposed to her giving a speech at St. Larry's, but she's been quite stubborn on that point."

I couldn't help smiling at the thought of Thea and Jill in a debate; they were both articulate, intelligent, and utterly pigheaded. "Has that been set up?"

Thea sighed. "Yes. Father Sikora was perfectly willing to offer the church for her lecture. It will be announced in the paper tomorrow.

And it won't just be a local event. An immigrant rights group has volunteered to stream it over the Internet."

"That's a lot of pressure on Jill."

"She told me the hard part was deciding to go public, but if her story is going to be out there, she wants it in her words, not filtered through the media. Gives her a greater sense of control."

"We need to give the other victims a heads-up about this story coming out tomorrow," I said. "Even though they won't be named, it will be a hell of a shock. I'll call the women I interviewed personally, and I'll pass the names of the others to a rape counselor I know so she can break it to them."

"The Miller family won't be blindsided. Apparently Az Abkerian is on fairly good terms with them. They confirmed that the police told them their daughter had likely been sexually assaulted; obviously, it's painful for them, but it wasn't their idea to withhold it from the press."

"We'd better let Chase Taylor know. Reporters will want to talk to him."

"I've already spoken with his aunt about it." She hesitated. "Tom Farrell is a bit of a wild card. What do you make of him?"

"I like him. What's your take?"

"He's a trifle . . . western in his attitude. He doesn't have any patience with all this legal folderol. I have a feeling he would rather administer some frontier justice. Do you suppose he owns a gun?"

"Probably several. He runs a shooting range."

"Dear God."

"Don't worry. I explained that handguns are illegal here, that you can't even transport a loaded weapon in your car in Illinois." I'd said it more for Jill's sake than his; she was the one who must be missing the familiar weight of a holster on her hip, but so far she hadn't let it show.

"They'll be staying at our house tonight. I've booked them into six different hotels for tomorrow night, after the lecture, to confuse the media. In fact, we have friends in Oak Park who will provide them a quiet place to stay for the next week. By then, let's hope the worst of it will be over."

I went back out to the waiting room and took a chair beside Jerry, who had fallen asleep, a magazine open across his lap, his tie loosened. He snorted and sat up. "Guess I was out for a while." He blinked at his watch. "Any luck with those work records?"

"It's amazing, Jerry. They totally match up."

"It's him."

"Yup. He's the one."

"Holy Christ." He closed his eyes for a moment, looking as if he was saying a prayer of thanks. But when he opened them he laughed. "First thing that comes into my head? This calls for a drink. I swear, it's on my mind every minute of the day."

"You did it, Jerry. You got him."

"Took me only twenty-three years. And it wasn't my doing."

"Give yourself some credit. I told Jill I couldn't have done this without you. And I meant it. If you hadn't reached out to me . . . After Kevin Casey found you passed out on the floor, I promised him I wouldn't talk to you again. I'm glad you wouldn't let me keep that promise."

"Kevin said that? When?"

"After I dropped in on you out of the blue to tell you I was working on your case."

"He said I was on the floor?"

"He told me you were in a bad state, that he thought he might have to call an ambulance. He was concerned, that's all. He didn't mean to embarrass you."

"Had a mother of a hangover, but not bad enough to call an ambulance." He nodded toward Jill and Az, who had just come out of the conference room. "Looks like our turn."

"Don't say anything to Az about Parchmann," I said under my breath.

"Do I look stupid?"

Jill appeared drained but strangely radiant, as if her skin had become more translucent, letting some inner light shine through. Az said something to her, tapping his notebook against his palm. She said something in return that made him laugh. She leaned over to give him a peck on the cheek.

"Got him eating out of her hand," Pozorski murmured. "Good girl."

"God, this is unprofessional," Az muttered as he waved us in. "Journalists shouldn't fall for their sources. But, boy, isn't she something?"

When Az finished with us and went off to confirm facts and gather "no comments," I made my phone calls. Three of the women who had come forward to tell me their stories accepted the news with a mix of stunned surprise and cautious gratitude; they were all happy to know progress had been made, but also realized their trauma would be dominating their lives again as police revisited their cases. The exception was Stacy Aldrich, who was giddy with excitement. I had to extract a promise that she wouldn't say a word to anyone until the story was published the next day.

"Do you know who did it?"

"We have a pretty good idea."

"Wow. Okay, I'll see you at St. Larry's. I'm bringing all my friends."

Pozorski and I headed to Clarke's for dinner. We ordered pie for dessert and took our time dallying over it. Pozorski talked about his daughters; I told him about Martin. Around 8:00 P.M. Pozorski looked at his watch and said he was going to head home, make an early night of it. He read something in my face. "Don't worry; I'll stay off the sauce."

"I didn't—"

"I know, but you were thinking it." He smiled to take the sting out of it.

As I drove him back to his apartment, Dugan called to say he was still officially in the doghouse, but unofficially things were getting interesting. When I asked for details, he said, "no comment."

The story appeared the next morning on the front page, the headline in an attention-getting font:

SALAZAR ARREST CALLED INTO QUESTION

Jill McKenzie, a professor at St. Vincent's College in Iowa, believes the man who killed Kathy Miller remains at large and is responsible for a dozen violent attacks on women, including a notorious rape in 1986. McKenzie is an authority on the Lincoln Park Rapist. She was his victim.

It was a long piece, carefully sourced. Az included quotes from Pozorski and me, with short recaps of our respective falls from grace. Sources within the department who would only speak on the condition of anonymity confirmed that a detective who had tried to raise the issue had been reprimanded and placed on desk duty. I was willing to bet some of those unnamed sources had the surname Dugan.

A police spokeswoman declined to comment other than to reiterate they were committed to finding justice for Kathy Miller. There was a vigorous denial from State's Attorney Peter Vogel, who insisted the professor's allegations had been investigated previously and dismissed; he insinuated that Jill was an attention-seeker with a political axe to grind.

We assembled at St. Larry's at six-thirty. Our cars were let into a fenced yard behind the church rectory to avoid the crush of journalists. While Jill chatted with Esperanza Ruiz in the vestry, Tom leaned against a wall, flipping idly through a hymnal. He had been silent most of the day, but I'd observed tense snatches of conversation between him and Jill, hostile body language. Something was not right between them.

Thea pointed to her watch: time for the curtain to go up. "Coming?" Jill said to Tom.

"Nope. This is your show." He didn't look up from his hymnal. Jill's mouth tightened, but she straightened her shoulders and went through the door into the sanctuary.

The church was packed with reporters, parishioners, supporters, and the curious. Several pews were filled with people wearing shirts with Kathy Miller's familiar face on them. I scanned the room, wondering if Otis Parchmann might have been drawn to the event, but I didn't see him. Kevin Casey stood among the crowd at the back, arms folded across his chest, skepticism all over his face. Stacy Aldrich beckoned from one of the front pews and pointed at a seat that she had saved for me. Though she had a dozen or more friends with her, it was my hand she gripped as Jill started to speak.

After a brief welcome from Father Sikora, Jill looked around the room and waited until it was completely silent. "When I was twenty years old, I took my dog for a walk early one morning," she began.

Later, I could never play the video of her speech all the way through. It left me feeling emotionally flayed, though on that night it also made me feel strangely uplifted. She wove together her story with those of a dozen women who were attacked by the same man. She recalled the fear that had gripped the city, letting a sixteen-year-old black man become the scapegoat for a host of anxieties. She didn't spell out the parallels with the arrest of a Mexican immigrant for Kathy Miller's murder, but they were too obvious to miss. She intercut her social analysis with the personal struggle she had faced to overcome her fear and rebuild her life. She talked about why she had kept her rape secret for all these years, and why she now had to speak up. Stacy's cheeks were wet with tears but her eyes glowed with triumph as she listened. She held my hand so tightly, her nails left dents.

Jill took questions when it was finished. She pointedly ignored the reporters who, forgetting it wasn't a press conference, started yelling out over each other. Instead she called on people who weren't holding notebooks or microphones. When one questioner wearing a Kathy Miller T-shirt insisted that the police had already arrested the killer, she gave a diplomatic answer that praised the hard work of the police while leaving no doubt that she thought they had made a mistake. The next questioner asked if she knew who was responsible. She hesitated before she answered. "Yes, I believe I do. We've provided the police with the evidence; now it's up to them. That's really all I can say at this point."

She took a few more questions, then skillfully drew things to a close. As the church thundered with applause, she slipped out the back and reporters raced for the door.

Thea and I had worked it out in advance: the pickup truck with Iowa tags drove out through the locked gates and headed downtown. The reporters who followed would find out the people in the truck, though they superficially resembled Tom and Jill, were actually associates of the Adelmans; the woman had even cut and dyed her hair to help with the subterfuge. Jill and Tom waited in Father Sikora's office in the community center next door until the press dispersed, then got into a rental car inside an attached garage and drove toward their safe house in Oak Park. With any luck, their temporary address would remain a secret.

But twenty minutes after they departed my cell phone rang. "Anni? Goddamn it. I need you to come get me."

"Tom? Where are you?"

"A gas station on the corner of Madison and something. Starts with an L. Leamington?"

"What are you doing there?"

"It's the only place I could find with a pay phone that works. My fucking cell's out of juice."

"No, I mean—why aren't you on your way to Oak Park?"

"You'd have to ask Jill that. She kicked me out of the car."

"She *what*?"

"She said she wanted to drive. When I got out to switch seats, she drove off without me. We had a fight, okay? Man, she not only dumped me, she dumped me in the ghetto. I have no idea where I am, but I don't exactly feel at home here."

"Tom, how could you let this happen? This is when she needs you."

"That's not what she thinks."

He was shamefaced when I pulled up. "Sorry. I didn't mean to drag you into this."

"Jill's not answering her phone."

"Probably turned it off so she won't have to talk to me. We've been having a rough time of it the last couple of days. She thinks I'm being overprotective. When did they make that a crime?"

I just shook my head and drove to the address in Oak Park. She wasn't there.

The police found the rental car two hours later. They didn't find Jill.

THIRTY

t felt as if I'd entered a parallel universe, one where time folded together and the same nightmares played over and over on the news.

Two detectives questioned me that night. It was obvious they were wondering if it was some stunt. But in the days following, they launched a full-scale search, one as thorough as that for Kathy Miller, with the FBI and state police in a five-state area assisting. Jill's parents flew in to speak with police on Wednesday morning. They filmed an appeal, asking for the safe return of their daughter. Standing side by side, they had the stolid straightforwardness of Midwesterners. Her father read from a piece of paper, haltingly. "We love our daughter. Please let her come home." At his side, her mother's eyes were staring and empty, as if this new tragedy had struck her blind.

Dugan and I spoke on the phone, but our conversations were frustratingly elliptical. Whatever was going on, he couldn't share it with me.

Thea gave me a new job: keeping an eye on Tom Farrell. After the police questioned him long into the night, he drove his pickup to the house in Oak Park. He barely spoke to his hosts, and politely refused the food they offered him. He just went upstairs and shut himself inside the guest room. He hadn't come out yet, but Thea wanted me to watch the house that night and make sure he didn't do anything reckless.

It was two in the morning when he slipped out the back door, got into his pickup truck, and drove out of the alley behind the house. I followed as he drove back and forth on the streets between Oak Park and the site of their argument. A couple of times he got out and walked aimlessly, kicking at trash. It was approaching 5:00 A.M. when he circled Garfield Park, then parked and got out. I pulled up behind his truck and followed him. He stopped by the lagoon and waited for me to catch up.

"I don't know where anything is. Is this one of the parks he was in?"

"Tom—"

"Simple question."

"Yes. He attacked a woman here four years ago."

"The one with a dog?"

"The police are doing everything they can."

"I bet you know where he lives."

I didn't respond. An El train rattled by on the tracks to the north, its windows glowing in the darkness. We stood there, listening to the rustling trees and the swish of traffic. Off in the distance, there were three pops, then three more. "That's not fireworks," he said to himself.

"Come on, Tom. It's not safe here."

He started to laugh. He laughed so hard, he lost his balance, stumbled against a tree, and sat on the ground. He wrapped his arms around his head and sat for a few minutes before he raised his head. "I don't know if I can do this," he said to himself.

"Let's go."

He ignored the hand I held out and pushed himself up, brushed off his jeans, and headed for his truck. As he unlocked the cab, I opened the passenger side and searched his glove compartment. Then I looked in the toolbox under the passenger seat. I showed him a 9mm Beretta. "Forgot it was in there," he said, not bothering to make it sound convincing.

"I'm taking this to the police. Go back to the house. I'll be right behind you."

He nodded. I followed him back to Oak Park. He didn't look in my direction as he climbed out of his truck and went inside.

t was a little after 6:00 A.M. when I called Dugan from the curb outside his aunt's Hyde Park house. He came to open the gate for me. "I took this from Tom Farrell." I handed him the gun. He looked at it as if I'd just handed him a grenade. Then he led me into his apartment, setting the gun on the kitchen table.

"You look done in."

"I was up all night."

"Coffee?"

I took the mug he filled and handed to me. "He kept driving back and forth. He wanted me to tell him where Otis Parchmann lives."

"Poor bastard."

"Have you arrested Parchmann yet?" Dugan looked away. "Oh, I forgot. You can't tell me anything." I was too tired to keep the bitterness out of my voice.

"We don't know where he is," he said.

I shook my head, unable to process it. "What are you saying?"

"We were going to bring him in on Tuesday, ask some questions. He wasn't where he was supposed to be working. He wasn't at his apartment. He isn't anywhere."

"So, he could have . . ." I felt hot coffee slop over my hand. He took the mug and set it on the table. "He figured it out. He must have been watching. Waiting."

"I don't know, but he has to be a lot smarter than anyone thought, to get away with this for so long."

"All these years, Jill's been keeping her secret, carrying a gun, looking over her shoulder, trying to protect herself from all this. Now she tells the world—and it all happens again."

"We don't know that. Maybe she took off. All that pressure—"

"She wouldn't do that to Tom." The floor seemed to be turning slowly clockwise. "God, Dugan. We have to find out what he did with her." My last words were muffled, my face pressed against his chest.

"I know." He held me, his chin on my head. "It's okay. Shhh."

"Crap," I said after a while. "I got your shirt all wet and snotty." I pushed out of his arms.

"It doesn't matter."

"Seriously, you'd better change. You're back on duty?" He nodded. "Good. Get a fresh shirt on and go find him."

The sound came to me like fingers plucking at my sleeve. I swam out of a strange and unpleasant dream that mingled the warm sensation of being wrapped close to Dugan, feeling his breath on my hair, mixed with blood-soaked scenes of brutality and violation. I sat up and groped for my phone.

"You got to help me out."

"Chase?" It took me a minute to figure out where I was. Dugan had left for work, but offered his guest room so I could get some sleep instead of fighting traffic to get home.

"They coming after me. You got to help me figure out what to do."

I kept my voice steady and calm. "Are you at your aunt's house?"

"No. I had to climb out the bathroom window. I think she called them on me. Man, I thought I could trust her."

"Chase, is she okay?"

"Nothing worse'n a bloody nose. She tried to stop me, so I had to hit her. What am I going to do?"

"Maybe I can work a deal with the police. Some kind of trade. You might know something that can help them out."

"Fuck that shit. They think I killed that woman, the one been on TV so much. They blow my head off 'fore they talk to me. Then they can say everything was my fault, they was right all along."

"They're looking at someone else for that."

"Then what they come to the house for? They had helmets and shit."

"What have you gotten yourself into, Chase?"

"Nothing. I was just doing a favor for a friend. He needed a place to store some stuff. He was going to give me a car. Now he's going to be all mad, 'cause I had to leave his stuff behind in my room."

"Where are you, Chase?"

"You know that A and W on Garfield, 'cross from the liquor store? No, wait. You going to tell the police."

"I'm glad you called me, Chase. I think I can help, but you have to tell me where you are."

"It's next door. A empty building, all boarded up. I called Raymond—" I heard him choke a little. "He told me I was on my own, he didn't have time for a loser like me." He had started to cry, a blubbering, gulping all-out meltdown. "I wanted that car so bad. But now everything's all fucked up."

"Hold on, Chase. We'll work something out."

I called his aunt as I headed to my car. Someone else answered the phone, a man with an abrupt voice. "I have an idea where Chase Taylor is," I told him.

"Who'm I talking to?"

"Anni Koskinen. I used to be on the job. Is Chase's aunt okay?"

"She'll live. You got something for us?"

"He left something in his bedroom. He told me he was holding it for a friend. Look, Do you want to bust a dealer, or just this small-stakes mule? If you want the dealer, you'll have to take this easy. He's scared out of his mind, but I think he'll cooperate if you play this right."

"Where's he at?"

"A boarded-up building next to the A and W on Garfield Boulevard."

There was some muttering in the background. "Across from the liquor store, right? Okay, we got it."

I t wasn't far from Dugan's house. I got there seconds before they did. As I parked on the street, four squad cars came screeching up behind me, two pulling up to the front of the building, two circling to the back. A group of kids hanging on the corner in front of the liquor store jeered and joked as the police barricaded the street and shooed them across the boulevard. An officer went into the A&W to clear it of customers. They were getting ready for a siege.

I looked for the officer who seemed to be in charge and approached him. "I'm the one who called. You're handling this all wrong."

"Ma'am, move on down the street or I'll have you arrested. I'm serious." He nodded at another officer, who tried to take my arm. I shook him off and walked away, seething.

I stopped down the block, in front of another derelict building. I pulled out my cell phone. "I'm sorry, Chase. They're being assholes."

"I see them." He sounded resigned now, no longer tearful. "You told on me." He hung up. I dialed again. It rang several times before he picked up.

"Chase? Don't hang up on me again. You need to stay cool, okay?

What you need to do is show them you're unarmed, that you don't want anybody hurt. I'll call Thea Adelman. We can still—"

Something smashed against the side of my head and I staggered. An arm snaked around my neck, pulling me back, a gun pressed to my temple.

"Who said I was unarmed?"

knew you'd call them," he said. "I ain't stupid."

My scalp burned from him pulling me by the hair up a staircase to a second-story flat that overlooked the street. One of the front windows was boarded up; the other was missing a pane of glass and pigeon droppings dotted the linoleum floor. The apartment was empty except for a couple of plastic milk crates, a filthy mattress, and a large wooden dresser with a cracked mirror. I saw myself reflected in it, fractured. "Chase, listen—"

"Shut the *fuck* up!" He raised the gun as if to strike me with it again. Then he tapped the barrel against the side of his head. "You been nice to me. I don't want to have to hurt you. Be quiet so I can think."

More squad cars were pulling up outside. Voices drifted up from the street. He peered down, rubbing his gun arm with the other hand. "Damn, it's cold. Didn't have time to get my coat." He glanced over at me, a flicker of irritation creasing his face. "What you looking at?"

"Nothing."

"Fuck. Can't think with your big eyes staring at me." He pointed with the gun barrel to a doorway across from the windows. "Go sit in there. Take one of them crates to sit on. The floor's all dirty."

I picked up one of the plastic crates and carried it through to the back room. The floor was littered with empty bottles and cans. The two windows were covered with plywood. "Don't come back out till

I say so. And don't say nothing, or I'll get mad at you." He closed the door, leaving me in darkness.

I had to get that gun away from him.

I set the crate down and groped my way over to the boarded-up windows. The plywood was fastened tightly, screwed down from the outside. I felt around the old-fashioned wood frame. A length of molding came off. I weighed it in my hands; it wasn't sturdy enough to do any good. I started to systematically feel my way around the room, looking for a heavy bottle with a neck long enough to grasp, but most of them were plastic; the only glass ones I found were small flasks. I could break one to get a sharp edge, but he would hear me and I wouldn't have a chance to surprise him.

Back at the window, I felt around the frame for a sturdier length of wood. The sill wouldn't give, but I managed to dig my fingers through the lath and plaster to grip one of the side panels. With as much energy as I could muster I bent it toward me. It cracked with a loud report and I waited, my heart pounding, for him to come back through the door. But he must have missed the noise over the commotion outside. Things were happening. I could hear someone speaking through a bullhorn.

The piece of wood that had broken off was too small, useless. I tossed it away and struggled to pry loose something more substantial. When I stopped to rest, my arms shaking from exertion, I remembered installing windows in my flat, old-fashioned sashes that I'd found at a secondhand store. Martin had tied weights to them, concealed behind the window frames. When I slid my arm into the gap where the piece of frame had broken off, my fingers found a long rough piece of cast iron, a rotten hank of rope still tied to one end.

I worked it out of its hole and hefted it. A foot-long iron bar; six pounds, at least. I envisioned Chase Taylor, standing by the window, rubbing his arm. He had carried the gun in his right hand. I went to stand by the door, the sash weight in my left hand.

After a few minutes I heard shouting. Chase paced in the next room muttering to himself. "Okay. Okay, now. This is it." A minute later, he pulled the door open. "Come out here. They seen me." He grabbed my right arm and pulled me toward him. I kept the weight beside my left leg as he gripped my hair and held the gun to my head and led me over to the window. "I got a hostage here," he yelled. Then he pulled me back to the center of the room.

The neck of his T-shirt was soaked with sweat, but he was shivering from the cold. I tried to read the sounds outside. A hostage changed things. They would be calling in a negotiator, reinforcements. A sniper.

Minutes passed. I felt his hand in my hair, shaking with tension. His gun hand must be getting tired. His eyes kept darting between the window and the door that led to the top of the stairs.

"Chase?"

"Shut up."

"We could push that dresser in front of the door."

I wasn't sure if he even heard me at first. But then I felt his hand relax in my hair. "Keep them out for a while. Only you got to do it. You strong enough?"

"I think so."

When he lowered the gun from my temple, I swung the sash weight with all my strength. I hear his wrist bone crack just before his scream. I scrabbled after the gun as it clattered to the floor, got it in my hands.

He held his wrist to his chest, bent over and crooning in pain. "Oh man, oh man. Can't believe you did that."

"Step over to the wall. The *wall*, Chase." He backed away from me. "Not there, Chase. *Chase!*"

He was only there for a moment, in front of the window, his eyes fixed on mine, knowing. The light picked up every pore of his skin, every drop of sweat. Then he jerked like a puppet as his head exploded in a billow of red mist.

I stumbled back, tripped, and sat down on the mattress. My front was soaked with his blood. I tried to unfasten my jacket. It took me a second to realize I could put the gun down and use both hands. I stripped it off as feet thundered up the stairs. Big men in body armor poured in, guns at the ready. I must have picked the pistol up again because they were yelling at me, but I couldn't think what to do. There was blood on my shirt, too. I started to unbutton it and then thought, no. That's stupid. Not in front of all these men. Besides, it was on my jeans, too. In my hair.

"Anni?" Dugan came toward me. "Oh, God. Did he—"

"*Drop it*!" someone bellowed.

"You didn't have to shoot him!" I was yelling myself, now, holding the gun up to show Dugan. "I got it away from him. I had it all under control."

t was late when I got home, dressed in a borrowed pair of sweats and a T-shirt from the 2006 FOP family picnic in Gaelic Park. My throat was still sore from screaming at Dugan when he tried to help me up from the mattress. Some officers had taken me to Wentworth Area Headquarters, where I'd showered off in the locker room, watching red run down the drain. I'd answered their questions, and when it was over they took me back to my car. My fingers were scraped and sore from tearing the window frame apart, but at least the shaking had stopped.

I dug a bottle of Grey Goose out of the freezer, where it had been lying for so long it was encased in frost. I couldn't remember who'd given it to me. I didn't care much for vodka, but I poured a glass and drank it down.

I called Thea and gave her a stumbling apology. She cut me off. "I heard what happened. He took you hostage; he held a gun to your head. I'm not wasting any sympathy on him."

"He was your client."

"So?" She sighed impatiently. "You've been through a hell of a trauma. Do you want Harvey to come get you? You could stay here tonight."

"No. I'm fine." It was funny how grumpy she sounded when she was trying to be nice. I opened the refrigerator to see if I had a lime.

"Did you hear about Otis Parchmann?"

"Dugan told me."

"At least you won't have to worry about watching Tom Farrell tonight."

"You got someone else to do it?" I found one, hiding in the back.

"There's no need anymore."

"I'm sorry. I'm not thinking too straight. Parchmann's missing, right?"

"So you didn't hear. They found him two hours ago, in a shipping yard just south of Little Village, shot in the back of the head."

"*What?* No. You mean . . ."

"He's dead."

"That can't be." I leaned against the counter, my head swimming. "I wanted to bring him in. All those women. He should be charged. He should face justice."

"I guess this is somebody's idea of justice."

"But it's not . . . *Shit!* It's not the same. Did this happen today?" While I was watching Chase Taylor's head come apart. I rubbed my eyes, willing the vision away.

"I'm not sure when he was shot. All I heard is they found his body."

I had taken a gun from Tom the night before, but I realized I hadn't searched the truck thoroughly. He could have had another pistol under his seat. "Did he stay at that house all day?"

"Who?"

"Tom. Did he go out?"

"I don't know. He's so difficult to read. When I told him Parchmann was dead, all he said was 'good.' No emotion at all."

"The police will want to talk to him."

"I doubt it," she said dryly. "The state's attorney has made it public that Parchmann was going to be a witness for the prosecution. The police are calling it a gang killing. They're blaming Diggy's friends."

"Jesus. I suppose nobody mentioned that he was a suspect in Kathy Miller's murder, that he was the man who raped Jill."

"They're still saying Chase Taylor was responsible for that."

I felt that red mist raining on me. I looked at my arm, expecting to see it there. "How do they explain Jill's disappearance? Abducted by aliens?"

"You'd have to ask Peter Vogel, but my guess is he'll eventually insinuate that Jill was emotionally unstable. That she couldn't face reality. He can't say that yet, not while her parents' appeal is still being broadcast."

"God. This is all wrong."

"Well, there's nothing we can do about it now. Let's talk tomorrow. You should get some rest."

I decided to get some more vodka, instead. It went down better with a twist of lime. With my third glass in hand, I called Pozorski. "Did you hear about Parchmann?"

"Thea told me."

"Did she tell you they're hanging it on Diggy's friends?"

"They're still using the old script. That'll change."

"You think?"

"She told me what happened to you, too. Are you okay?"

"I got pissed off at Dugan again. I said some awful things to him. After they shot Chase, I was pretty freaked out and Dugan was all, you know: let me take care of you."

"Is that a bad thing?"

"It mixes me all up. I like him a lot, but what if . . . I don't want to ruin it."

"I don't think there's much chance of that. He's nuts about you."

"How do you know? Was he talking about us?"

"No, I got eyes, that's all. Are you sure you're all right? You sound funny."

"I'm a little drunk. I should be over at your place, so you can talk me out of it. Maybe I'll drive over."

"*No.* Don't do that."

"I'm safe to drive."

"Doesn't sound like it to me, and I should know. Besides, I got company coming."

"Your daughters?"

"No, not my daughters." He sounded infinitely sad. "What you need to do is drink a big glass of water and go to bed. No more whiskey."

"Vodka."

"Whatever. And say, would you do me a favor? Check on the cats tomorrow?"

"Sure. Why?"

"You never know." I heard a buzzer for the door, heard leather creaking as he got out of his recliner. "It was good, working on this thing with you. Getting a second crack at it meant a lot to me."

"But now it's all messed up."

"Drink that water and go to bed."

I capped the vodka and put what was left in the freezer. I filled a tumbler with water and drank it down. It wasn't until I was setting the glass in the sink that it occurred to me: why was he speaking in the past tense?

The cold water that I splashed on my face didn't help much. The streets looked strange as I drove, corners looming too suddenly, meaning lagging behind sights and sounds, a weird Doppler effect. Parking was hopeless, as usual, so I left my Corolla in the middle of the street. I pushed the button for the manager's apartment. No response. I pushed all the buttons I could, holding them down until someone buzzed the outer door open.

The basement steps were steeper than they used to be. I was gripping the railing, trying to get my balance when I heard the shot. I stumbled down the stairs and pounded on the door. "Jerry?"

"Jesus Christ!" It wasn't his voice. "Jerry, God, no. Oh, fuck."

I kicked the door open. Kevin Casey was crouched over Pozorski, pressing his hands to his chest, red seeping between his fingers. "Call nine-one-one. Hurry."

I made the call, but didn't know the address. Casey reached for the phone, almost losing it with his slick hands as we traded places and I held back the blood. "Stay with me, Jerry."

"Here, use this."

Casey was holding out a folded dishcloth. I took it and pressed it down, hard. Tried to hold Pozorski's eyes with mine. "Don't you dare. You have to stay with me."

"It hurts," he got out between chattering teeth.

"I know. They're on their way."

"Could use—" He gripped his lip with his teeth, bit back a howl. "*God.*"

"Hang on, Jerry."

"Use a drink." He was trying to smile as tears of pain rolled down the sides of his face. He clamped his teeth together, a high, thin sound escaping.

The police arrived first. I sensed one of them crouching beside me. "He's a police officer," I told him. "Go out front. Make sure they know where to come." I heard him on his radio as he clattered back up the stairs.

"Can you tell me what happened here?" the other one asked Casey.

"I tried to get the gun away from him. It must have gone off."

"He was holding the gun?"

"His service weapon. I didn't realize he still had it."

"He was going to use it on you?"

"Christ, no. He's my best friend. We're very close."

"So, the gun . . ."

"He has a problem with alcohol; he didn't mean it, not really."

"Can you just tell me what happened?"

"He was distraught. He had it up under his chin. I grabbed his arm, tried to pry it away, but I guess, I guess—Christ, would you hurry up?"

The EMTs nudged me away and went to work. My hands were red. So were Casey's, and there was a feather of blood on his cheek where he'd wiped it. He looked at me, pleading. "I tried to stop him."

I summoned up everything I had and knocked him across the room.

THIRTY-TWO

hate hospitals."

"They're not so bad," Pozorski said. "This morphine's great."

"People die in hospitals."

"I'm not going to die."

"But you could have, you big dope." I watched him drift off to sleep, then noticed Dugan standing in the doorway.

"How's he doing?"

"High as a kite on the drugs they're giving him." It looked bad, all the tubes, monitors massed around him, but the bullet had passed through muscle, dinged a bone, and traveled out the other side without hitting anything important. He'd been in surgery for three hours and would be sore for a while, but he would live.

"You've been here all day?" Dugan pulled a chair up next to mine.

"Since they brought him in last night. What's Casey saying?"

"Nothing. You broke his jaw."

"Good." I flexed my hand. It was still swollen and sore, two knuckles scabbed over. My leg ached, too, from kicking in the door. I'd never done that before.

"He's writing a lot of notes to his lawyer, though, trying to save his ass. You were right about the gun. Jerry's wife took it from him years ago, when he was in the dumps after that shooting. She gave it to Casey for safekeeping."

"He could have gotten away with it."

"Except for bad aim. And this." Dugan queued something up on his iPod, handed it to me. "Jerry had a recorder in his pocket. The ER nurses found it when they cut his clothes off."

I put the earbuds in, heard Casey say hello and try some small talk before Pozorski cut him off. "You killed him, didn't you?"

"You been drinking again."

"How long did you know?"

"Jerry, what the fuck is this?"

"Did you help him hide Kathy Miller's body? Or did you do that all by yourself?"

"Christ. You really think I'd do something like that?"

"I don't know anymore."

"I never would. What that family went through, how can you think that?"

"What kind of appointment is Vogel going to give you when he's governor?"

"I don't believe this shit."

"Think it will be worth it?"

"Fuck you, Jerry."

"You did kill him, though. Parchmann. Had to keep your case on track."

"So what if I did? Theoretically."

"It's murder."

"Ah, Jerry. You're making it so complicated. He did all those women. He told me."

"When did you know?"

"Not till I saw that. You knew before I did."

"Of course. You have a key."

"And you were passed out cold, as usual. You're a sad bastard, you know that?"

"Kevin." Pozorski sounded tired. "Don't."

"You think I want to do this? I swear, you don't know me at all."

I jumped when I heard the shot. I felt Dugan take the iPod from my trembling hands. I leaned into him. He put an arm around me, rubbed his fingers up and down my spine.

"What we know for sure," Dugan said. "Casey went to the apartment building last Thursday night when a tenant had a problem and Jerry'd had too much to drink. We're guessing he let himself into Jerry's apartment and saw all the stuff on the wall, realized the case his future was riding on was about to fall apart."

"When did he shoot Parchmann?"

"T.O.D. was early Saturday morning."

"Before Jill disappeared."

"Casey probably figured it was the best way to hang onto the case against Salazar: claim the Latin Kings took Parchmann out to prevent him testifying. He's the one who got the bogus complaint filed against me so I'd be pulled off the case. And it looks like he told Raymond Ashe you were stirring up trouble, damaging his political chances. He probably hoped Ashe would do something to discourage you from pursuing the case. Maybe do more than discourage you."

"But the one who really had him worried was Jerry."

"Right. Vogel's distancing himself from the whole thing, of course. He's calling for a new investigation. You'd think it was all his idea."

"Casey was at the church. He was at Jill's talk."

"He's denying he had anything to do with her disappearance. He's denying everything at this point."

My head fit against his shoulder as if the hollow under his collarbone was custom made for it. He stroked my hair. "Dugan, do you think Jerry wanted to die?"

"I don't know. He wanted to set things right."

"I'm sorry I said those things to you yesterday."

"You were upset. Had a right to be."

Pozorski stirred in his bed. His hand groped his gown, feeling for the pump pinned to it. He thumbed more morphine into his bloodstream. For a moment his eyes opened. "Aw. That's nice." He gave us a wobbly smile before drifting off. I wasn't sure if he was talking about seeing us snuggled together or the drugs.

"I should take you home," Dugan murmured after a while. His fingers moving through my hair had put me in a trance.

"Do you have to go back to work?"

"Not until tomorrow."

"Stay with me."

His fingers stopped moving. "You sure?"

"I'm sure."

"Okay." When I sat up, I saw he had a big dumb grin on his face. I couldn't resist kissing it. It took a while.

As we walked past the nurses' station, two girls were standing there while someone looked up a room number. I recognized them from the photo in Jerry's apartment. My vision went blurry, and I blinked back tears. He would be so happy to see his daughters when he woke up.

I studied Dugan in the morning light that spilled through the windows, memorizing moles, freckles. He was sprawled on his stomach, his breath moving steadily, a whisper of sound against the sheet. There was a furled scar running across his ribs, the result of a childhood mishap. I'd felt it last night, exploring it with my fingertips as he explored me with his tongue. I wanted to run my finger along it again, but I didn't want to wake him up. He would have to go to work, and I wanted to lie beside him for as long as I could, preserving this moment. It scared me, to be this happy.

My phone rang. I managed to snatch it before it rang again. "Hello?"

"Why are you whispering?" It was Sophie.

"There's someone here." I carried the phone to the other side of the flat.

"A man? Oh, my God, is it that cop? The one with the bent nose?"

"What do you want, Sophie?"

"I tried to call you last night, but you weren't answering your phone." She packed a load of insinuation into the words.

"I was at the hospital with a friend."

"Yeah, right."

Dugan stretched, swung his legs out of the bed, picked up his watch, and winced at the time. He started to gather up his clothes.

"Sophie, was there something you wanted?"

"You're in the papers this morning. It says this guy took you hostage. Sounds scary."

"It was. Listen, I really have to go."

"Okay. I just wanted to see if you're all right. But I guess you are."

"Yeah, I am."

As Dugan passed me, on his way to the bathroom, I reached out and ran my finger down his scar. "Hey, that tickles." He swatted at my hand.

Sophie was snickering as I hung up.

fter a few days, I could go out without being ambushed by a camera; after a week I stopped getting calls from reporters. The publicity was beginning to die down, but not until Az had set a new personal record: he'd scored the front page six days in a row.

It was hard not to think about Jill, but work kept me busy. One of my kids had disappeared from home during a manic episode; another had walked away from his rehab program. When I wasn't busy with paying work, I went back to that stretch of Madison Street where Amira had last been seen, handed out flyers and talked to the women who worked there.

It paid off, eventually. I got a phone call one night from a woman who said a body had been found behind a building on Jackson around the end of July. Might have been the girl on the posters. Nobody knew who she was. They took her away in a bag.

I called Harrison and asked to speak to someone in the morgue detail; said I might have an identity for a Jane Doe. The person who answered the phone said the computers were down but he'd take my information and call back. But he didn't. The slip of paper he'd written my number on had most likely been lost, just like Amira. I finally realized I would have to call back, but I dreaded it. I decided instead that enough time had passed; I would drive to Iowa and see Tom Farrell.

I found him sitting on the front steps of a rusty mobile home at the otherwise empty shooting range, throwing a ball for Jill's dogs. "How're you doing?" I asked him.

"Surviving." He hadn't shaved in a few days, and there were circles under his eyes. He nodded at a mug beside him. "Want some coffee?"

"No thanks."

"Good call. It tastes like crap. Jill does something with it . . . did something. Always tasted better than mine." He got up abruptly to pick up a dead branch lying on the grass. He cracked it in two and tossed it on top of a massive woodpile. "What brings you out here?"

"They haven't made any progress on the search."

"Long trip to tell me something I already knew."

"Don't you think it's time to end this?"

He picked up another branch, then stared out at the distance until one of the dogs started tugging on the stick playfully. He threw it in a high arc, tumbling end over end. The dogs romped after it. "Maybe. I miss her something awful. How'd you figure it out?"

"Something Thea said. When she told you Otis Parchmann had been found dead, you said 'good.' She thought it was an odd reaction, not showing more emotion. I thought it was odd that you didn't say, 'we just lost our only chance to find out what he did with her.' You're a good actor, Tom, but that line was off."

"There goes that career."

"Will you take me to her?"

"Depends. You bring a passport?"

had my passport, and he had a pilot's license and part-ownership of a small plane. We flew north, stopping at a small airfield in Manitoba to gas up and go through Canadian customs, which turned out to be a clipboard in a shed. Then north again, across a vast sea of trees and lakes, using a pontoon plane for the last leg of the journey, flown by a taciturn man named Renny. It crunched through a skin of ice as we docked at the fishing camp where Tom and Renny worked in the summers. Jill had come out of a cabin when she heard the engine and was waiting on the dock. Tom caught her up in a big hug and spun her around. "Christ, I missed you." She smiled and rubbed a palm across his whiskers.

Inside the tiny cabin it was warm and smelled of wood smoke. We ate canned stew, sitting close to the woodstove, then Tom went out to help Renny with some repairs. A raccoon had gotten into one of the cabins, and another building needed its roof patched.

"I can see why he likes to come here," Jill said. "It's so beautiful, so remote. Miles and miles of wilderness."

"It's terrifying. No roads. No cell reception. We're in this little plane that gets pushed around by every gust of wind and Tom tells me there's not even any radar coverage up here. You could disappear without a trace."

"Exactly." She grinned and stretched her feet toward the stove to warm them. "It's been odd, knowing that my picture has been on television, in the papers. I suppose if I did a Google search right now there would be thousands of hits on my name."

"More than that. The lecture you gave is still one of the top videos on YouTube. It just was edged out of the top ten by an exploding toilet."

She laughed. "Good to know what's really important. None of that seems real. Up here, I'm nobody. Nothing. Just a speck."

"Sooner or later you'll have to face the cameras."

"Tomorrow. I'll be flying out with you. I couldn't stay here much longer, anyway. The lake is starting to freeze over."

"How are you going to explain your disappearance to people?"

"Simple. A man had attacked women for over twenty years and nobody noticed. Nothing gets the public's attention like a missing blonde. I suppose I may face charges for causing all that fuss."

"At least you know a good lawyer. How'd you pull this off? Tom tried to explain, but I couldn't hear over the engine."

"One of Tom's friends went to Mexico for a few months. He'd left his car parked at the range, so Tom took it to the city while I drove in his truck. We picked out a good place to leave it ahead of time using satellite maps, somewhere we could park his friend's car overnight and I could make the switch the next day without being noticed. That was the trickiest part. After that, it was just a matter of driving a long way and paying cash for everything so there wouldn't be a paper trail. Tom, of course, had to pretend. And my parents. They were in on it."

"They were amazingly convincing. I'm surprised you weren't recognized."

"It wasn't hard. I wore a down coat that I've never liked because it makes me look fat. And there's no better disguise than being bundled up for cold weather in a stocking cap and scarf. All of which has come in handy up here."

"How'd you get across the border?"

"Renny knows places in North Dakota where it's safe to cross. Don't tell the authorities, but when he's not working up here, he makes money smuggling cigarettes. Once we reached Canada, he flew me up here and made sure I had enough firewood and food and a sidearm. For animals; don't have to worry about people up here. Now, your turn. Tom said Otis Parchmann was dead. How did that happen?"

"He was shot in the back of the head by Kevin Casey, a man who'd worked on your case and ended up as an investigator for the SA's office. He had weaseled his way into Peter Vogel's good graces over the past few years and was counting on his good buddy being elected governor. He didn't want your case or the one against Salazar discredited because it would mess up his plans for getting rich in a patronage job."

I explained how he'd made Parchmann's murder look like a gang killing and got a resident of the county jail to file a complaint against a detective who was asking awkward questions. I told her that he warned Raymond Ashe that I had been checking up on him, goading Ashe to see me as a threat, hoping he would scare me off the case. I told her about Chase Taylor. And then I explained what happened when Jerry Pozorski confronted Casey.

We listened to the fire crackle for a while. "If he'd been killed, I would have had a hard time forgiving myself for setting all this in motion," Jill finally said.

"Setting this in motion might be what saved him."

"You think? I was shocked when I saw him. He'd changed so much."

"He's had a few rough years, but he's the same guy inside." He'd have a long road ahead, getting a handle on his drinking, but at least his finances were looking up. One of Dugan's brothers, the one who worked in the organized crime section, was skilled at following the money. At Dugan's urging, he examined the records of the real estate partnership that had taken Pozorski's life savings. It looked as if Casey had funneled rental income into his own bank account while using Pozorski's investment to pay off bills. It would take a while to sort it all out, but when it was untangled, Pozorski might end up holding the title to some prime Chicago real estate. Meanwhile, he was wearing himself out, maintaining three apartment buildings while his wound was still healing, but it kept him busy, and busy was just what he needed.

"I feel bad about Chase Taylor," Jill said. "I'd hoped it would end differently for him. If only I hadn't pointed to his picture."

"He never blamed you. The deck was stacked against him before he was even born."

We sat there quietly for a while, listening to the fire snap and hiss.

"That girl, Esperanza," Jill asked, rousing herself to open the stove and shove in a couple of sticks of wood. "Is she still taking sanctuary in the church?"

"For now. She's getting tired of it. Diggy still has several years to serve for the liquor store robbery, but I don't see her waiting for him. I give her a couple of months at most before she surrenders to the feds."

"Then what?"

"She'll be deported. Father Sikora knows people in Mexico who will help her get on her feet." I looked around. Night pressed against the cabin's windows, and I sensed the miles of wilderness surrounding us. "You think those guys are okay? It's awful dark out there."

"There's a full moon. Last night it was bright enough to cast a shadow." She got up and tossed me my jacket. "Let's go outside. You've never seen stars like these."

———

The next day we were met at the airfield in Iowa by two FBI agents, tipped off by US customs. Az Abkerian had been tipped off, too, as soon as my cell phone started to work. He had managed to talk his boss into paying for a charter to the tiny airfield to get an exclusive.

I left the next morning, early, before the tidal wave of media broke. Jill seemed ready for it, as if two weeks of being a speck in the middle of nowhere had given her new courage. A little of that courage must have rubbed off on me, because I went straight to Harrison and, after some confusion, got my hands on the file for the Jane Doe found curled up on some cardboard under the back steps of an apartment building on Jackson. The morgue photo looked different than the one Aisha had given me, but there was no question it was the same girl.

I found Aisha at Olivia's house. We went onto the back porch and sat on the steps. "I have bad news about your sister. She died not too long after you last saw her."

"From drugs?"

"An overdose."

"She said she was kicking, but I guess it was too hard." She looked straight ahead, her chin firm.

"I'm sorry, Aisha."

"Least you found her. I lied to you. It was her boyfriend that beat her up. I didn't know any other way to find out what happened to her, so I lied."

"That's okay."

A tear rolled down her cheek. She wiped it away impatiently. "Where's she at?"

"A place called Homewood. Where my mom was buried."

"You know if any buses go out that way?"

"It's a sad place, Aisha. You don't want to go there. But there'll be a service for her in the spring. For her and all the people they've buried out there. That's a better way to remember her. I go to the service every year. We can go together."

"All right. I better go tell my momma."

"I'll do that. I did it a lot when I was a police officer. I'm used to it."

"Let's go, then. I'm getting cold."

told Dugan about it that night. "She was so calm it was scary. Their mother should be hospitalized and they should be somewhere where they don't have to worry about keeping warm and getting enough to eat."

"Foster care."

"I'm going to get things rolling tomorrow. They can't keep going the way they are. Even Aisha's beginning to understand that. Mm, that feels good." I had discovered that Dugan was great at back rubs, though they tended to turn into something else that felt good, too.

"What you thinking?" he murmured later, his lips against my shoulder.

"I thought you were asleep." I ran my fingers through his hair.

"Come on. What?"

"That I'm happy." He frowned at me, being a tough interrogator. Finally, I said, "I'm scared."

"What are you scared of?"

"That it'll end. That it'll be over and you'll be gone, and I don't think I could stand it."

He turned on his back and scratched the line of hair just below his belly button as he stared up at the ceiling. "You want to get married?" he asked at last.

"Christ, no. Do you?"

"Nope. I just thought maybe that's what you were getting at."

"I just . . . I want it to stay like this."

"Me, too." He got up on his knees on the bed and took my hand, kissed my knuckles. "Anni Koskinen, I love you. Will you not marry me?"

"Yes. I won't."

"You've made me a happy man." He stretched himself beside me again. "Only, there's something I need to tell you. I've been putting this off for too long."

"What?"

"This not-married thing, it's for better and for worse, right?"

"What is it?"

"Don't get mad, okay?"

"Tell me."

"You sure you're ready for this?"

"Dugan, I'm going to hit you."

He took a deep breath, pressed his forehead to mine, looked into my eyes. "My mother wants to meet you."